HERS TO PROTECT

A BLACKTHORNE SECURITY NOVEL

NICOLE VIDAL

COPYRIGHT

TABLE OF CONTENTS

KEEP IN TOUCH WITH NV

Visit me on social media or online to learn about my newest releases:

Facebook (http://fb.me/NicoleVidalAuthor)

Instagram (http://instragram.com/nicolevidal_author)

My website (www.nicolevidal.com)

Goodreads (https://bit.ly/NVGoodreads)

Amazon (https://amzn.to/2XCLSlR)

Pinterest (http://pinterest.com/NicoleVidal_Author)

CHAPTER ONE

ALEJANDRA

"Great job, Lisa!" I praise the newest member of the club. Aside from my job, I volunteer at this gym as often as possible. The owners, Kim and Steve, donate space and training expertise four or five times a week to teach self-defense tactics to survivors of domestic abuse—a club I never wanted to be a member of, but nonetheless, I am. I shift my focus from my past to the ladies in this room fighting for their future. My hard work and dedication with training and therapy helped me come out on the other side. These ladies can too. With knowledge and confidence, I can protect myself and others, mostly anyway. As I walk around the room, I correct the form of a few attendees and then join the class from the back of the room.

"Hey, Alex. It's been a while since you attended class," Kim calls me out hard as the class ends.

"Hi. I've been traveling for work and unable to make it here when the classes are running."

"As long as you're training, I'm good," Kim offers.

"It may be crazy early or at the end of a long day, but I train daily regardless of where I am."

"Glad to hear it. You're a great example for the students. You prove survival is possible."

Kim only knows the physical part of my story. My inability to protect myself from my ex has since been corrected. The mental healing is a work in progress, especially with romantic relationships. "Thank you."

I chat with a few of the other women, pack up, and head to my condo. I don't own it, but it's where I live with my roommate and coworker, Maia. After almost a year of searching for a position with a good fit, I joined Blackthorne Security. I tried bank security and private building security, but I was working on my recovery and couldn't handle the idle hours. My application to Blackthorne was a prayer. While I met the requirements as set out in the posting, I wasn't confident I would be truly considered. It isn't a reflection on the owner Jacob Blackthorne or his partners, but of my own insecurities. Much to my surprise, I did get the job, and I haven't been this happy in a long time, at least work wise.

I park and head inside. "Maia?" I don't get an answer, but her car is in the garage. When I started at Blackthorne, housing wasn't offered as an option, like previous new hires, due to lack of space. The company has a bunkhouse at the farm since we travel frequently. Paying rent simply doesn't make sense. However, Connor, my team leader, offered his condo to the older employees. Maia took him up on his offer, but Nolan, her best friend and potential other half, declined. Then Connor suggested I take a bedroom. I'm glad I did.

The condo has three bedrooms and a massive rooftop patio, which I adore. The furnishings are cozy. Connor's decorator has skills. As I climb the extra set of stairs, I find Maia reading.

"Hey, Alex. How was class?"

"Good. It's nice to have time to see the girls. When did you get back?" I haven't shared every detail with Maia, but she knows the basics about my ex. I would bet only Jake and Connor have read my entire file, which includes the details of my background check. I immensely appreciate their attention to employee privacy. Only those who need to, or those I've told, know about my history with Ramon.

"Early afternoon." Maia has been on assignment for about three weeks overseas with one of our uber-hot, A-list actor clients.

"When is your next assignment?" she asks.

I shrug. "Don't have one on the books right now. I'll find out in the morning at our team meeting."

"Same. What do you say to a cheesy movie and some sushi?" Maia suggests.

"I'm in after a quick shower."

Maia sets her book on the glass table and sits up. "The usual work?"

"Yup."

"I'll meet you in the living room." Maia smiles.

I bound downstairs and head straight for the shower. By the time I finish, Maia is setting up the movie and our drinks are poured. Twenty minutes into the film, our dinner arrives. We each take a corner of the massive couch, laugh our way through a romantic comedy, and turn in relatively early.

Near eight the next morning, I climb the stairs from the basement gym and find Maia making coffee in the kitchen.

"Our meeting is at ten, right?" Maia asks.

"Yeah. Want to ride over together?" I suggest.

"Can't. I'm going to run some errands and shop for a dress for Nolan's sister's engagement party afterward."

"You decided to go as his date?" This is news. Despite her more-than-friends feelings, Maia has been pushing Nolan off.

I have plenty of reasons to avoid men—well, not men but romantic relationships with men. Maia, not so much. Yet she refuses to give him a chance.

"Yes, I agreed to attend as his plus-one. It isn't a date. We're just friends."

"Oh girl, you're so wrong. Don't you see the way he looks at you or feel how intense his stare is?" Two things I have never experienced once in my entire life.

Maia's olive skin turns a bright shade of red. "I plead the fifth on both."

"Of course you do. You should give him a chance."

"Admittedly, I don't know your entire history, but perhaps you should take your own advice."

A deflection. "I agree. Frankly, I haven't put myself out there, nor have there been any men I'm willing to take the risk on."

Maia gives me a side hug. "If you want me and the guys to screen a date or two, let me know."

"Thanks. I'll keep it in mind." It isn't as if I don't want to share my life with someone. I'm still working on how and when to let someone in on the whole truth of me, Alejandra Mejia. My truth still scares me some nights, never mind a potential partner. It's going to take a strong and patient man to pull me out of my fortified fortress. The sky-high walls around my heart, body, and soul rose from the ground on my third attempt to press charges. I suppose it makes my situation better than average. Since Ramon's trial, I've learned it takes five attempts on average for a woman to leave her abuser. I push those thoughts away for a later time and get ready for the team meeting.

"Maia, I'm heading out. I'll see you there," I call out from the garage entrance.

With a flourish, Maia is standing beside me ready to go. "I'm here."

Laughing, we open our car doors and head to the Blackthorne office in town. Crescent Bay is a quaint town with Main Street exactly as you would picture it. There's a hardware store owned by the same family for generations, a family-owned general store, a florist, and a candy store. Next door to the office is Norah's bookstore. I'm not sure it's a bookstore exactly. The Nook is a store where you can grab a cup of coffee, browse shelves of books, and actually read them. You can purchase books too, but she wanted everyone to be able to enjoy the space regardless of their ability to pay. Norah is married to my boss Jake. They have a young son named Ben and two highly trained dogs, Tank and Sabre.

I follow Maia into the office, and we're greeted by the office manager. "Hi, ladies. There are breakfast staples on the table, and coffee is set up in the kitchen." Gemma is in her mid-twenties. Her dad was the commanding officer for the bosses and Cruz, I think.

"Thanks, Gemma. You're the best!"

She shrugs and answers the ringing phone, and we make our way into the conference room. We grab two seats near the far edge of the table. Jake, Connor, and Christoph are talking about assignments and personnel.

"Morning," Connor greets us.

"Morning," we reply at once.

Over the next ten minutes, the rest of the team who isn't on assignment filters into the room. Nolan sits between Maia and Finn. Cruz is a newer addition to the team, along with Lane and Barrett. Cruz and Barrett were caught up in a cold case from Cruz's days with the NYPD. Cruz also served with Jake and Connor in the military. Barrett is currently suspended from taking assignments while the boss men decide how to handle his actions, including sharing intel and endangering Jillian Blackthorne who married Cruz last weekend. The clincher is he took those actions to protect his teenage daughter. I can understand why he made the choice. The bigger question is how to deal with it.

"I won't make this longer than necessary. Here's the schedule as of this morning. Those of you unassigned are on call, except if you have already requested personal time." Jake gives us a few minutes to peruse the schedule.

I'm unassigned for the next two weeks. It's unsettling, but perhaps I can use the time to visit my brother. My gut clenches when I consider going *home* so soon—not soon, not really. It feels recent though. I visited over the holidays, and it was pleasant enough. However, I made the trip as quick as possible and avoided every location that might trigger a bad memory.

My brother, Miguel, is four years younger and serving in the army. He stood by me when my life went to hell as best he could. Ramon is lucky Miguel was deployed when I finally pressed charges. He might not have lived to see the inside of a jail cell. I settle my thoughts and refocus on Jake.

"Please make sure you provide your expense reports to Gemma by the end of the week, or you'll have to wait an extra month for reimbursement. Does anyone have any concerns to be addressed?"

Not surprisingly, the room is silent.

"Everyone except Alex is dismissed," Connor announces.

With a bit of laughter and boyish revelry, the guys grab more food and hustle out the door. Maia nods and leaves immediately after Nolan.

"What's up, Connor?"

He glances at Christoph and nods.

Christoph addresses me. "Madeleine is working with a client who may be traded to this area. A decision will be made in the next few days." His fiancée is a high-powered agent, and they share a young daughter.

What does her client have to do with me?

He continues, "Without sharing many specifics, the assignment would require you to pose as his daughter's nanny and provide care as well. We realize it's a bit outside of the norm."

Oh.

"We wanted to give you the option to decline the assignment given the parameters we set when you joined the team." I requested no assignments where the client was male and required me to live in. Jake and Connor agreed.

"If I don't take the assignment, it would go to Maia?"

"It's an option," Connor replies. "Our intention isn't to pressure you into changing your mind. Given Madeleine's long-term relationship with the client, we feel you're the best fit. I realize the details are a little cryptic, but I can't divulge more until he hires us."

"I understand. Can I take some time to consider it?"

Christoph answers, "Yes, of course. We appreciate you not turning us down flat."

"You're welcome." Silence blankets the room. "Is there anything else?"

"No, we're set," Jake answers.

"I'll give it some thought and get back to you soon." I make my way out of the conference room and wave to Gemma who is on the phone again. Instead of heading home, I make my way to the shoreline. Connor showed me a spot near the rear of his parents' property soon after I joined. The serenity of the lapping water and peacefulness will give me clarity for deciding. Deep down, I know taking the assignment is the right choice for me to make more progress in my recovery. I'm merely preparing myself to say the words.

CHAPTER TWO

JORDAN

Near the end of last season, I succumbed to a few nagging injuries. Nothing serious, but it caused concern for my old team. As such, I need a new place to hang my helmet on Sundays.

My life wasn't always roses. For the most part, I pulled myself out. My history and the location of this potential new team gives me pause. My agent, Madeleine Wilton, is a pit bull for her clients. She has worked tirelessly for me since I hired her. There have been numerous lucrative offers including the one team I was purposely avoiding.

I haven't been back to the DC area since I left for college. Avoiding the area made the most sense, and my troubled youth remained in my rearview mirror. However, this team would be the best place for me to play and succeed. I granted Madeleine the ability to share my childhood stupidity with the owners as necessary with the caveat it remain private. So far, it has been kept out of the media. I need my personal history to remain confidential for me and my daughter.

"Reese, we need to leave."

She shuffles toward me. "I'm ready."

"Good job." We exit the hotel and meet our driver to the team facility.

"Are you going to like this team?" she asks.

My stomach twists in knots. Reese has no idea about my past and the reasons the area concerns me. "I'm not sure. We'll see."

"Is Miss Madeleine coming? Someday I want to be like her."

I smile at my daughter. She's precocious and wise beyond her nine years. Being a single parent isn't easy. Add in professional football and no reliable, trustworthy family, and she grew up faster than most girls her age. Too fast in my opinion. "Yes, Miss Madeleine will be there. Do you remember Christoph?"

"The really tall guy who was hovering in her office when she was pregnant?"

I bite back a laugh. "Yes, he's her fiancé and will be joining us today as well. You know what it means, right?"

"They're getting married."

I give her the side-eye and decide not to worry her with the probability we—mostly she—will gain a shadow if I select this team.

She snickers. "I've got a book. I'll be fine."

I kiss the top of her head and stare at the team facility unfolding as we drive along the road. This facility is newer than a few others I've toured in my search for a new team. The stadium age isn't a deal maker or breaker for me. As long as I mesh with the quarterback, head coach, and offensive coordinator, I can make the rest work.

"Hi, Reese. Nice to see you again. You remember Christoph?" Madeleine greets my daughter when we arrive.

"You too, Miss Madeleine. Mr. Christoph."

Christoph offers his fist, and Reese bumps it.

"Morning, Jordan. Are you ready for this?" Madeleine greets me. There are at most five people who know the full story of my life. Madeleine and Christoph account for two of them. Madeleine is discreet when she shares and how much.

I nod cautiously.

"The offer sheet is the better of the remaining two, but I understand your hesitancy," she states.

"I know. Fear is a strong motivator."

Before she can answer, we're greeted by the head coach and general manager of the team, and they whisk us down to the field. While Madeleine and I go to talk with the team representatives, Christoph and Reese toss a football at midfield.

The director of player personnel speaks first. "In all honesty, we need your expertise, Mr. Devereaux. We're willing to pay for it, as our offer sheet shows. This team will make you the highest-paid wide receiver in the league."

Despite my childhood, I've been mostly smart with my earnings. "The value of the contract is not my concern."

He nods in acknowledgment without outwardly saying he's aware of my history. "We understand. As such, we provided contact information for two of the best security companies in the area and the best private schools for your daughter to Miss Wilton."

"I appreciate your attention to detail." We continue to discuss the parameters of the contract until the quarterback of the team joins us on the field. Preston Jameson is a sixth-year quarterback and has lost twice in the big game in the last four years. Hence the team is willing to pay a hefty price for my services, especially considering my former team won the Super Bowl both times Jameson lost. We chat a bit, and he throws about ten passes to me. It's an easy game of catch, but his arm is smooth and his throws on point—exactly as I would expect given his success by most metrics short of championships rings.

We spend another few hours touring the facility and meeting with other members of the staff. About hour two Reese and Christoph begged off and camped out in the cafeteria. I don't blame them. Overall, the morning is successful. If I can get over my fears about being this close to *home*, this team would be an excellent fit for me. Reese is my main concern. Madeleine and I walk to the cafeteria.

"All set?" Christoph asks when we join them.

"Yes, thank you for keeping her company."

"Anytime. Reese is awesome! We have some space on our Thanksgiving Day family football team if she wants to join."

A huge smile graces her face. "Really?"

"Of course. The catch is whether your dad is playing on Thanksgiving or not."

Reese purses her lips. "Good point. If you aren't playing and we're here, can we join Christoph and his family for dinner? I would really like to meet his new baby, Liz."

A strange feeling overtakes me. Family has always been a fluid concept to me until Reese was born. Then it became the two of us against the world. It hasn't been easy, but it has been worth it. "It's definitely a possibility."

Reese throws her arms around me. "Sweet. What do you think of this team? Jameson is really good."

"How do you know about Preston Jameson?"

My daughter rolls her eyes at me. "I have internet access, Dad." The sass in her tone is strong today. "I know your stats and your opponents' stats for the last few years."

Madeleine laughs.

Reese wasn't kidding when she declared she wants to be an agent like Madeleine. "I see. We'll talk more about the team when we get to the hotel." The ride to the hotel is mostly quiet. "What's on your mind?"

"I can wait like you asked."

"Okay, thank you." Once we're back in our room, I order a huge spread from room service. For the short term, I don't want to make any outward shows of my presence in the area, at least not without security in place for Reese. I'm less worried about myself. I'm keenly aware of my surroundings. I may have straightened up and made much better choices in my life, but I haven't lost my ability to protect myself. When we're on the road, I play the game and return to my room. There's no barhopping or clubbing. Keeping the lowest profile possible regardless of my prowess on the field is the best way I can protect my family.

With our food spread out in front of us, I ask Reese for her opinion. "What did you think?"

"The people I met were nice, but they always are. The team failed to win the Super Bowl two years ago because the defense of your old team shut them down. Your skill set is better than their receivers. It's why they want you. What are you worried about?"

Never discount the intuition of a woman or child. "Thanks. It would mean a new school and probably some security for you."

"I figured when Christoph stayed with me instead of you. Is it because this is where you're from?"

"Yeah."

My daughter knows I'm a product of the foster care system in this area. She doesn't know the extent of the trouble I got myself into when I was younger. Reese knows nearly nothing about her mother. She believes her mother couldn't care for her and left her with me.

"What are we talking about specifically?"

I push out a breath. *Am I really considering this?* It's a lucrative offer, and the team has potential, especially with the other roster moves the director of player personnel alluded to during our meeting today. I'm not foolish enough to believe each one will happen, but even if it's half, the upside could be enormous. "Until school starts, someone would be with you or us when I'm not working. Depending on the school, someone would at least drop you off and pick you up for me or with me."

"Okay, not terrible. What about away games?"

Our situation gets tricky there. Her nanny gave her notice so she could go away to finish her college degree. I'm hiring personal security, not a babysitter. Although whoever her security is would act as a nanny, kind of. While she's mature for her age, she certainly can't be alone overnight. Yet I don't have a family member who can care for Reese while I travel, and she needs to be in school. "It's an aspect of this I'm still working on."

"This is a huge opportunity for you, Dad. You should take it. We'll figure it out. We always do." Her resilience astounds me.

"You're right. We do."

Reese finishes eating and takes her book onto the balcony. Unfortunately, it's raining and the private pool at this hotel is out of the question. I join her on the balcony and contemplate the offer. If I can secure Reese, there's no reason for me not to take it. After nearly two hours of weighing my options, I head back inside and call Madeleine.

Hearing soft cries of an infant in the background, I attempt to end my call immediately. "Sorry to bother you. I can call back later."

"Hi, Jordan. She'll soothe momentarily. What can I do for you?" As if Liz stops crying on cue, the infant sounds cease.

"I need to secure Reese, and then I'll sign the DC contract."

"Okay. When are you free?"

I glance at Reese curled up with the tablet. "I'm free whenever necessary."

"Let me talk to Gemma at Blackthorne, and we'll make arrangements."

"Thank you, Madeleine."

"Of course."

I end the call and release a jagged breath. I'm terrified of making a mistake with Reese's safety. The measures I had in place in New England were fine. Kirsten was her nanny and handled school drop-off and pickup as well as care while I was at an away game. Barring crazy weather or plan issues, it's only one night, which was fine. With this team, the proximity makes me anxious. One never knows when vengeance or an old grudge will resurface.

After another hotel meal, Reese selects a movie and promptly falls asleep. Not ready to get some shut-eye yet, I boot my laptop and search the list of private schools the team provided for Reese. The list is longer than I anticipated. A few hours later, I shut down without much progress toward finding a school for my daughter.

Near ten the next morning, Christoph and another man arrive to escort us to the Blackthorne office.

"Morning. Cruz, meet Jordan and Reese," Christoph introduces him to us.

I extend my hand to him, and he takes it. "Morning." Then he offers his fist to Reese. She bumps it, and we head out.

"The ride is about twenty miles. How long it'll take will depend on traffic," Christoph informs us.

I nod and settle into the back seat beside Reese. "Thanks." As we drive, the landscape changes from big city to a small, quaint town. The town feels idyllic. "Where are we?"

Christoph answers, "We're near the center of Crescent Bay, Maryland."

Reese interjects, "It's super cute, Dad."

Yeah, it is. In New England, we lived about an hour away from the team facility in the opposite direction of the nearest big city. Her school was small and private. Christoph pulls into a narrow driveway and parks behind a brick building and leads us toward the rear door.

"What is the Nook?" Reese asks. The rear door has a placard indicating it's next door.

Christoph smiles. "It's a bookstore owned by Norah Blackthorne."

Excitement bubbles within my daughter. A store filled with books is always a pleasure for her. "Can I go, Dad?"

I look up at Christoph who nods tightly.

"Sure, but you have to stay in the bookstore until my meeting is over."

Giddiness overtakes her. "Piece of cake. I'll have a stack of books to buy when you're finished."

I shake my head. The stack may be as tall as her by the time I get there.

"I'll walk her over and introduce her to Norah," Cruz offers.

"Thanks. I appreciate it."

Once they're out of earshot, Christoph adds, "She'll be fine. Norah may not work for Blackthorne, but she can take care of herself." There's a story there. I feel better about allowing her to go alone with that bit of information.

He's perceptive. I shouldn't be surprised. "Thanks."

"My daughter is young, but I understand the inclination to keep her close wholeheartedly." Christoph leads me into a conference room. Already seated at the table is a fit man with dark hair and eyes as well as a stunning woman with long, dark hair and big, brown eyes. "Jordan Devereaux, this is Jacob Blackthorne and one of our team members, Alex."

I extend my hand to Jake only because he was introduced first and then to Alex. As her hand slides into mine, ribbons of heat streak up my arm. I've never felt anything like it ever before. "Pleasure to meet you both," I manage. I slowly withdraw my hand from hers and take a seat.

CHAPTER THREE

ALEJANDRA

Jake called me late last night, inquiring about the potential assignment, indicating it is definite now. I agreed to take the client. Over the phone he provided a cursory overview of the file and the client as well as the fact her father is a professional athlete. This morning the client, well, one of them, just walked into the Blackthorne office. He's tall, built, and has striking cobalt eyes. Each of those attributes would make any woman weak in the knees. I can set aside the fact he's obscenely attractive. However, the lightning bolt of awareness coursing through me when he takes my hand is another matter entirely. I've never felt a spark ever before.

Jake opens the meeting. "Thank you for coming in, Mr. Devereaux."

"Jordan, please."

Jake acknowledges his request. "Jordan. I thought your daughter was coming?"

"She did. She's making a dent in my wallet next door with your wife."

A bookworm, I like his daughter already.

Jake continues, "Madeleine indicated you need security for your daughter when she isn't with you and overnight care for away games. Depending on the school you select, security during the school day as well. Correct?"

Jake and Christoph didn't mention which sport. I'm guessing he plays either professional soccer or football. Maybe baseball I suppose, but the season has already started at this point.

"Yes, for the most part."

Cruz joins the meeting and takes a seat beside me.

"Alex will be with Reese almost exclusively. If necessary, Cruz may be present as well, especially if Reese attends games at the stadium."

Jordan's eyes shift to Cruz. "Understood. I would prefer Alex handle the away games."

His request isn't surprising. Hell, it would be hard for me to leave my child with a caregiver overnight.

Christoph glances in my direction, and I nod tightly. "Alex will accommodate your request."

Jordan looks in my direction. The relief and twinge of sadness in his eyes makes my stomach knot up before he states, "Thank you."

"You're welcome," I mumble.

Christoph speaks next. "Have you selected a school yet?"

Jordan drops his head. "Do you have recommendations? Honestly, the options are overwhelming."

"What about Oak Hills?" Cruz suggests. "It's a private school and has an exceptional curriculum, which Reese needs given her voracious appetite for books. The security is top notch, and we've worked with the staff before."

It's an excellent suggestion. Jillian Blackthorne Cruz is on staff there.

"I'm open to a visit. Is a visit something you can arrange?"

"Absolutely. I'll reach out when we're done here today. I'm sure Jill would be happy to give you and your daughter a tour," Jake offers.

Christoph pushes the discussion forward. "What about in the meantime? What is your schedule?"

Jordan pins his gaze to Christoph. "During preseason, we have strength and conditioning daily plus meetings. Then we move to workouts during the four weeks before the first preseason game. My focus is a smooth transition for Reese. She's my priority. The team will need to deal with my need for more time, if necessary. During the season, the schedule is static. Monday, we have weight training or therapy for injuries, if necessary, followed by team meetings. Tuesday is our off day. Wednesday and Thursday, we have morning practice. Then we discuss a prospective game plan for our upcoming opponent. Friday is a short day with a light practice and refining the plan for our upcoming opponent. If we're home, Saturday we have a walkthrough. If we're away, we leave for our game, typically, in the morning. On game day, we eat as a team, warm up, and go head-to-head with our opponent. If we're away, we hustle to the airport, return home, and begin the process again for the next sixteen weeks or more if we make it into the playoffs."

The schedule sounds grueling. Being a single dad at the same time can't be easy. Not once while sharing his schedule did he mention how difficult it would be on him. Something about this team or this area troubles him. I'm not sure if it's his matter-of-fact sharing of his schedule or the fact he put Reese and her needs before considering his own.

"Alex, do you have any questions for Jordan?" Jake's question interrupts my thoughts.

Jordan's gaze shifts from Jake to me, and I feel tension. The same tension I see when Nolan looks at Maia. He's being respectful by looking at me when I speak, yet I could melt into a puddle from the underlying attraction. *No bueno, Alejandra. You're working with his daughter.*

"Not right now. I would like to introduce myself to Reese today, if you don't mind. Maybe grab a bite to eat and get to know each other a little before you join the team."

He pauses before replying, "I would appreciate that. Is there a deli or diner nearby?"

Jake rattles off a few options. "Do you need assistance with anything else?"

"Do you happen to know a discreet realtor? I need a permanent address."

"Yes. I'll email his information to you as soon as we're done," Jake replies.

"Great. Thank you for meeting with me and making this process smooth and more pleasant than I anticipated."

"You're welcome. Alex, here's his file. Grab a set of keys for a company SUV on your way out. I'll have Gemma handle the paperwork," Jake instructs.

"Will do," I reply and head out toward Gemma. On the way and as discreetly as possible, I input his name into a search engine on my phone. The first result reads "Jordan Devereaux, top wide receiver in the NFL." *Football.* I scan through his date of birth, height, weight, and college information. "Hey, Gemma."

"What's up, Alex?"

"Jake sent me for keys. He said he would handle the paperwork."

She reaches into the key box behind her and lofts a set of keys in my direction.

I catch them and say, "Thanks."

I return to the conference room. "Ready, Jordan?"

"Yes." His response sounds nervous and clipped.

I follow him to the sidewalk outside the Blackthorne office. "Jordan." My hand briefly skims his forearm to capture his attention. The slight touch sends heat surging through me again. My attraction to Jordan isn't a wrinkle I need for this assignment. Yet ignoring the pull of him seems virtually impossible. "Has Reese had a security detail before?"

"No, but she had a nanny."

"Jake gave me a copy of your file, but I prefer my clients fill me in on the background. Later, when we can have a private conversation, will you share with me what troubles you about this area?" Our investigator, Blaine, is thorough, but his reports lack emotion and don't exude the depth of the person requiring our services.

His demeanor softens a tiny amount as if my observation is on point. "Yes, I will. Reese doesn't know the full story, and I would like to keep it that way."

"I understand." He turns to enter the bookstore and pauses when I speak again. "Jordan, I will protect her." Assurance for him, and me, if I'm being honest.

He nods and steps inside.

A young girl with bouncy, brown curls and the same piercing blue eyes runs toward him. "Dad, Miss Norah is awesome! She owns this store, and maybe I might want to be a combo of her and Miss Madeleine."

Excellent choices, Reese.

"It astonishes me how many words you get out in one breath, peanut. This is Alex."

I extend my hand to her, and she takes it. "Nice to meet you, Reese."

"You're way too pretty to have a boy's name."

Kids never mince words. Reese is no exception. "Thank you. My name is Alejandra, but I go by Alex. It's shorter and easier for most people to say."

Norah approaches with her son, Ben, swaddled against her. "You must be Jordan. Pleasure to meet you. Your daughter has exceptional taste in books."

"Nice to meet you, Norah. Yes, she does. I have a feeling we'll be here regularly."

Norah winks at Reese. "I'll make sure to have the next ones in the series ready for you."

"Thanks, Miss Norah."

"You're welcome. Jessa has your books at the front to check out whenever you're ready."

Jordan smiles. It's the first genuine smile I've seen since we met—not surprising given the reason I'm here. "What do you say to paying for your first stack of books and grabbing sandwiches with Alex?"

"Sounds perfect, Dad."

After checking out, the three of us cross the street and order lunch from the deli. Once we exit, I suggest the gazebo near the edge of the village. The gazebo is in the center of the smaller town green along a man-made pond with a decorative fountain in the center. Apparently, Reese does most everything with gusto. I don't even get a question in before she's deep into her sandwich.

When she takes a breath, she asks, "How long have you been a bodyguard?"

"A few years."

"What about before?"

"I served in the marines."

Surprise crosses Jordan's face. Obviously, he didn't read my profile before our meeting this morning.

"Cool. Are all the women around here awesome, Dad?"

He shifts his line of sight from his daughter to me. "It seems to be the case, doesn't it?" Jordan is certainly raising her well on his own. She recognizes women who are badass at what they choose to pursue. The thought leads me to wonder about her mother and other family in their life.

"Alex is going to be with me every day like Kirsten, except she's more than my nanny?" Reese observes.

"Something like that," Jordan answers.

"What about school?" Reese asks.

"We're going to tour a school either tomorrow or the next day."

"Will Alex follow me around in the building or...?"

"Undetermined. At a minimum, she'll bring you to school and pick you up on days I'm at work. We're also going to look for a new place to live."

Reese jumps up from the bench and throws her arms around her dad's neck. "Can I make a few requests?"

He laughs. "You can ask."

I'm intrigued by what a nearly ten-year-old girl wants in her home.

Reese ticks off her requests. "I would appreciate my own bathroom, space in your office to store my books, and an awesome patio, backyard, or both. Can it be near here? This town is super cute and like our old one."

"That's all?"

I can't stifle a laugh.

"I'll keep your requests in mind," Jordan replies.

"Thanks. When are you moving in, Alex?" Reese asks.

"Not sure yet. Once everything is in place and your dad needs to be at the training facility, then I'll be with you."

Jordan acknowledges my judicious response and excuses himself to answer his phone.

I watch him take a few steps away.

"He always takes his calls in private. Don't be offended."

Her observation shouldn't surprise me. "You guys don't know me well. I would take mine in private too. How do you feel about moving?"

"The contract with this team is the best one. I watch ESPN. The sportscasters say he would be crazy to turn this team down. Dad is one of the best wide receivers in the league. His former offensive coordinator didn't know how to best use his skill set. The job is time-consuming, and he doesn't like the hours away from me, but he's a great dad."

She idolizes her father. I vaguely recall the feeling. I was her a long time ago. My ex may have turned out to be less than ideal, but my father was good to me. "What is your favorite part of his job?"

Reese barely takes a moment to think about her answer. "Game day. The rush of the fans at the stadium and the thrill when the team wins. It's awesome. Have you ever been to a football game, Alex?"

"Not a professional one."

"Cool. You're going to love it."

Jordan returns as Reese finishes her statement. "She's going to love what?"

"Football Sundays."

Jordan shares the content of his call with Reese. "The caller was the realtor Jake suggested. We're going to look for a home tomorrow afternoon. He's going to find a few options for us."

"Awesome. Are we going to the team facility tomorrow for you to sign too?" Reese has been through this process before, or Jordan has properly prepared her, probably the latter.

Jordan smirks at his daughter. "Miss Madeleine is still working out the finer details of my new contract."

Reese smiles and starts digging for information about the homes they will be viewing tomorrow, but Jordan responds, "Sorry, I don't have actual listings yet. I'll share them when I get them."

"Okay. What else is there to do around here, Alex?"

"There's a fair next month and other town events, but the events happen mostly on the weekends. Millie has tours of her chocolate factory over there." I point to Millie's store up the block from the office. "The general store hosts kid construction events too."

"Can we get those schedules?" Reese asks both of us.

I raise an eyebrow at Jordan to make sure he has no objections. The boundaries for her activities is another topic we still need to discuss.

"Alex and I will work out the schedule for you," Jordan replies to his daughter.

"Now?"

He shakes his head. "I'm sure Alex has other things she needs to do today, and I promised you could swim this afternoon."

"Fine," Reese replies and gathers her trash.

"Where are we heading?" I ask as we walk toward the Blackthorne parking lot, and Jordan shares their hotel information. The ride is filled with Reese chatting about how cute Crescent Bay is. If her plan is to remind Jordan of her opinion, she's doing a great job. It's affecting me, and I already live here. I escort them to their door.

"Would you like to come in?" Jordan offers.

I step into their suite. It isn't over the top as one may expect. I need to learn more about his profession, and fast.

Reese rushes toward the dresser and rummages for her swimsuit. "It was a pleasure meeting you, Alex. I'll see you soon."

"You as well, Reese. Have fun at the pool."

She waves and hurries into the bathroom.

Jordan asks, "Are you free early tonight for a call about her schedule, perhaps seven?"

"Sure." I reach into my back pocket and extend my unlocked phone to him. "Why don't you text yourself from my phone, then you'll have my number."

He takes the phone, seemingly careful to avoid unnecessarily touching my hand. Can't say I blame him. A relationship outside of the professional with Jordan isn't possible. *Wait, what?* I haven't considered a date with a man since… let alone a relationship. I push the stray thought away. His notification tone pulls my thoughts back to the present.

He hands me my phone back. "I'll call you tonight. I appreciate you waiting for me to share my circumstances personally."

"You're welcome. Have fun at the pool." A river of unspoken words flow between us before I force my feet out the door he opens for me.

CHAPTER FOUR

JORDAN

With Reese beside me, I key us into the private pool, and she dives into the deep end as fast as she can shed her coverup. My focus should be on Reese, but it isn't. The chaos of signing with a new team is a lot. Since my daughter will be adequately protected, I can focus on the rest of the details. I'm surprised Reese didn't ask why Alex doesn't need to stay with us yet. For starters, I haven't officially signed anything. The pundits and sportscasters haven't brought attention to my travels either. After the season started in New England, the people and photographers left us alone. However, it was before we won the Super Bowl, and before I became a household name for most people except Alex.

Like some celebrities with their children, more in recent memory, I protect Reese from social media. There are no posts of her face or details of her life. It not only protects her but keeps the wolves like her mother at bay. Moving back here could make it more difficult to keep the hard line between Reese and my childhood. The other major issue swirling in my head right now is Alex. I haven't looked at a woman as a potential anything in longer than I wish to admit. Yet the woman tasked with protecting my daughter spikes my heart rate and other physical responses like no one else. Even if I could set aside the heat from her hand in mine, which frankly I want more of, not less, Alejandra embodies each physical attribute I would select for my woman. Her chestnut hair cascades down her back in waves, and her eyes are a unique shade of hazel. At first glance, they look brown, but when she handed me her phone, I noticed swirls of green. She's fit but feminine. Her body could fuel every one of my lascivious dreams. Her sultry voice surrounds me like a cozy blanket. Yet in the brief time I've been with her, I can tell many additional layers exist below her carefully constructed façade. It's that woman, the real Alejandra beneath the surface, I want to know. Getting personally involved with Alex would be a mistake, right?

A few drops of water yank me out of my thoughts. *How long have I been daydreaming about Alex?* Too long apparently. I glance at the clock and realize we've been here for nearly an hour.

"Dad, I'm set."

"Okay, peanut. Shower, then dinner?"

"Sounds good."

We laugh our way back to the room. Reese showers and throws on some pajamas. After we eat, she curls up on the bed and starts one of her new books. Barely a second after she opens the cover, she asks, "Are any of the houses in Crescent Bay?"

"Probably, why?"

Reese smiles. "The people are nice, and it feels… I'm not sure of the right word, comfortable maybe."

"I agree. We'll see what the realtor finds. I'm going out to the balcony to make a few calls."

I take a seat and position myself so Reese won't be able to see the screen of my phone. Necessary? Probably not, but I take the precaution anyway. I mentally prepare myself to share my story before calling. I remind myself Alex needs to know everything to adequately protect Reese. Right before seven, I press the video call link and wait for her to answer.

"Hey, Alex. Thank you for taking my call. I'm sure you have better things to do."

"No problem."

She looks like she's atop a mountain surrounded by trees and greenery. "Before I get started, where are you?"

"My condo—well, not mine—but where I live has this amazing rooftop patio. I love it up here. It's private but outdoors."

"I can imagine. Thank you for sharing. I know you signed a nondisclosure, but I want you to know, aside from your team, at most five other people outside of the court system know these details."

"I won't betray your confidence, Jordan."

I scrub my hand down my face. "I didn't mean it that way. I would share with you even without the agreement."

"Why?"

"I'm drawn to you. I can't explain it. We just met today, yet you feel safe for Reese and, more so, me."

She hesitates to respond. "Thank you. I'm…." She doesn't finish her sentence.

I don't know Alex well—yet—but the attraction isn't one-sided. "I know. It shocks me too."

Silence falls between us. I catalog her features as best I can from the screen.

She tilts her face skyward as if she needs to regain her composure. I understand completely. "Please continue when you're ready," she suggests.

"The details I know of my early childhood are slim. My mother was a high-end escort in the DC area. My caseworker gleaned my father was one of her johns. She left me at the fire station less than twelve hours after she was discharged from the hospital. I bounced around the foster care system for the first eleven years of my life. I stopped counting how many different parents and siblings I had over the years. At age eleven, I was physically abused by a foster father. Another kid reported him; then I was placed in a group home. It wasn't pleasant, but I had been in worse conditions."

"I'm sorry, Jordan."

"Thank you. Unfortunately, it gets worse. To escape the conditions, I fell in with the wrong crowd. More accurately, I chose to run drugs to raise my standard of living to palpable levels. I wasn't in search of the newest Nikes or…. I merely wanted enough to eat and clothes without holes and stains." Ironically, Nike sponsors me now, and a few new pairs arrive at least quarterly.

"Shouldn't the home have provided necessities?"

"Should have, but the director was more interested in padding her bank account."

"Taking advantage of innocent children is despicable."

"I appreciate your disdain for Ms. Chinto. I still harbor some as well."

Alex intently listens as I share my life story to this point. No judgment crosses her face—perhaps some sympathy and a dash of awe, considering where I am now. I would go so far as to say she feels empathy as well, which makes me want to learn more about Alejandra Mejia. It's the first time I've shared my story and the listener didn't judge me on the spot.

I push out a harsh breath and continue. "As I'm sure you can surmise, I got caught. A few days before I turned fourteen, I blindly followed my supplier, Trey, and his partner, Smith, into a sting operation. Rather than heed the police, Trey opened fire. The officers returned fire. Smith was shot twice and bled out on scene. Trey was shot once in the arm. He continued to fire until he exhausted his ammunition. Then he attempted to use me as a human shield to evade capture. The betrayal I felt in that moment was as effective as an ice bucket dumped over my head. The shock was instant and the effects long-lasting. Trey and Smith were only out for themselves and their wallets, despite their words of family and brotherhood. The kicker is they knew exactly what I needed to hear because I was an orphan like them."

"Oh, Jordan, I don't know what to say. 'I'm sorry' doesn't seem adequate, nor does 'you were lucky to survive,' but I'm glad you did."

I drop my head for a moment. Her anger on my behalf is genuine. The sound of my name with a rolling R makes her more tempting. "I appreciate it."

Reese appears on the other side of the sliding door.

"Can you give me a moment, Alex?"

"Sure."

I turn the screen away from my daughter as she opens the door. "I'm going to sleep. Love you to the moon," Reese shares.

"Good night, Reese. Love you to the moon and back."

I return to my call with Alex. "Thank you."

"You're welcome."

"Where was I? My age and the fact the district attorney could only prove I handled one drop-off on the night in question was my saving grace. Smith and Trey were both eighteen. Trey was charged as an adult with a slew of crimes from drug distribution to firearms possession without a permit. He's currently serving up to thirty years. I spent nearly a year in juvie. My counselor, Mr. Generali, gave me two choices: straighten up or don't. If I chose the former, he would assist me as much as he could. He enrolled me in the youth football program with Coach Apple. I learned near the end of my stay that Coach was a foster kid like me. To this day, he's still one of my biggest supporters. Coach pushed me to play high school football. He worked with my high school coaches and prepared a training and recruitment plan for college and beyond. Those two men are the reason I made it to where I am today."

"You're wrong," Alex accuses.

Surprised at her sharp response, I ask, "I am?"

"You did the hard work. You made today happen."

No one has ever given me credit for my success. I don't give myself full credit. Then again, nearly no one truly knows my whole story. "Thank you."

"You're welcome. Do you want to keep going or stop for tonight?"

My chest tightens. Alex is perceptive. Over the video call, she sees the conversation is difficult for me. "I'll finish this part, and we can talk about Reese tomorrow."

"Okay. You're concerned Trey will learn about your proximity and enlist someone to come for you."

"Yes."

"I see you're point, but you served your time."

"Trey may not agree with you. In his mind, I'm responsible for Smith's death, despite not having a weapon. I never had one."

She attempts to speak but pauses and bites down some of the anger in her response. "That's bull."

"Perhaps, but it's a fact I'll always have in the back of my mind. He's lurking in the shadows, and I'll do everything in my power to protect Reese from him and...."

She frowns. "There's a disconnect though."

"What disconnect?"

"You only retained us for Reese. Why don't you believe you need security as well?"

"I can protect myself. Plus, I don't go anywhere other than work. I don't go clubbing or out with the guys. I haven't since Reese was born. The team facility has a security team and limits access to the player/personnel areas."

"Okay. Will you at least talk to Christoph about his observations from his visit to the team facility?"

I hadn't considered the possibility of gaps in security at the facility. "I will."

She continues, "Thank you. Reese knows none of the information you just shared."

It was a statement but begs for confirmation. "Correct."

Alex pauses a little too long for my liking. She wants to ask something.

I speak first. "What are you concerned about asking?"

She exhales sharply. The reason for the hitch in her breath is unclear. "Would you be opposed to me teaching her basic self-defense?"

"No, not at all. In fact, I would welcome it. I want her to be prepared but never need to use the skills."

A flicker of sadness materializes in her eyes. She recovers quickly, but I saw it. Now isn't the time to press her. It merely solidifies my position. Alejandra, the real her, is buried. I ache to unearth her, slowly and with precision. The challenge will be worth it.

"Don't worry, she'll think it's fun."

"I'm not worried. Will you be joining us tomorrow or will it be Cruz?"

"Both of us will be there for the school tour."

"Why both?"

Alex laughs softly. "Cruz will volunteer for any detail where his wife will be."

"There's a story there."

"Yeah, I'll let Cruz share it though. It's his to tell."

"Fair. I appreciate your discretion, Alex."

"No problem."

I consider whether it's appropriate for me to ask, then decide I don't care. "Can I ask you a personal question?"

A shade of fear mars her flawless face. "What is your question?"

"You don't have to answer."

"Okay."

"Why do you choose to be called Alex? I'm not buying the story you fed Reese."

She sighs. "When I enlisted, there were two people in my unit with the same last name. Generally, in the military we're addressed by our last names. My first drill sergeant convinced me I would be better off using Alex instead of Alejandra if I wanted to be taken seriously as a marine."

Damn! I'm more impressed by her. "What did you do after the military but before working for Blackthorne?"

"I was a personal trainer for… a little while." She's leaving out an important detail there. "Then I tried other security jobs before applying to Blackthorne."

"I'm glad Madeleine recommended your team. It's only been a day, but I'm confident it was the correct choice for my family."

She yawns politely. "I should turn in. We'll pick you up at your door at 8:30 tomorrow morning."

"Good night, Alejandra."

Her breath hitches before she replies, "Good night, Jordan."

A satisfied smile grows on my face. Aside from the wall fortifying her heart, we need to get over the fact she's working for me to protect the most important person in my life. It's a risk—one I'm willing to take, if she'll have us. *Baby steps, Jordan.*

The following morning Cruz and Alex meet us as expected. The tour of the school is exceptional. Jill is exactly as advertised. She's knowledgeable about not only the school and the advanced curricula for Reese but Blackthorne's inner workings given her brother is an owner and her husband works there. There was something about her that struck me deeper than usual when meeting someone new. Perhaps it's the fact her school will be perfect for my daughter. Reese is giddy by the time we return to the SUV.

"Ohmigod! The school is awesome! Did you see the library?" A huge grin covers my daughter's face.

Finding a school for her was easier than I anticipated with Blackthorne's assistance. I thought Madeleine was overselling the company given her fiancé is one of the partners, but she wasn't.

"Would you like to grab some food before house hunting?" Alex offers.

"Yes, please," Reese begs.

After inhaling sandwiches from a cute café near the school, we make our way to the first of four homes for viewing. I discount the first two almost immediately upon arrival. The third one is close to perfect. The issue is the owners won't be available to close for about a month. According to Cruz, the fourth one is a security nightmare. With those considerations in mind, I have the realtor inquire if the owners would rent the third property to me until they return from their international travel.

The only remaining thing to be addressed is signing a contract with my new team, which is set for two days from now.

CHAPTER FIVE

ALEJANDRA

Nearly a week has passed since I took the assignment for Reese. While I have been with them daily, today is moving day for all of us. Initially Jake's plan allowed for me to travel home each night, considering the proximity of their new home. Then I would stay overnight when Jordan travels. However, there was a scuffle at his "welcome to the team" press conference amongst the reporters and photographers. Out of an abundance of caution, I'm living with them until the media frenzy dies down... if it dies down.

When I arrive at the house, a flurry of activity has already started. The owners were accommodating and allowed Jordan and Reese to move in before closing with a hefty deposit and an indemnity agreement. I park at the end of the driveway near the gate. The home is beautiful. The newer colonial has five bedrooms and a wraparound porch that overlooks lushly landscaped grounds. It also checks off all Reese's requests. She has her own bathroom, space for her books, a patio, and a large yard that abuts an expansive inground pool.

Reese spots me from her perch near the front door. "Hi, Alex."

I check my watch, knowing I'm early. "Morning, Reese. I thought they were starting at nine."

Jordan steps out after the movers pass through with a cup of coffee in his hand, which he extends toward me. "I wasn't sure how you take this."

I graciously take the cup he purchased on his way here. "Thank you." I sip the coffee, and it has the perfect amount of cream and sugar. I don't recall telling him I drink coffee like a fiend or how I take it.

Jordan continues, "To answer your question, they were waiting for me when I got here. Why don't we walk while they move things inside? Then we can start the real work."

"What's the real work?" Reese asks.

I laugh. "Putting it all away."

Jordan smiles. "What she said."

Reese frowns, and we take a leisurely stroll around the house. I walked the property with Jake and Connor for security system purposes after the seller accepted his offer. The team will be here later today or tomorrow to install a state-of-the-art system complete with a panic button in a cute necklace for Reese, which is mostly for during school hours. The layout of the building and the safety protocols in place will allow me to walk her inside in the morning and escort her out in the afternoon. Plus, she knows Jill is part of Blackthorne if something seems off.

Nearly two hours later, we head inside and assist Reese setting up her room.

Jordan starts with assembling her bed. "You don't have to help with this," he reminds me.

My initial reaction is to bristle. Despite the brief time frame, I like spending time with Reese—not just Reese—even though it's my job. "I don't mind. It isn't in my nature to sit around and watch others work."

"I appreciate the help."

"You're welcome." Seamlessly, we work to assemble and make Reese's bed while she unpacks her clothes and books. Once we finish there, we move into the master bedroom, then the guest suite, repeating the same process. It isn't until we're nearly done with the guest bed does his proximity start to unravel my resolve. The tension in his arms holding the frame up while I turn the Allen wrench to secure the rail rivets my attention. I fail miserably at my attempt to ignore my desire to feel again. No one since Ramon made me desire a man's touch... until Jordan. Not true. How I feel toward Jordan is significantly different than my ex. The emotions skating through me are strong and all encompassing. It's exponentially more than what I thought was love with Ramon, and we haven't....

"Alejandra."

I hear my name and lift my gaze to meet his. My full name has never sounded as sinful as it does when Jordan says it. The electricity between us is palpable and impossible to ignore. "Yes?"

"I asked if you would join us for dinner," Jordan reiterates his request I didn't hear.

"I would like that." I expected to make myself scarce once Jordan arrives home from work starting next week.

"Then we can discuss Reese and her schedule after she turns in."

"Sure."

Jordan rises to his full height and extends his hand to me. When I take it, the same awareness streaks up my arm as I stand. I'm slightly above average height, but I feel small around him. The urge to step closer and kiss him has me doing the exact opposite. The brush of my fingers as I slip out of his grasp doesn't soothe me. I want more. *No, you work for him!*

"Alej—"

Reese rushes through the open door. "Dad, our house is awesome! I'm starrrvvving though!"

I can only imagine what he wants to say. Perhaps acknowledging our attraction to one another is a good place to start. Regardless of our feelings, we can't act on them. We laugh at once, and Jordan informs her we were discussing dinner options.

"We don't have any food to cook," she reminds her father.

"I know. We're going to have takeout and order groceries for delivery early tomorrow."

"What's good around here, Alex?"

I look over at Reese. "Depends on what you guys like. There's exceptional Thai, excellent pizza, and decent Chinese takeout within ten miles."

Jordan and Reese stare at one another and smile. Each balls up their fist and taps it on their other hand while saying, "I want…." It looks similar to rock, paper, scissors.

Jordan says, "Thai."

Reese says, "Pizza."

Both laugh out loud.

"Again, or let Alex pick?" Jordan asks his daughter.

I'm already shaking my head. "Nope, not getting in the middle at all."

"Chicken," Reese chides.

I grin at her being comfortable enough to call me names already. "Nope, not happening. I won't cave. I'm not taking a tiebreaker role on night one. You two need to decide."

"Not budging, huh?" Jordan accuses.

"Nope."

Jordan decides, "Chinese it is."

Secretly, I would've voted the same way. We place both orders and set up the kitchen while we wait. Our dinner arrives, and we chow down in relative silence until the cartons are mostly empty.

"This is miles better than the one near our last home," Reese states.

Jordan shakes his head merely because his mouth is full. These two are super cute and have an amazing relationship. It makes me wonder how they got here—details I'm sure Jordan will share later.

We chat a bit before Reese heads back to her room. "I'm going to finish setting up my room."

"I'll come up closer to bedtime. Tomorrow we'll talk about your schedule until school and then your school schedule," Jordan states.

"Okay. What are we doing tomorrow?"

Jordan pins his gaze to mine. "Not sure yet. It's my last day before reporting for preseason training. I'm sure we'll come up with something fun."

We? I ignore the undertone of his words. There can't be a "we" while I work for him, and Reese needs security. It's not a smart move.

"Want to sit outside?" he asks me.

I nod. Reese is perfectly fine in the house, and she won't leave. Either way, I verify the front door is locked and deadbolted as well as the door to the garage. I consider rechecking the walkout basement sliders, but I'll have a clear view from where we're sitting. I curl up in the corner of the rattan patio furniture that the previous owners left. Rather than sit across from me, Jordan takes the other corner of the couch facing me.

"Thank you for helping today. It's above and beyond your job description."

"You're welcome. Like I said, I can't watch others work."

He tilts his head skyward.

"You don't have to share. I can read your file if it's difficult."

Jordan meets my gaze. "It isn't that. While sharing my youthful stupidity is one thing, how I ended up a single father isn't pretty. Some choices I made were in her best interest, not necessarily mine. Despite how I got here and how hard it was, Reese is the most important person in my life. I'll forgo everything else if it means she's safe and happy." He inhales sharply and exhales slowly. "As you know, I was in the foster care system. Coach Apple saw potential in me and pushed me to strive to be my best at football. It was a way for me to make something of myself. He only had one rule. I had to complete my degree before going to the NFL."

"What did you major in?"

"I have a degree in elementary education with a focus on special needs."

"Impressive. Jill too. Her students have developmental disabilities."

"Jake's sister and Cruz's wife, right?" Then he frowns. "Except Jake and Jill don't look alike at all. They're opposites in every way."

He isn't wrong. Jill is blonde and fair while Jake has olive skin and dark hair. I consider if sharing the information is a violation of their privacy but decide he would understand more than anyone. "Jake, Jill, and their brother Cameron are adopted."

He nods as the seemingly incongruent pieces fit together.

Immediately, I want to pull back my last statement. Not because I violated Jake and his sibling's privacy but…. "I'm sorry."

"For?"

"Did it bother you other kids were adopted but you weren't?"

"It did until I was around six or so."

"Why?"

"It's the kid threshold. The chances of adoption after going to school are slim."

"I never thought of it that way."

He shrugs and returns to sharing about Reese's mother. "During my sophomore year in college, I met Christie. It took me too long to realize she was chasing my jersey. When I reinforced my intention not to seriously date anyone while I was in college, she tampered with the condoms and stopped taking birth control. A few months later, she was pregnant and demanded an engagement ring. When I refused, she threatened to terminate her pregnancy."

Hatred bubbles in my veins. I hope I'm never face-to-face with Christie. I understand not wanting a child, and choosing not to carry is a woman's choice, but to threaten termination when Jordan was willing to care for his child is unacceptable. "I'm not a fan."

A look I can't decipher crosses his face, but he continues. "In the end, she got some of what she wanted. I paid her a settlement from my rookie signing bonus to carry Reese and walk away. Not only did she take the money, but she willingly terminated her parental rights. To be fair it was after the fact, but she followed through."

I can't stifle the urge to comfort him. My hand is curving around his forearm before I think better of it. I fight the urge to pull my hand back when the familiar warmth of his skin meets mine. "What do you mean?"

"Reese was born at the beginning of my senior year of college. Christie had to wait until the draft to get her money. I thank my lucky stars daily I wasn't seriously injured, or I don't know how I would've fulfilled the agreement I made with her."

"Aside from Trey, you're worried she might resurface and make demands to see Reese or ask for more money, especially with the media coverage and sheer astronomical amount of your new contract."

"Yes."

"Didn't you go to college in Florida though?"

Surprise crosses his face. "I thought you didn't read my file yet?"

"I didn't."

Realization jumps to his gorgeous face. "You googled me?"

I attempt to pull my hand away and hide the blush creeping into my skin, but he stops me by covering my hand with his. "Didn't have a choice. I had no idea who you were when we met at the office. I saw an insanely hot man with soulful eyes who needed personal security for his daughter. Also, I know barely the basics about football."

"Don't be embarrassed. It makes me like you more."

Like me? We're on the same page there. "Which part?"

"All of it—your fiery disdain for Christie, you met Jordan and Reese not NFL superstar wide receiver Jordan Devereaux and his amazing daughter, and the fact you have no idea how exciting football is."

"Is it?"

"Hell yes! Is it easy? No, it's hard work, but…. You'll see when you bring Reese to the first home game."

I arch an eyebrow.

"I promise you'll like it. If you don't, Reese's exuberance will rub off on you."

"Okay." Speaking of Reese, I slowly pull my hand from beneath his as she approaches from our left.

"I'm going to sleep. Do I need an alarm?"

"No. We haven't made any plans for tomorrow yet."

She rounds the couch and hugs Jordan. "Night, Dad. Alex."

"Night," we reply in unison.

Reese slips back inside and slides the French door closed.

After a few moments of silence, I ask, "Do you have any restrictions on where I can take Reese during the day while you're at work?"

"I trust Madeleine completely and, by extension, Blackthorne and you. She has been my agent from the beginning and never steered me wrong. I don't mean she's a pushover. In fact, she's the opposite. She's tenacious and a fierce negotiator. If you believe she's safe, then it's fine with me. Where are you considering?"

"Norah's store, the town green, the farm, and maybe a tour of Millie's before school starts."

"The farm?"

I laugh. "The farm is Jake's home. It's more like a compound. Connor and his family also have a home there. They have an exceptionally large parcel with hiking trails, horses, a few dogs, and I think Norah added some chickens as well. There's a gym too."

"Sounds fine to me."

"Anything in particular you want to do tomorrow?"

"Would you mind taking me to the farm? It sounds peaceful, and it's the only place I haven't been that you suggested."

"Not at all. I'll text Jake to let him know before I turn in. Do either of you know how to ride a horse?"

"No. Do you?"

"I've had a few basic lessons with Norah since I started with Blackthorne." I scan the property casually to remind myself why I'm here. It isn't to learn more about Jordan than necessary to protect Reese. Yet I want to know it all.

Jordan shifts the conversation to the personal. "Can we talk about the tension between us?"

My eyelids drift closed. "You feel it too?"

"Yes."

When I open my eyes, he's closer to me. "Addressing it won't change the facts."

"Which are?"

"I'm here for Reese. I won't deny I'm drawn to you, but my focus needs to be her. I won't risk her safety for my own personal desires."

"You kind of like me," he asserts.

I drop my head. "Yes, more than I would care to admit for how long I've known you."

"I've never met anyone like you. I don't know you well—yet—but there's a depth to you I ache to know."

Speechless. No one, especially a man, has ever made me feel the truth in his words. "Not all my depths are pretty, Jordan."

"Don't have to be. That fact alone makes me yearn to know even more. Mine aren't either. I still want to know you."

It's taking significant resolve not to lean forward and succumb to his wordless offer. "As much as I want to say yes, I can't. Not while I'm here for Reese."

Instead of backing away, he eliminates most of the space between our bodies. His crisp cologne surrounds me. His mouth is a mere inch away from mine. His nearness causes seemingly opposed reactions—butterflies flutter in my belly and my body tenses. *Breathe. Ramon can't hurt me. Jordan won't hurt me. I have the skills to protect myself now.*

"Your inclination to put Reese before yourself makes you exponentially more intriguing, Alejandra."

If I wasn't already melting into a puddle from his proximity, his words would've finished the job. Fighting my attraction to Jordan and maintaining a boundary between my personal and professional life is going to be harder than I anticipated. The real question is how long we can ignore the heat between us before it combusts. Will I be able to hold it together long enough to share my story with him? It'll be a true test of his resolve to understand the real me. When he knows, will I need to remove myself from this assignment for Reese, for me, or both?

"I'll reach out to Jake about a visit tomorrow," I offer to end our conversation.

"Good night, Alejandra," he whispers, draws back, and rises to his full height.

"Night, Jordan," I manage.

After composing myself, I recheck the locks. As I pass her room, I check on Reese. She's sound asleep in her bed. Reese needs to be my focus, not her sexy-beyond-words father. I text Jake and turn in for the night.

CHAPTER SIX

JORDAN

Our day at the farm was relaxing. Reese learned to care for a horse from Norah and rode Trix around the corral for a short time. According to Norah, learning care and feeding is the first step. We hiked to the point with four dogs, Cora and Cleo, who belong to Connor and his wife, Callie, as well as Tank and Sabre. By the time we reached the end of our hike, Reese was begging for a puppy or three. I wouldn't mind having one or more, but we need to settle in first.

The entire day was fun and light. It shocks me how easy it is to be around Alex. Although dating her wouldn't be the smartest move ever, I can't help but think about her. I want to laugh while preparing dinner, see her beside us on a family outing like today, and under me in this bed. I push the last notion away and get some sleep. Tomorrow, I need to report for preseason training, and I'm getting a later start than the rest of my teammates. One saving grace is two of my college teammates are on the roster. At least I'll have a few familiar faces greeting me.

When I wake, the house is eerily quiet. I dress and make my way to the coffee maker. I notice the French doors to the patio are open, but the screen is latched in place. Concern rushes through me as I approach. My worry is squashed by what I see on the flat grassy area beyond the stone patio. Alex is moving through some type of martial arts positions with precise cadence and grace. I lean against the doorframe and watch like the captive audience I am. The more I learn about her, the more I yearn to know. Too many minutes than I care to admit pass before the alarm on my phone pulls me back into the kitchen. I need to hustle through the rest of my morning routine to be on time. With my protein shake, snack, and gear in hand, I see Alex slip inside.

She looks content, for lack of a better word, despite just completing her workout. "Morning. I hope I didn't wake you."

"No, I like to report at least thirty minutes before I'm required."

"Understood."

"Ideally, I'll be back by six. I would prefer to eat dinner together if you don't mind."

"Of course. Any preference?"

"Just pick a protein, I'll handle the rest."

She laughs. "Will do. Good luck."

"Thanks."

With my stuff stowed in the trunk, I pull out of the garage and head to the stadium. The drive passes quickly. I glide to the gate and produce my license.

"Good morning, Mr. Devereaux. Welcome to the team."

"Morning, Bill," I address the security guard by name.

"Follow the left lane around the corner of the building. There are plenty of spots near the team entrance. Have a great day!"

"Thank you. You as well." I follow his instructions and make my way inside. Within seconds, I'm greeted by my college teammates, Cameron Beau and Tyson Beck. Cam is a tight end and has been with the DC team since draft day. Ty is a safety and has moved around a few times.

Cam greets me first. "Dude! How are you? Long time!" Cam and Ty both bro hug me.

"I'm well and you?"

Ty replies, "Happy to have you on board. How is Little Miss?"

I smile. Cam and Ty were both beside me when I found out about Reese. Cam was in the waiting room at the hospital when she was born. "She's amazing." I pull out my phone and show them a photo or ten.

"She's huge. I haven't seen her since last summer," Cam states.

"Same," Ty adds.

"Where is she now?"

Instead of an image of my amazing daughter, a flash of Alex passes through my mind first. "She's home with a caregiver until school starts."

"Is this caregiver hot?" Cam inquires. Cam is a player of epic proportions. Rather than abstain, he has a firm "love 'em and leave 'em policy," which is known upfront before anything happens between him and said lucky lady.

"His silence speaks volumes," Ty quips. Ty's a serial monogamist, which is to say he sleeps with a woman until he gets bored or she demands things a professional athlete can provide. I think his longest fling, as he calls them, was nearly eight months.

Cam tilts his head. "You like her."

"Even if I did, she works for me and is taking care of Reese. It's a line I shouldn't cross."

Ty accuses, "Yet you want to. How hot is she on the Ty scale?"

Off the chart. "I don't recall the scale. It doesn't matter."

Cam laughs. "We'll continue this conversation later. Now we need to get focused on the playbook and our training session, which starts in ten minutes."

"It's great to be here. I'm looking forward to sharing the field with you guys again." We fly through our college handshake and make our way to the training room.

Nearly four hours later, we break for lunch. I scan through my phone and find a text from Alex.

Alex: Hey there! Reese wanted to send photos of our morning activities.

The image is of Reese and a baby playing outside. I'm surmising it's Ben Blackthorne considering Norah is in the background. The next one is Reese scouring over what looks like a book catalog in an office. The last is my daughter in one of the positions I saw Alex in this morning.

Me: Glad your first morning is going well.

Alex: What about you?

Me: Overall, promising.

Alex: Good.

I scroll back to the first image to look at them again in more detail.

Cam leans over my shoulder. "Is that her? She's hot."

I can readily admit Norah is beautiful and a badass girl boss much like Madeleine, but she doesn't capture my attention like Alex. "No, she owns a bookstore where Reese was earlier this morning."

"How are you holding up getting a later start than the rest of us? Any issues with the injuries?"

"Nah, haven't had any since a week after the end of last season. I might be sore tomorrow, but overall, I'm ready to go. You?"

"Same. Want to come over tonight for a beer?"

I shake my head. "You know better. Other than some time passing, nothing has changed. I need to get home."

"She has someone with her though."

"It isn't different from college or my first few years in the league either. I didn't leave Reese with Trudie, during college or my early days in the league, or Kirsten longer than necessary, and I won't with Alex."

Cam raises his hands in surrender before adding, "I would hurry home if my nanny was hot."

I ignore his comment and finish eating. The second half of the day is easier. We have meetings with the offensive coordinator and then break off into small groups and meet with the wide receiver coach. The meeting with the offensive coordinator was shorter than anticipated.

I step out of the large meeting room and make my way to the smaller room to meet with Wide Receiver Coach Denver.

"Devereaux, great to see you again."

"Thanks. Happy to be here." The rest of the wide receivers file in, and I have a quick meet and greet with them before Coach takes over. Two hours later, I sit in front of my locker and unpack the rest of my stuff. It's a surreal feeling having my name embossed with #88 in garnet and gold instead of blue and red.

Ty enters after the defensive backs meeting and plops down beside me. "Want to join me for a beer?"

"No, thanks. I have dinner plans with Reese. Plus, you know I don't drink during the season."

"Still?"

Not sure why he's surprised. "Yup. See you tomorrow." I make my way to my car and wave to Bill as I head out. Overall, I'm happy with my first day with the team. As I drive out of the facility, I note a dark-tinted SUV following me. Rather than head straight home, I take a circuitous route. By the fifth extra turn, my concern increases. My initial instinct is to call Alex and check on Reese, but I'm confident she's fine. Instead, I call Jake.

"Good evening, Jordan. How can I help?"

"I'm being followed. At least I'm fairly certain I am."

"Can you give me the plate?"

I rattle off the plate.

"Do you recall how to get to the farm?"

"Yeah."

Jake replies, "Good. Drive here. If my hunch is correct, the driver will peel off before you have time to park at the gate."

"Will do. Care to share what your hunch is?"

"Paparazzi."

I exhale and drive toward the farm. "I'll call you back. Alex is trying to reach me."

"Understood." Jake ends the call.

"Hi, Alex. Everything okay?"

"Hi, Dad." *Reese.* "I'm fine. I wanted to share about my first day with Alex, and I didn't want to wait until you get home."

"I'm glad, and I want to hear the finer details the photos you sent didn't convey. Is Alex there?"

"Duh, Dad. This is her phone."

The sass is strong today. "I should be home within the hour. Let's talk in person."

"'kay."

Pushing off Reese isn't usually as easy as today. "Can I speak with Alex please?" I attempt to maintain a steady tone.

"Hey, Jordan."

I hear concern in her tone. I offer before she asks. "I'm fine. I have a tail. Jake seems to think it's photogs. Please don't take offense, but is everything good there?"

"None taken. Yes."

"I appreciate your discretion. I'm sure my daughter is beside you begging for your phone back."

Alex laughs. "You're welcome and on point."

I grin though she can't see me. I turn down a narrow road toward the farm, and the SUV continues on as Jake predicted. "They kept going. I'm going to call Jake back and then head home."

"Okay. See you soon."

As I end the call, Jake rings through. He confirms they were in fact photogs and suggests a few ways to avoid them. I thank him and drive home. I set down my bag and toe off my sneakers in the garage. "Hey, Reese. I'm home."

My daughter runs around the corner and spills the itinerary of her day, most of which I'm already aware of from the photos Alex sent at lunch. With a nod, Alex withdraws down the hall. While Reese talks, I glide a knife over an array of veggies and fixings for dinner to go with the chicken Alex has defrosting in the fridge. It takes nearly fifteen minutes for Reese to finish her rendition of the day's events.

"Sounds like a busy day."

Excitedly she smiles. "It was perfect. Alex is awesome, less teacherish than Kirsten."

"Cool." Alex did say she would make teaching her fun. I'm glad Reese agrees. Ten minutes later, I slide dinner into the oven.

"Please set the table and wash up while I find Alex."

"'Kay." Reese locates the dishes she needs for dinner as I step away.

I lift my hand and knock on her door. I wait a minute or more. Then I knock again. Initially, she doesn't answer. As I'm about to knock a third time, the door flies open. Ignoring my attraction to Alex is difficult. She's wearing leggings and a fitted tee. Her clothes don't flaunt her figure in any way, and yet I find myself running through the playbook to stave off my physical reaction to her.

"Hey. How was your first day?"

"It was great to catch up with a few of my college teammates. Would you join us for dinner?"

She shakes her head. "It isn't necessary. I don't want to intrude."

The only reason for her to beg off is me and our conversation. I intend to respect the line she's drawn, but it doesn't mean we can't share meals. "You wouldn't be intruding. It's dinner. Please join us."

Most of the tension leaves her frame before she states, "I'll be right there."

"Thank you."

When I return to the kitchen, Reese has the table set for three, and my drink and hers are ready to go.

"What would you like to drink, Alex?" Reese asks her.

"I can get it. Thanks." Alex retrieves the glass Reese put out and steps into the kitchen after setting the glass on the island. She opens the fridge and opts for iced tea. With the pitcher in hand, Alex turns in the opposite direction I expect, and we crash into one another. The glass pitcher plummets to the floor and shatters, iced tea splashes on the floor, the lower cabinets, and our legs and feet.

My arms instinctively surround Alex. Her curves flush against me has my mind spinning with possibilities. Possibilities I promised her I wouldn't pursue. "Don't move." I glance down and notice a line of blood on the top of Alex's foot.

While seeking a safe path, I feel Alex trembling, and her breaths are jagged. I lean closer so only she can hear me. "Breathe. It's only iced tea."

She takes a shallow inhale and exhales slowly.

"Again," I whisper. Her breathing regulates somewhat, but she's still shaking. "Please don't move. I don't want you to get any more cuts."

She doesn't acknowledge my words at all.

"Alejandra." I wait until she looks at me.

The expression in her eyes is a mixture of trepidation and desire. It makes absolutely no sense. Then I realize she's in my arms, but it goes deeper than unwanted, unexpected touch. She's scared to be close to me. Is it me or men? I table my thought and murmur her name again. "Alejandra."

In a hushed voice, she answers, "I won't move, Jordan."

I nod and slowly release her from my embrace. Despite the concern I have for her, I feel as if I lost grip of something significant. I step backward and grab paper towels for the floor. I clean around her feet and set a clean towel over the cut on the top of her foot before clearing a path for her. Rising, I extend a hand to her and lead her away from the rest of the glass.

Reese rounds the island and rushes down the hall. In less than a minute, she returns with bandages and peroxide. While I finish a cursory clean of the sticky liquid and glass, Reese assists as Alex cleans the cut on her foot and secures a bandage on it.

"Let's eat!" I announce and bring the food to the dining table. Reese takes her seat, and Alex follows silently behind her. After another trip into the kitchen, I prepare more iced tea for Alex. She accepts graciously, but I get the impression she didn't want or expect me to make more. Our meal passes with a little small talk. We clear the table and successfully wash the dishes.

"Where can I find a mop?" Alex asks.

"It's in the closet around the corner, but I'll mop when we're finished."

She shakes her head and retrieves it from the closet. Reese excuses herself to read.

Instead of addressing her adamance about mopping, I step closer to her. It takes everything in me not to pull her into my arms again without permission. She felt as if she belonged there. "Are you okay?"

"Yes, of course." Her reply is clipped and defensive. The walls around her are firmly back in place despite the progress I thought we made.

"When you're ready to share your story, I'll listen. When you're ready to share why you were afraid to spill a drink or break a pitcher, I'll listen. You and all your depths are safe with me."

She starts to speak but fails.

"The parts you're afraid to share won't change how I see you."

Her eyes flutter closed, and she wraps her arms around herself.

"Can I hold you?"

Her hand extends forward and presses firmly on my chest. The heat of her fingers seeps through my shirt. "I can't."

I heed her request, take a step back, and reach for the mop. When I turn back, she's gone. I finish the floor, wash the lower cabinets more thoroughly, then set the mop outside to dry. The sun is nearly set in the distance. As difficult as it is, I need to wait for her to realize my words are sincere. I concede it won't be today and head back inside. When I turn into the living room, Alex is checking the front door.

She nods and continues rechecking the locks. "Are you staying inside?"

"Yes."

Inputting the code to our newly upgraded security system, she sets the alarm before turning down the hall. She pauses and looks back over her shoulder. "Night, Jordan."

"Good night, Alejandra."

CHAPTER SEVEN

ALEJANDRA

The first three weeks have passed with few issues, at least security wise, to the point where I considered asking to go home each evening. Ignoring the pull of Jordan is the worst form of torture. Despite the passing time, his words echo in my head almost daily. I trust Jordan, but the fear of letting him truly know me is fathoms deeper than I imagined. I believe *he* believes my story won't change his opinion, but I know better. Only once before did I share my story with a potential boyfriend. *Boyfriend?* He exited the restaurant before our appetizers were served and left me to pay the check. The notion they could be perfect to build a family with terrifies me.

Me: Are you free to chat?

Maia: I'll call you in a few.

I peek my head into the living room. Unfortunately, it's pouring today, so Reese and I are staying indoors. We've trained, watched a movie, and played cards before lunch. Now Reese is reading the next book in the Nancy Drew series.

My phone vibrates in my hand. I step into the office but leave the door ajar. While boxes still litter the edge of the room, it's the room that is mostly Jordan in the house—although I haven't been into the master since I assisted with building his bed. "Hey, girl!"

"Hey. I miss you."

"Same."

"Well?" Maia asks without asking.

"Well nothing."

"What happened with the gorgeous Mr. Devereaux?" She knows me quite well. Maia and I are roommates, coworkers, and besties. I don't need advice on how to do my job, and she sees right through my call. True, I miss my girl time with her, but she has a sense my call is about Jordan, and she's correct.

I explain what happened with the iced tea, how I froze up when he held me to prevent further injury, and then shut him out.

When I share his reaction, Maia answers true to form.

"Oh, Alex. You won't know for sure until you share. I'm sure he trusted you with his baggage."

Instantly I defend myself. "He didn't have a choice. I needed to know to do my job. I do have a choice whether or not to share about Ramon."

"Do you?" Maia questions me. "You know as well as I do the only way forward is to act."

"Says you who is keeping her best friend, coworker, and potential love match in the friend zone."

Maia scoffs, "That's different."

"No, it isn't."

"Your fears are earned. Mine are shields to protect myself from losing my best friend. Are you attracted to him?"

No sense in denying it. "You know I am."

"What are you afraid of?"

"Losing them." I hope she doesn't catch I said "them."

"Alex, you shouldn't forgo the chance to be happy simply because you have a past or you're assigned to Reese. The boss men will understand."

I shake my head. "It's better—"

"For who? You or them?"

I wrinkle my nose. If I can protect Reese from Jordan's past, why can't I do the same for my own. I'm more worried about Ramon coming for me—sending someone for me, not them. "You're right."

Maia chuckles. "Can you repeat that? I thought you said I was right."

"Very funny. I did."

"Woo-hoo!"

"Jake is calling. Let's talk again soon."

Maia replies, "You deserve to be happy in your personal life too, Alex."

"Thanks, Maia." I click over and answer Jake's call. "Jake."

"Are you home with Reese?"

Concern rushes through me. "Yes, why?" A bit faster than casually, I walk from the office toward her room just to make sure. Reese has her nose in her book. She looks up, smiles, then returns to her fictional sleuthing world.

Jake continues, "I assume by now you have either discussed his history or read his entire file."

"Yes."

"Good. Blaine has uncovered some threats levied by his former friend Trey Edson at the prison, and Christie is searching for Reese. According to Blaine, Christie Wingate's history shows she been keeping tabs on Reese as best as possible since soon after her payday." Blaine is our investigator. The title doesn't come close to adequately cover the skills he possesses. It's rumored he was once the best white hat hacker in the world. Perhaps he still is. Yet Blaine is elusive. If I recall, only Jake and Peter Harpin know where he lives and what he looks like.

"Okay. What do you suggest?"

"For now, please stay at the house. If you need to leave for some reason, let me know and I'll arrange additional support. While you're more than capable, another set of eyes and ears won't hurt."

"Understood. Reese has an orientation and teacher meet-up scheduled for Friday afternoon. If Cruz is free, I'm sure he won't mind accompanying us."

Jake laughs. "No, he won't. I'll check his schedule and let you know."

"Thanks. Does Jordan know any of this yet?"

"No. My call when straight to voice mail. I requested he reach out when he receives the message."

"We're fine here. Thanks for the call, Jake." I end the call and consider the new information in more depth. It makes my stomach twist in knots. Everything Jordan was worried about is coming to fruition. Frankly, I don't know how he'll handle the news. I don't have much time to process Jake's information before Jordan rushes through the front door.

"Reese," he calls out while toeing off his Nikes. He all but runs down the hall to verify for himself that she's safe. I don't blame him. A few minutes later, he calmly returns to the kitchen.

"I assume you heard the voice mail from Jake."

"Yes. Why didn't you call me?"

At first, I'm taken aback by his tone, but I shove it aside. "I got off the phone with Jake within the last few minutes. I also knew you already had a voice mail from him, and I didn't want to unnecessarily alarm you further."

He squeezes the bridge of his nose, closes his eyes, and takes a deep breath. "I'm sorry. This is the very reason I didn't want to move here."

I set my hand on his forearm to make him look at me. Once he does, I reluctantly slide it off slower than necessary. "I understand. Blackthorne is the best in the country for a reason."

He drops his head. "I didn't mean to…."

"I didn't take it that way. She's fine. The team will adjust as necessary. For now, we stay here."

"What about the orientation and teacher meet and greet?"

"Jake and Connor are working on a plan to provide additional support for Reese."

A small smile curls at the corner of his mouth. It's devastatingly sexy despite the tenor of this conversation. "Cruz?"

I laugh softly. "Probably Cruz or Christoph."

"Want to choose the takeout this time, or shall I throw down with Reese?"

I smile at the memory from my first night with them. "I'm not picky, but pizza works on a cold, rainy day like today."

"Pizza and a movie sound perfect. I'll order."

He passes me and pulls out the takeout menus stashed in the island. With a flourish, he orders more food than the three of us could possibly consume. "We have about forty-five minutes. I'll tell Reese."

I nod and move near the French doors. The sky is gray, and heavy rain pelts the glass. The weather is indicative of the storm swirling in my head and my heart if I'm being honest. Maia is right; I need to own my story. All of it. I overcame my inability to protect myself and now teach other women in the same situation. However, learning to trust a man with the real truth of Alejandra… I have tried and failed. Jordan claims he isn't like the rest, but the only way for me to truly be sure is to put the entire truth out there and hope for the best. My deeper concern is Reese. I don't want sharing my story with Jordan to impact her. She's special, and I refuse to allow my personal life to cloud my job.

Apparently, pizza gets more leeway than other meals. Not only are we consuming tons of food but were eating in front of the massive television in the living room. The room that was barren and sparse on moving day is now cozy and warm since the new furnishings arrived. Jordan has fabulous taste as far as décor. He decorates to foster a home not a museum.

Jordan asks, "What are we thinking for a movie, Reese?"

I look between the two of them. "No fancy way to figure this out?"

Reese giggles. "Most of the movies Dad would watch, I won't like. He prefers suspense and drama films, usually older ones too. I pick most of the time."

"Good to know."

She wrinkles her nose. "Let's go with *Harry Potter and the Chamber of Secrets*. Have you read the books, Alex?"

"No, I haven't."

"What about the movies?"

"I've seen clips here and there, but I haven't watched the entire series."

Reese reconsiders. "Let's start at the beginning so it'll make sense to Alex."

"You don't have to go backwards for me. I'm sure I can follow along."

Reese shakes her head. "The movies build on the ones before, like the books. It's no problem."

"*Sorcerer's Stone* then?" Jordan asks.

"Okay," I reply.

I cross my legs in front of me and snuggle deeper into the couch with my plate in my lap. While we eat the amazing pizza, my attention is riveted to the movie. Half-blood, muggles, wizards, and weird pets capture my imagination. An owl and a rat as a pet is quite unique. Jordan pauses the movie for a short break to clean up the pizza and shift to the desserts he purchased. He passes one to Reese. A sliver of surprise passes over me when I see the chocolate confection.

"Should you be eating this during preseason training? Until tonight, you have been eating perfectly balanced and portioned meals." After the question leaves my lips, I realize how he could take it wrong. "I mean…."

He smiles, which leads me to believe he isn't offended. "It's for you."

I know my preference for chocolate over everything else has never been discussed. "Thank you." I nearly moan as the first bite of the chocolate on chocolate with a warm chocolate center melts in my mouth. "Would you like some?"

He winks at me before replying, "Can't. I need to maintain a strict diet for the season."

"Dad! One bite won't mess up your training plan." Reese scolds him before I catch the sarcasm and levity in his voice.

I appreciate the example Jordan has set for Reese. Overall, she eats well for her age. It can't be easy parenting an opposite-gender child alone.

"Good point. Yes, I would like to try your dessert, Alex."

The underlying innuendo hits me square in the chest. Whether he intended to lace his response or simply calling it as it is, I'm affected either way. Thankfully, Reese misses the tension completely. I scoop a bite and extend my spoon in his direction. He took the opposite corner of the couch when he returned to the room. Initially, he reaches for my wrist to steady my hand, but allows it to fall away without touching me. Part of me is disheartened, but the rest is encouraged by his steadfast demeanor and adherence to his word.

His eyes close briefly as he savors the bite. "It's amazing."

"It is." Despite my efforts to avoid touching him, our fingers graze one another as he returns the spoon. I lift my gaze to his. The fiery lust in our stare is impossible to miss. I partake in another bite of the cake and then refocus my complete attention on the movie.

As the credits roll, Reese asks, "What did you think?"

"It was really good. Do you have the books?"

Reese scoffs. "Of course! I'll get the first two for you. Be right back." Reese rushes to her stash of literary pleasure.

"I think you just cemented your status as Reese's BFF," Jordan quips.

"I disagree. At best I'll always be second to you, which is as it should be until she starts dating obviously."

"She isn't dating until she's twenty."

I laugh. Then the expression on his face makes me realize he isn't joking. "Jordan, not a realistic plan!"

"Don't care. I know how guys are."

I'm rescued from addressing his statement further when Reese bounds back into the living room.

"Here are the first two. I've read the entire series more than once. If you have any questions about the houses—I'm definitely Gryffindor—spells, or potions, let me know." She's breathless with excitement.

"Thanks, Reese."

"It's late. You should get some sleep," Jordan addresses his daughter.

"Night, Dad. Good night, Alex."

At once we reply, "Good night, Reese."

"Want to watch the next one?"

I consider this for a bit too long.

"I don't mean to push."

I set my hand over his. "You're not. I was deciding whether reading first makes more sense."

"Oh," he replies.

"Either way, I owe you an apology."

He twists to face me more fully. "I don't believe you do. If anything, I owe you one."

"You don't. You did nothing wrong. Actually, you did everything perfectly right. What does your day off look like for you during the regular season?"

A confused look graces his gorgeous, chiseled face. "I usually do a moderate recovery workout and take care of stuff around the house. Why?"

I steel myself with a deep breath. "Which would start next week, right?"

"Yes."

"Based on some sound advice I received after the iced tea spill, which is innocuous to most, I…." Involuntarily, my eyes flutter closed and a chill cascades over me. A memory of spilling milk in Ramon's presence and the beating that followed flashes through my mind. Seemingly simple things set him off. I never knew what it would be from day to day. That day it was wasting money. *He isn't here. You can protect yourself now.*

The cushion of the couch shifts as Jordan scoots closer and holds my hand in both of his. "Take your time."

The only way to know if he can handle me is to let him in. I look at my hand before Jordan. His face is serene but concerned. "I want—no, I need to share why I reacted how I did with the spill and you. However, it isn't going to be easy, and I need to make sure I have enough time to compose myself before picking Reese up from school."

"Thank you for considering trusting me with your story."

"Thank you for asking and waiting until I'm able to share with you."

He lifts my hand near his mouth. "May I?"

I drop my head in permission and inhale sharply in preparation. The touch of his hand sends heat streaking through me; the softness of his lips on my skin is infinitely more. My chest tightens, and my heart palpitates.

"I meant what I said. I'll listen when you're ready to share. However, you need to know I want all of you, soul deep and stripped bare, Alejandra."

Wow! "It might take quite some time."

"I'm an insanely patient man." He leans forward, eliminating most of the space between us, and waits.

I drop my chin, acquiescing to his proximity. He sets a lingering kiss to my forehead. My body is on fire. No man has ever kissed me there before.

It feels sweet and deeply intimate. Before I can garner the courage to kiss him, he's on his feet with a hand extended in my direction. As I take it, all the air leaves my lungs, and I find myself standing close enough to feel desire rolling off him.

"Good night, Alejandra."

"Good night, Jordan."

CHAPTER EIGHT

JORDAN

As soon as Coach blows the whistle for the end of practice, I take off at a brisk pace to the locker room. By the time the rest of the guys make it inside, I'm heading back to my locker dripping from a shower.

"Where's the fire?" Cam asks as he plops down beside me.

"Going to see the hot caregiver," Ty accuses. He doesn't know the half of it.

Yes. Sort of. "No, Reese has orientation at school. I would prefer to arrive with her rather than meet her at school."

Cam replies, "You can't keep the little miss waiting. Hustle up!"

I laugh, finish dressing, and take off down the tunnel toward the parking lot. With a quick wave to Bill, I hurry home. Luckily, the traffic is sparse, and I don't have a tail today. I have no doubt the lack of photographers is Jake's doing. The firm is worth every penny. Once the thankfulness exits my mind, Alex filters in. Whatever she needs to share about her past isn't pretty. I can handle not pretty, but not having a shot at all isn't in the cards. She speaks to me on a cellular and carnal level. I would double down Alex feels the same way.

The sparks are inexplicable. The type fairy tales are made of. I never had an example of a solid marriage or relationship outside of fiction. Madeleine and Christoph seem to be stable, but they aren't married yet.

From the small amount I've learned about Jake and Connor and their wives, the same seems to hold true. My main goal is to learn as much about Alex as she's willing to share, ideally before Tuesday.

I pull into the driveway and straight into the open garage. With barely a minute to spare, I set my bag near the door and slide into the back seat with Reese and Alex.

"You made it!" Reese exclaims.

"You doubted me?" I catch Alex stifling a smile and wink at her.

My daughter rolls her eyes. "Doubt is a strong word. I knew you would make it to the school. Home first, I wasn't sure."

Home. I'm glad my daughter is comfortable here. I am too. "Glad to keep you on your toes. Hi, Alex. Cruz."

"Good to see you again, Jordan," Cruz replies and backs out of the garage.

I turn my gaze toward Alex.

"Hi. How was practice?" Her words sound strained.

"Fine. Today's workout was light. How was your morning?"

Reese answers before Alex can compose her response. "It was great. We trained first thing, had breakfast, and then we talked about Harry Potter, and we built more of the puzzle. Right, Alex?"

Her head moves in agreement. "Good summary, Reese." Still she isn't her usual self. It takes me too long to realize it's because the three of us aren't alone. We pull into the lot at the school, and Cruz parks.

We enter the school, and Jill greets us. "Welcome, Reese. Are you ready for this?"

"Hello, Miss Jill. Yes, so ready."

Jill smiles. "Here's the map and the scavenger hunt to learn the building layout. You have thirty minutes to follow the map to your teachers."

"Cool. Let's go, Dad and Alex."

"What about me?" Cruz feigns rejection.

Reese giggles. "I think you should keep Mrs. Cruz company."

Cruz raises his hand for a high-five. "Thanks, Reese."

"Anytime." She turns in a circle and orients herself and the map.

"Are we helping?" I ask.

"Nope, I've got this." She takes off down the hall.

Alex and I follow. Reese enters a room and returns promptly with a red card. Reese continues down the next corridor.

I take the opportunity to talk to Alex. "Are you okay?"

"Of course, why?"

With a shrug, I continue, "You seem different today. Then I realized it could be because Cruz is with us, but honestly, I'm afraid you're pulling back a bit." While we chat, Reese has secured two more cards and dashed into the gym.

Alex sighs softly.

Spot on.

"I'm not pulling back exactly. I haven't shared my entire story with a man in a long time, and frankly it didn't go well. I'm not suggesting you're like him, but—"

"I'm not."

Reese snags another card and states, "Two more to go! Come on, slowpokes."

I laugh, and Alex smiles, but it doesn't reach her eyes. Alex murmurs, "Thank you."

"You're welcome. For?"

"Being true to your word, even if you don't know my full story yet."

I glance ahead at Reese and behind where Cruz would approach from, finding the coast clear. Guiding Alex beneath one of the archways, I eliminate the space between us and whisper near her ear, "I will never lie to you. I like you more than I should considering your role in my life. The reality is I don't care. I wouldn't say I believe in fate per se, but our meeting was serendipitous. We were meant to meet, and I intend to embrace the chance we have to chase whatever we could be."

I have rendered her momentarily speechless. "I want to as well, but—"

"No buts. We can figure it out."

She drops her head in agreement.

"Good. We'll learn more tonight."

Her eyebrow rises into an arch.

"We're going to share more about ourselves later."

A small smile graces her face. "Like?"

"Everything you're willing to share." I grin at her, take her hand, and lead her toward Reese. Once we approach my daughter, Alex slips her hand from mine. I feel disconnected from her, and I don't like it.

We slide behind Reese who doesn't appear to have noticed our private conversation. Alex fades into the background while Reese and I meet her teachers, which unsettles me. She's becoming a huge part of our life. Hiding in the shadows won't work for me. Except, it's her job, her only role in our life. I'm impressed by the faculty and the anonymity I seem to be enjoying. If they know my profession, it doesn't matter regarding my daughter, and I'm grateful.

Reese is bouncing on cloud nine as we make our way back to the SUV over an hour later. "Dad, it's awesome here. I can't wait until Monday."

"Happy to hear it." Changing schools is tough. I'm glad she loves this one. It'll make my transition a little easier. Cruz meets us at the front entrance and escorts us home. After dinner, Reese and Alex curl up outside and read by the firepit while I attempt to tackle my inbox. I fail miserably. I spend most of the time waffling between questions to ask Alex.

Reese pokes her head into my office. "I'm going to sleep." She rounds my desk and hugs me. "Love you to the moon."

"I love you to the moon and back." I shut down my laptop and seek Alex. She hasn't moved from her cozy reading spot, but she isn't reading any more. "Want to stay out here?"

"Sure."

"Need anything?" I offer.

"No."

I join her on the rattan couch and bend my leg in front of me, facing her. "How's the book?"

She smiles. "It's good. Have you read them?"

"Yes."

"Is it something you enjoy or because she asked?"

I smirk at her. "I prefer biographies or philosophy, but if Reese suggests a book, I'll read it. What about you?"

"My parents didn't emphasize education. The plan was to take over the store after high school graduation."

Yet she served in the marines and works in private security.

"It was a bodega beneath our apartment." She pauses and gazes skyward.

"What happened to your family?" I murmur and inch closer to her.

She takes a deep breath before answering. "My parents met in high school and became fast friends. When they immigrated here from Columbia, they weren't a couple. The bodega was the only place willing to hire them. They worked long, hard hours but made the best of it. They married within six months of moving to the United States. I was born three years after they married. My brother, Miguel, followed four years later. When Sal was ready to retire, he sold the store to my parents. More accurately, owner financed the store so he could have income and not work. It worked well for them until it didn't. The bodega, not the purchase." She pauses again.

What she needs to share on Tuesday has nothing to do with her parents. However, this topic is difficult for her as well. "While I didn't know my biological parents growing up, I understand the impact of a parental figure on your life, good or bad."

"Against their wishes, I enlisted to earn money for college."

"What would you have chosen as your major?"

Her gaze settles on mine. "What will my major tell you?"

"Just a little more insight into who you are."

A small smile curls at the corner of her lip. "Political science."

"A lawyer?" I suggest.

She wrinkles her nose. It's cute and endearing. "An immigration lawyer."

"Was it difficult for your parents to immigrate here?"

She shakes her head furiously. "No, but in the years after, it became more difficult for other family members to follow them."

"Makes sense." I wait her out. It doesn't take a huge leap to surmise something terrible happened to them.

"My parents were executed by two armed robbers within days of my brother's high school graduation."

Without hesitation, I draw her against me. "I'm sorry." Though similar in quickness as the last time I held her, she isn't tense.

Her arms curve around me and flatten on my back. "Thank you." Her words tickle my neck. I tamp down the urge to kiss away her pain. She remains tucked against me until her phone vibrates in her pocket. "I need to check. It could be Jake."

Reluctantly, I release her.

She reaches into her pocket and checks her phone. "It's Maia. I'll answer her later."

I shift and set my bent leg on the stamped concrete. "Want to stop?"

"No, but I appreciate the offer. Around the time of their deaths, I needed to decide if reenlisting was the best choice for me. I decided against it and finished my contract within three months of their deaths. I went home and ran the bodega on my own. We sold the bodega, and Miguel enlisted in the army. The new owners kept me on as the manager for almost a year after the sale."

"How did you get from there to Blackthorne?"

"Those answers will have to wait. Please share something else about you."

I'm partially disappointed, only because we're making progress. Much like mine, her life hasn't been a cakewalk. In fact, it was anything but easy. "Like what? My favorite pizza topping?"

She grins. "I already know your favorite."

"Enlighten me," I goad her.

"Pepperoni and sausage."

Correct. "Okay, care to guess my favorite color?"

"It isn't something obvious like blue or orange. You're...."

"I'm what?"

"Unlike any man I've ever met. A sparse few would willingly take on single parenthood. Sprinkle in your lack of support and demanding career, it's admirable."

"After my childhood, I could never allow Reese to suffer the same way I did. The rest is determination to be the best father possible and intricate planning. The infant days during football season my senior year were rough. There were days I went without sleep to make sure I met my obligations to Reese and the team."

"It paid off. Your favorite color is turquoise."

Disbelief filters through me. "How?"

A soft smile curls up on her face. "I'm a good guesser. What is your biggest regret?"

"I'll answer your question, but then it's my turn. I get two questions in a row."

She drops her head in tacit agreement.

"Falling in with Trey and Smith. Looking back, I only had to make it a few more years with Ms. Chinto. There were likely other options as well. I could've reached out to my caseworker. I had a few over the years. My last one was the best one. I didn't give her a chance to work her magic though."

"What was her name?"

"Joyce. I think her last name began with an M. Either way, she was assigned my case when I was nearing fourteen. I had a meeting scheduled with her two days after I got arrested. She met me once at juvenile detention. Somehow, she culled through my file and got me placed with Mr. Generali and, in turn, Coach Apple. I haven't been able to find her again."

Alex is unusually quiet after my answer. I can see her mind spinning, but I don't call her on it.

I press on. "Time for my—"

"Can I ask one more? You can choose not to answer this one."

"Okay."

"Would you want to learn about your birth parents, if you could?"

Silence falls between us. "I suppose if I wanted to know, I have the resources to find out. Truthfully, I never truly thought about it either way."

"Thank you."

"You answered a few tough ones already. Let's see, a simple one first. Where would you travel if time and money were of no consequence?"

A genuine smile materializes on her face. "Colombia. More specifically Ciénaga, Magdalena."

I was wrong about the rolling Rs. Even the name of a town in Spanish slipping between her pouty lips is…. "You speaking Spanish is sexy as hell."

Surprisingly, she looks away from me. I set two fingers beneath her chin and turn her gaze back to mine. "Hasn't any man ever told you how exquisite you are?"

Her eyelids flutter closed, her head moves ever so slightly left to right, and she doesn't open her eyes.

"Fools, every last one."

"The list is tiny, Jordan."

"Doesn't matter. Alejandra, please look at me."

Her striking eyes meet mine again.

"I may not know your entire story... yet. However, I'm sure of a few things. You've suffered tremendous personal loss and pain. You're a fighter. You're smart. If I sat down and tailored my dream woman, you would be her, right down to how you wrinkle your nose when I'm right. Even deeper, you make me believe a stable, happy life is possible."

Silence surrounds us for an achingly long minute. "You can't possibly know—"

"I can and I do. When you shook my hand, my world shifted on its axis. It has never happened with any other woman. Are there obstacles for us? Yes, more than I would like. I'm asking you to trust me with all of you and know when you're able to share the rest, I won't run away. I'll walk beside you."

"Sharing the rest is a huge leap for me. I can't bear being wrong again. Please don't make me regret it."

I draw her close again and murmur near the shell of her ear, "I won't."

For the second time today, Alejandra is in my arms, and I don't feel any fear or tension. I'm taking it as a step forward.

CHAPTER NINE

ALEJANDRA

Reese joined me for training at six and is now showering before school. I grab a water and pad down the hall toward my room. As I pass Jordan's bedroom, his door flies open. I casually scan him from head to toe. Should I be taking an active interest in his physical appearance? No. Do I care? Only to the extent it may impact my job. If he's offended, it's carefully disguised.

"Morning."

"Morning. Done training already?"

I smile. "Reese is an early bird. She was waiting for me this morning."

"I'm glad she's following through. Want a cup of coffee?"

I shouldn't be taken aback by the offer. He has been taking care of me since he hired me for Reese. It's unsettling and unfamiliar but surprisingly welcome. "Sure. I need to shower and dress first though."

"Okay. Fifteen minutes work?"

"Yes."

When I return to the kitchen, Reese and Jordan are laughing loudly. "What are you two laughing about?"

Reese points to the television and rewinds about thirty seconds. "Look."

I turn my attention to the screen. Jordan appears onscreen in his old team's uniform in a compilation of his missed receptions last season. It isn't long, but it's funny because each time, the creator put a roll of duct tape on the ball to help him catch the next one. Obviously, he fails. I can't help but join in the laughter as well. I grab a stool at the island, and Jordan slides a coffee and a breakfast burrito in my direction.

"Thank you." It isn't until then do I see an empty plate in front of him and Reese. I should attempt to get up earlier from now on, at least on Tuesdays.

"You're welcome."

I glance at the clock and note we have fifteen minutes to be out the door. I savor the first bite. This assignment has seriously impacted my food choices. Jordan eats well, and it's tasty. "Are you set to go, Reese?"

"Yup. Waiting on you." She smirks at me.

"Very funny. Perhaps you could be a little faster in the shower."

"You have your own shower," she reminds me.

She isn't wrong. I was working out my seemingly inappropriate thoughts about my boss of sorts.

I take two more huge bites before we make our way to the garage. As I round the SUV to the driver's side, Jordan steps behind me. Goose bumps rise on my skin from his nearness, and a sliver of a memory creeps into my mind. *Jordan has never hurt me. His closeness feels... exhilarating.* "You're coming?" I manage.

He leans even closer. In a whisper, he says, "I see you, Alejandra."

I know. It's fantastic and terrifying at the same time.

Then he adds space between us. Loud enough for Reese to hear, he says, "Of course I am."

Reese giggles, and I turn to face him. Face-to-face is equally as intense. "You want to drive?"

"Yes, unless it's against the rules."

I shake my head. "No, not against the rules." I slide away and take the long way around the SUV, composing myself as best as possible. Not only do I fail, but Jordan is keenly aware of my reason to extend my walk.

Reese chatters the entire ride to the school. I direct Jordan to the staff parking lot beside the building where Principal Platt allows me to park before escorting Reese into the building. I round the car and open Reese's door. She slides to the ground between me and the door like I requested yesterday. It's overly cautious, but for now I'm keeping my guard up. Jordan is watching us but says nothing. He unknowingly stands in the perfect position with Reese between us in a staggered grouping. I scan the parking lot. Then we walk the ramp and enter the building. After a brief greeting with the staff at the entrance, Reese hugs us both and scampers off to class.

"I guess she likes this school," Jordan opines.

I laugh softly. "It's only day two, but school seems like a safe and happy place for her."

He acknowledges my statement. "It is."

We walk side by side out the main entrance and back to the car. Jordan remains beside me at the passenger side of the car. We reach for the door handle at the same time.

The familiar spark runs up my arm. I take a breath before saying, "I can get my door."

Jordan ignores my statement and opens the door for me. After I sit, he replies, "I know you can. However, you deserve to have it opened for you. I would've in the garage except you seemed to need time to handle how being physically close to me affects you."

It's evident somewhere along the way Jordan learned manners and how to treat women with respect. I'm grateful to whomever instilled those values in him. I would surmise it was Mr. Generali or Coach Apple. He has been instilling them in Reese as well. "Thank you."

"You're welcome. Where to?"

"Let's grab a coffee, and then I'll direct you."

After we glide through the drive-thru for coffee, I direct Jordan to the river's edge near the Michelson's home.

"Where are we?"

"Connor's parents live there." I point to the massive colonial slightly more than an acre away from where we are.

"It's peaceful."

"It is." Fear skyrockets through me. I clench and unclench my fists a few times.

Jordan stops walking beside me, turns into my path, and takes my hands in his. He doesn't speak until I lift my gaze to his. "Take all the time you need. I meant what I said; I won't run. I won't make you regret sharing with me."

No one, man or woman, family or friend, has ever been as attuned to me as Jordan. "I believe you. It's harder than I thought to trust again. Yet I blindly trusted you without you knowing." I force myself forward. With a blanket from the box spread on the platform, we take a seat.

Once he's settled, Jordan retakes my hands in his. "What do you mean?"

"When I joined Blackthorne, I requested no assignments where the client was male and required me to live in. Jake and Connor accepted my conditions. For Reese, they gave me a choice to walk away due to the parameters I set." He takes a few moments and processes my words.

His entire body tenses from his tightening jaw to his hands around mine. "Who hurt you? Is that why you protect people? Because you couldn't protect yourself at one point."

Fear should be coursing through me given the nature and tone of his words. It's not. Despite my acquired skills, Jordan will never force me to defend myself against him. "Yes." I sharply inhale and slowly exhale before continuing. "I met Ramon at the bodega while I was the manager. At first, it was great. He treated me like a queen, his idea of a queen anyway. He moved in after nearly eight months of dating." I allow my eyelids to flutter closed briefly.

Jordan scoots closer to me and twines our fingers together. "I'm right here."

His words reassuring, I share more. "It was little things at first. The apartment wasn't clean enough, and he would berate me. One morning, he deemed the jeans I chose for work were too tight and the top overly revealing. He blocked the door until I chose what he felt was appropriate clothing. The cycle continued for a while. He would do something or say something rude and destructive, but he would apologize profusely as soon as he arrived home from work. I could gauge how bad he felt by whether he came home with a gift or took me to dinner." I open my eyes slowly.

Jordan's expression is comforting. He's listening and controlling his temper at the same time. Not against me, but for me against Ramon. "You spilled something at one point," he prods.

"Yes. There was a time when he was laid off and money was tight on my wages alone. I spilled milk on the floor." My hands start to shake as if I'm in my dank apartment all over again instead of this serene spot near the water.

Jordan releases one hand and slides his to cup my face. His thumb moving along my cheek, I lean into his touch. This moment is the first time I've been unguarded with a man since I met Ramon. It's tender and in complete opposition to the feelings rushing through me. I know Ramon can't hurt me anymore, but the memories are powerful.

"It was the first time he physically assaulted me. His remorse was nearly immediate. He begged for forgiveness and nursed me back to health. For about a month following the incident, he turned back into the same guy he was at the beginning of our relationship. He treated me well and helped around the apartment since he was laid off."

"What triggered him next?"

"I'm sure you don't need to hear the rest, Jordan."

"I do. I can't avoid missteps if I don't know where they are."

"My reactions are on me, not you. Nothing about you concerns me for my safety."

His brow furrows, and he asks, "What about me gives you pause?"

"You're a nearly perfect example of the man I would create for myself if I could."

"Only nearly. What else do you need?" He winks at me.

I've never been affected by a man as much as him. I drop my head. It seems all I need to do is ask. If it can be accomplished, Jordan would pull it off. "I don't know everything yet. I need to leave some wiggle room. The information I know is beyond expectation."

"Fair enough. Will you share how you got out of your relationship and how you got to today?"

I organize my thoughts and share the rest of my sordid story. "I've learned it takes the average victim five attempts to leave their abuser. The first two times, I was dazed at the circumstance of my relationship, but didn't seek help. It was the third time for me. He arrived home at nearly 10:00 p.m., buzzed and belligerent. I attempted to coax him into bed to sleep it off. He mistook me removing his shirt for interest in sleeping with him. When I rebuffed his advances, he slapped me across the face and held me tightly against him. When he realized we were both still clothed, he set me on the floor, and I refused him again. He pinned me against the closet door and ripped—" Despite Jordan's comforting presence, my body tenses at the memory and chills race down my spine.

"Breathe, Alejandra. You needed medical attention from a professional?"

I'm grateful he's fine with a few blanks for now. I lower my head to his shoulder, and he pulls me against him, his strong arms holding me as close as he can and as tightly as possible. Close enough for me to feel his heart beating beneath my palm splayed on his sculpted chest. For the first time in a long time, I feel protected by a man and dangerously aroused.

He murmurs against my head, "You're safe with me."

"I know." I savor his crisp, fresh cologne before finishing my story. "Yes, it was the first time I sought medical intervention for my injuries. When he literally saw my blood on his hands, he ran out of the apartment. I crawled to the phone and called an ambulance." I don't miss him shudder as I share. "My nurse, Mel, was an angel. She knew the signs the moment I was wheeled into the emergency room. She convinced me to press charges and documented all my injuries."

"Where is he now?"

"In jail."

Jordan nods curtly. "Where he belongs. How did you get to Blackthorne?"

I sigh and add some space between our bodies. "I took a bunch of security-type jobs at a bank, at a mall, etc. Mel encouraged me to join her gym. It's for women who survive domestic violence. The classes were great, but not enough for me to keep my mind and body busy. The nights alone in my apartment were torturous. I applied to Blackthorne on a prayer."

"Did you not meet the qualifications?"

"I did. I was concerned recent life events would impact my hiring. Part of the application process is a deep, thorough background check."

"Understandable."

"I thought my history with Ramon would disqualify me somehow. Who would hire me to protect someone else when I couldn't protect myself? Jake and Connor interviewed me with care, and I shared most of what I told you with them and made my request about assignments. They hired me on the spot and recommended a local gym that hosts the same type of classes as Mel's in Texas. I teach classes when I'm not on assignment."

"How many people know about Ramon, the whole story?"

"Mel, Kim, and you. Well, you know more than they do. Only Mel knows the full extent of my injuries."

"Who's Kim?"

"She runs the local gym where I teach self-defense classes." I lean forward. He's a magnet for my heart and soul. Our lips are a mere hairsbreadth apart. I turn my head at the last second and set my forehead on his shoulder.

Jordan whispers, "What are you afraid of right now?" His hands move in opposite directions along my back.

Falling for both of you. "It's just... it's my job to protect Reese. I refuse to fail her because I miss something. I let my guard down when you're near me."

"Reese isn't here."

I lift my head and stare at his gorgeous face. He swipes the remnants of a few fallen tears from my cheeks. "Not now, but she was this morning."

"I'm drawn to you inexplicably more now. How I feel is impossible to ignore. Thank you for trusting me. You're more exceptional than I already thought. Please don't misunderstand my next statement. I want to date you. I want to build a relationship with you. I understand a relationship is complicated because you technically work for me. I don't want you to quit; you're amazing with Reese. She may like you more than she likes me."

I giggle softly.

"However, if I need to request an additional team member for you to feel comfortable to date me, I will."

"Jordan" is all I can manage before his soft lips skim across mine. The kiss is light and perfect. The small taste of him makes me yearn for more. Then I hear a crunching sound and extricate myself from Jordan's arms. I turn toward the noise and find Mr. Michelson approaching. "Hi, Ed." We rise to our feet.

Ed is similarly built as his son except for the gray hair and portly abdomen. "Alex, great to see you again."

"Jordan, please meet Connor's father."

Jordan extends his hand, and Ed takes it. "Pleasure."

"Likewise. I was just out for a lunchtime walk. Have a great afternoon."

"You as well. Please say hi to your wife for me," I request. In this moment, Jordan's story and his caseworker flash through my mind again. His story is eerily similar to Jill's. Considering it more deeply, so are his physical features.

"Will do." Ed continues past us and disappears around the bend of the shoreline.

"What do you say to lunch before we pick up Reese?" Jordan suggests.

"Okay."

He folds the blanket and returns it to the container. As he walks back, his smile hits me square in the chest. I take his offered arm, and we walk to the SUV. He holds open my door and waits for me to sit.

Jordan takes my hand in his. "Alejandra, will you at least consider going on a date with me?"

"Yes, I'll consider it."

"Thank you." He rounds the car and settles into the driver's seat.

We grab sandwiches in town and talk for over an hour until it's time to pick up Reese. While she regales Jordan with the highs and lows of her day, I take a call from Jake on the patio.

"What's up, Jake?"

"Hi, Alex. How is it going with Miss Devereaux?"

I laugh. "So formal. Reese is great. Principal Platt has been supportive and helpful so far."

"Good. Nothing new has popped up regarding Christie Wingate or Trey Edson. Based on Blaine's intel, Christie lives in Georgia, and her cell phone and credits cards have been used there in the last twenty-four hours. Nothing indicates her intentions to see her biological daughter any time soon. As far as Trey, there haven't been any new threats, and he seems to be all talk, but please remain vigilant when you are out and about."

"Understood. I have a potentially delicate statement.... When I spoke with Jordan about his early childhood, he mentioned a few things, and it's strikingly similar to Jill's story. He also stated his last caseworker's name was Joyce. I didn't press him. Blaine can determine if there's a connection, right? I don't know about Jordan yet, but Jill would want to know."

"Yes, she would. I can have him check discreetly and determine the best course after he finishes digging."

"Thanks, Jake."

"You're welcome. How are you, Alex?"

"I'm good." My words are a boldface, all-caps lie, but Jake doesn't need to know about my growing feelings for Jordan yet. Does he? *No.* "I appreciate you and Connor for giving me the choice to beg off this assignment. Taking it has helped me make progress."

"Glad to hear it. I'll contact you if anything comes up or I have pertinent information."

"Have a good night, Jake." I end the call and step back inside.

"Everything good?" Jordan asks.

"Yes."

He doesn't press, and we get started on cooking dinner while Reese tackles her homework at the dining room table. Jordan sets a cutting board and veggies in front of me, and I dutifully chop while he prepares the beef for dinner. It has been too long since I felt like part of a family. While Blackthorne offers a family-like atmosphere among its employees, Jordan and Reese could become my entire world.

CHAPTER TEN

JORDAN

A few days later, I'm still wrapped up in my observations of Alex and her brash survival to this point. She's exceptional. Not only does she see me, but she wants me and Reese. Alejandra never saw my bank account or my professional athlete status. She met Jordan and his amazing daughter.

"Dude, you good?" Ty slaps his hand on my shoulder.

"Yeah. Focused on our game." *Complete lie.*

"Is Little Miss attending?"

I shake my head. "No, she'll be at our first home game."

Ty replies, "Cool. Either way, I want to say hi."

"We can get together after the game for dinner," I suggest.

"What dinner?" Cam asks as he joins us near my locker.

"After our first home game, dinner out with Reese."

"Sweet. I can't wait to give her a huge hug."

I smile. These guys were always on my side with the Christie debacle during college. Hell, both watched Reese at times when I needed to meet my lawyer or attend a meeting with the coaching staff. "See you tomorrow."

"Later," they reply in unison.

I make my way through the gate and wave to Bill. The drive is uneventful. When I arrive home, I hear giggling coming from the kitchen.

I call out for my daughter and my... not accurate. Alejandra isn't mine... yet. "Reese. Alex." When I turn the corner, all laughter ceases. The island is a disaster. The sink is full of dishes, and there's a rack of something cooling to the right of the oven. "What kind of trouble are my ladies in today?" *My.* I said it, and I'm owning it.

Reese faux hugs me because her clothes are covered with smears of who knows what. "Hey, Dad. We made cookies, healthy cookies."

"I see. What makes them healthy?" My gaze is pinned on Alex while my daughter replies. The only thing different is the woman in my kitchen is the real Alejandra, unguarded and, dare I say, happy. "Hi," I mouth.

"Hi," she mouths back and tilts her head in Reese's direction.

"Right?"

I steal a quick glance at Alex who nods in agreement with my daughter's statement. "Right."

"We can try these after dinner," Alex suggests. "First, we need to clean this mess up, Reese."

"On it," she states and rushes past us to the cleaning supplies in the hall closet.

I step close enough to Alex that, if she were to take a deep breath, her breasts would skim my chest. "Hi. How was your day here?"

Goose bumps erupt on her arms from my proximity. "Good. I'm sure Reese will give you the rundown at dinner. How was practice?"

"Not too bad. We ran some plays half speed." An idea forms in my head. "You know what? How hungry are you?"

Alex raises her shoulders. "Not very."

"Reese, how hungry are you?"

My daughter rounds the corner with the cleaning supplies. "I'm not yet. Why?"

"What do you think about cleaning this up and teaching Alex about football in the backyard before we start dinner?"

Reese's eyes widen and double in size. "Oh yes! Let's do it!"

"Should I be scared?" Alex asks her.

"No, it's going to be fun. Are we teaching her plays and everything, Dad?"

"Yup."

"Sweet. Let's clean up fast." In less than twenty minutes, the kitchen is sparkling clean and we're heading outside to the large area of the yard beyond the pool.

"How much do you know about football, Alex?" Reese asks before I can.

"Basic stuff."

"Like what?" Reese presses.

"I understand the downs and some of the stats, like an interception or reception and how many points you get for a touchdown and a field goal," Alex replies.

"Not terrible." Reese grabs some pool noodles and lays them out to mark the endzone while I retrieve a football from the container on the patio. "'Kay. I'm going to be the quarterback and throw the ball to the wide receiver, aka Dad. You're going to be the cornerback and stop him from catching the ball."

I see concern cross Alex's face. Instead of allowing her to bow out, I extend a hand to her. "Come on. I'll show you where to line up." Her hand slides into mine, and I lead her about twenty yards away from Reese and the line of scrimmage. "What are you worried about?"

"There isn't a chance in hell I can cover you."

"Probably not, but it'll be fun to watch you try. You never know, I might simply allow you to tackle me."

"Why would you do that?"

I flash my signature grin at her. With my hands gripping her hips, I turn her to face Reese, hustle back, and line up.

"Ready, Alex?" Reese shouts.

"As ready as I'm going to be."

"Gators. One. Two. Hike."

I run a post route too far from my quarterback, and the pass falls two feet in front of me.

Alex is about two steps short of tackling me.

"What is that one called?" Alex asks.

"A post route," Reese informs her.

"Is there a chart or something?"

Reese chuckles.

I toss the ball back to Reese and walk Alex back to her position. "It's hot as hell you want a route chart."

A faint blush creeps onto her gorgeous face. "Football is important to you. It won't be fast, but I would like to learn."

"Not nearly as important as you and Reese."

Her steps falter slightly after registering my words.

"I probably have a spare in my office. If not, I'll draw one out for you."

Alex's gaze is toward the grass. "Thanks."

"Think you can catch me this time?" I goad her.

"I'll do my best."

"Reese, same play."

The play will give Alex a head start of sorts since she knows where I'm going to end up.

My daughter beams over at me as I take my spot. "Gators. One. Two. Hike."

I take off and run the same route a tiny bit shallower this time and catch the pass from Reese. As I secure the ball, Alex's arm slides along my waist, but she doesn't stop in time. She glides past me and falls to the grass. With a flick of my wrist, I toss the ball back to Reese, then help Alex up.

We spend the next hour showing Alex different routes and running plays I three of us laughing and having a blast. As we near the end of our impromptu football session, Alex successfully tackles me at the end of a slant route. I miss the ball completely, and we roll twice on the lawn. You would think winning my sports biggest game is the highest I've ever felt. It isn't. Seeing Reese happy in life is the best feeling I've ever felt until this moment right here. Having Alex caged beneath me, her eyes pinned to mine, and her curves against me is beyond comprehension. She ties Reese without question. "Are you okay?"

"No."

I frown and raise an eyebrow at her.

"I was going for the interception."

I laugh and lower my mouth near her ear. "I want to kiss you right now."

"We have an audience," Alex reminds me.

"I wanted you to know."

She exhales slowly. "When you have an appropriate opportunity, you should take it."

Surprised at her words, I pull back to fully look at her face. Before I can respond, Reese charges up beside us.

"Are you hurt, Alex?"

I rock back onto my heels, to my feet, and extend my hand to her.

"Just my pride, Reese." She takes my hand.

I steady her in front of me before slowly drawing my hand away.

"No worries. You made great progress today, and you didn't give up. That's most important," she offers.

"Are you sure about her age?" Alex questions me.

"Yes. She's wise beyond her years."

Reese giggles. "You taught me, Dad."

"I suppose I did. Dinner, ladies?"

"Yes! I'm starving!"

Alex laughs. "Are you both always hungry?"

We both emphatically answer, "Yes!"

After a delicious stir-fry dinner, Reese suggests the next Harry Potter movie since Alex finished the first two books. With popcorn and water, the three of us curl up on the couch.

Their attention is rapt on the screen. It allows me to focus on Alex longer than I would normally be able to with Reese present. Her words replay in my head. *When you have an appropriate opportunity, you should take it.* I would prefer to create an opportunity rather than stumble upon one. Yet a public date with Alex isn't likely anytime soon. A plan forms in my mind how to court Alex properly and respectfully, keeping in mind her job and her fears. Now, I need to ask her. Perhaps I won't call it a date, but time alone with her.

Reese is sound asleep in the chair before the movie ends.

"What did you think?" I whisper.

"It's close to the picture I have in my head."

"I agree. Are you free on Tuesday?"

Her nose crinkles up. It's cute and endearing. "I'm teaching a class after I drop off Reese. Then I'm free."

A small hitch, but not unrecoverable. "Can I come with you?"

"No." Her response is harsh and unwavering.

"Oh." I drop my head.

Her small hand slides along my jaw, tilting it upward. "I would welcome you, but you can't. The class is for women only. It makes the newer students feel safe knowing there are no men around. Not even Kim's husband, the co-owner of the gym, is there at those times."

"I understand. Can we—"

Her hand slides away from my face. Instantly, I miss her warmth on my skin.

"I missed it?" Reese sits up and rubs her eyes.

"You've seen it at least ten times, peanut."

She stretches and turns her attention to Alex. "True. What did you think?"

"I liked it. Close to what I imagined while I was reading. Can you lend me the next two in the morning?"

"Sure." She rises from her seat and hugs us both. "Good night. Have a great game, Dad, in case I sleep in tomorrow."

"Thanks. Night."

"Good night, Reese," Alex offers as my daughter shuffles toward her bedroom. Then she turns back to me. "Please finish your question."

"Will you hang out with me after your class?"

"Yes."

I lean closer and press a kiss to her forehead. "Thank you."

She takes a settling breath and replies, "You're welcome."

Drawing back slightly, I catch her staring at my mouth. "Alejandra." I slide my hand up her arm, around her neck, and eliminate nearly all space between us. I lean forward and anticipate feeling her lips against mine for the second time.

"Dad," Reese calls.

My shoulders sink. "I'm sorry."

"Don't be. We have plenty of time."

Reluctantly, I walk down the hall to see what Reese needs. Nearly twenty minutes later, I return.

"Is she okay?"

"Yeah. I forgot about our pregame ritual. She reminded me."

"Which is?"

"We pick apart the other's teams defense and look for weaknesses I can exploit."

"Oh." A note of rejection is present in her voice.

"You're welcome to join us next week."

She lifts her shoulder in question. "I may not be much help, but I would like to join you."

"Will you sit outside with me for a little while?"

"Sure." She checks the locks again before following me to the patio.

I flick on the firepit and settle into the corner of the couch with open arms. With only a hint of reluctance, Alex nestles against me. "What are you worried about?"

"Failing at my job because I'm interested in seeing what we could have."

"I meant what I said. I can talk to Jake on Monday."

Her eyes widen. "No, it'll only diminish the time we have alone together, which is already in short supply. Plus, I don't want to make more changes for Reese."

"What do you recommend?"

"Slow and steady progress for all of us."

"I can work with progress. If you need to get backup, let me know."

"I will," she replies.

We stay snuggled together until it's time to turn in. I know it's soon, but watching Alex disappear into her room strikes differently tonight. I want to spend every free minute with her—including sound asleep.

CHAPTER ELEVEN

ALEJANDRA

The first preseason game is in the books. Jordan and his teammates lost. Reese shared it isn't a big deal. She explained the starters only played the first quarter. At the end of the first quarter, the team was ahead fourteen to zero. By the end of the game, they lost by six.

We finished training this morning, and I hurried through the shower.

Jordan joins me in the kitchen. He verifies Reese is still in her room before pressing a quick kiss to my cheek. "Morning."

His lips are soft, and I want more. So much more. *Baby steps, Alex.* "Morning. I made coffee."

"Thanks. I'm grabbing breakfast with Cam and Ty at the facility."

Reese rounds the corner, and I find myself backing away from him. "When can I see them?"

"I think we're going out for dinner after the first home game."

"Yay! You're going to love them, Alex. Cam is huge and funny. Ty is a prankster. Be prepared."

"Noted." A dinner out with his teammates? "We should talk about those details when you get home tonight, Jordan."

"Sure, no problem. I gotta go. Have a great day at school, Reese."

"You too, Dad."

"Bye, Alex."

I wave at his back, and he's gone. "We have about twenty minutes before we need to leave, Reese."

"No problem. I'm ready except for breakfast."

I wander over to the large window near the front of the house and stare outside while sipping my coffee. Truthfully, I'm processing the inner turmoil I feel. I wanted to kiss him goodbye. *First, you should probably kiss him properly and thoroughly.* Daydreaming about Jordan isn't a good idea right now. *Focus on your job.* The tug I feel between being prepared for Reese and how Jordan makes me believe I'm worthy of him is heavy. Pulling myself out of my head, I rinse my cup and bring Reese to school.

"Have a great day, Reese."

She hugs me and rushes down the hall, her words trailing behind her. "You too. See you later."

I make my way to the SUV and to the office right on time for the morning meeting. "Hey, Gemma."

"Hi, Alex. How's it going with Mr. Devereaux?"

"He isn't my client. His daughter is."

She has a dreamy look on her face. I completely understand. Jordan is disgustingly easy on the eyes. His arms were made for holding me, and I want to allow myself to believe every word he says. It isn't on him. It's on me.

She shrugs as Connor calls me into the conference room. "Morning."

"Morning, Connor." I greet the rest of the team and slide into the chair beside Maia.

"Hey, girl. We need to catch up after this meeting."

I nod and focus on the boss men. Frankly, I don't need to be here. I'm assigned to Reese until my presence is no longer necessary. It's been nearly six weeks, and I can't imagine not sharing space with them. One of my biggest fears realized. I care about both of them.

"Does anyone have any issues to be addressed?" Christoph asks.

"I might," I state.

Silence blankets the room.

"Everyone is dismissed except Alex."

Maia leans closer and whispers, "I'll grab you a coffee and meet you next door."

"Thanks. You're the best."

She smiles and replies, "I know." With a soft chuckle, she heads out.

After everyone leaves, I speak. "Christoph."

"Hey. I wanted to see how you're doing with the assignment."

"It was a step toward personal progress for me. Reese is awesome."

Connor asks, "What about Mr. Devereaux?"

"What about him?" *Easy, Alex. Let's not tip our hand so soon.* "He's a great dad and consummate professional."

"Good. What is the issue to be discussed?"

"Jordan wants Reese to attend as many home games as possible, at least the 1:00 p.m. and 4:00 p.m. starts. There's one in the evening, which she'll likely not attend. Will Cruz still be joining us?"

"Yes. He'll meet you and Reese at the house and join you at the home games," Connor answers.

"Fine. I'll work out the details of travel and arrival with Jordan and then Cruz beforehand. Also, Jordan plans to take Reese out for dinner with a few of his teammates after the first home game. He indicated they were teammates in college and Reese wants to see her "uncles" as well. Do you think additional personnel will be necessary?"

"Which teammates?" Jake inquires.

"Cameron Beau and Tyson Beck."

Jake flips open the file in his hand and scans the associates page. Each Blackthorne client file includes a check on those the principal foresees himself or herself spending time with while working with the company. "We checked out both when Jordan hired us. My only concern would be photographers, although they've seemed to back off since his arrival."

"I agree. I'll check with Jordan where he plans to go and see if there's a private space or at least a private entrance the guys can use."

"If he hasn't selected a place and he's open to suggestion, Bistro on Bank and Chez Michel have worked well in the past," Christoph offers.

"I'll talk to him tonight and let you know. Also, I'll touch base with Cruz about the home games as it gets closer. I have a little more time as the first regular season game is away."

"Anything else?" Jake asks.

"Not at this time." A sliver of guilt stabs through me. Then I remind myself nothing has happened... yet.

"Perfect. I'll keep you in the loop when Blaine finishes your request," Jake shares.

"Thanks. See you next week." I wave to Gemma as I pass by and hurry next door to meet Maia.

"I didn't wait for you to drink my coffee," she admits. "Everything okay?"

"Yeah. Jordan has a few outings he wants to take Reese on, and I wanted to get their opinion on whether we need additional security."

"Jordan, huh?"

I've never been able to hide my feelings from Maia. "He very well may be perfect."

"Did you…?"

"Did I what?"

Maia rolls her eyes.

I answer to avoid her filling the blanks herself. "I shared about Ramon. The entire story, more than I told the boss men."

"I'm proud of you. How did he take it?"

I am too. "Thanks. Better than I expected. His response falls into the too-good-to-be-true category."

"Meaning?"

"He asked me on a date."

Glee casts on my friend's face. "Did you say yes?"

"Not exactly."

"Oh, Alex. The man is smoking hot, a great dad, he knows your darkest personal secret, and he wants to date you. What is holding you back?"

"Reese."

"You have a problem with him being a single dad?"

I shake my head furiously. "No. Not even a little. Reese is smart, intuitive, and fun. I don't want to fail her because I'm interested in Jordan too."

"I see. If anyone would understand, it would be the bosses. Connor fell for Callie while he was assigned as her security. Christoph and Jake were slightly different, but the outcome is the same."

"You don't think I'm crazy for wanting to say yes?" *I already agreed to spend time with him tomorrow, but it isn't a date. Is it?*

"No, not at all."

"Enough about me for now. How as the engagement party? Did you let Nolan out of the friend zone?"

Maia blushes something fierce.

"Ohmigod! Did you?"

"Maybe," she buries her face in her hands.

I scan the room, mostly for Norah, but she would keep Maia's business to herself either way. "You slept with Nolan?"

Maia doesn't answer the question immediately, then lifts her head. "Things got complicated. His family assumed we're a couple. His hand in mine and his arms around me while we were dancing at the party were so...."

"Why didn't you call me? How did you and Nolan leave everything?"

"I need to handle the ramifications with him. I haven't seen him since we got back. He went out on assignment with Angelica Swisher for a few months."

"Have you talked to him?"

"Yes, but it's strained."

"Strained isn't unfixable. Do you want to fix it?"

"Yes."

"Do you want to do it again?"

Maia's olive skin turns a darker shade of red. "Unequivocally, yes."

"All right. Does he feel the same?"

"I'm not sure."

I hug my roomie. "You know what you have to do."

"I'm terrified."

"Why?"

"Not only were we miles beyond what I've felt before, I don't want to lose my best friend."

"Aside from talking to him while he's gone, you need to make sure he knows you want to discuss things as soon as he gets home."

"I know. Doesn't make it any less scary though."

"I love you, Maia, but it's Nolan. He's your best guy friend. You two can figure anything out."

Maia smiles. "Thanks. Love you too. Now, back to Mr. Devereaux. You need to own your attraction to him and figure out how to separate your feelings for him and your duty to Reese."

"Is it that simple?"

"In my opinion, yes."

Upon Maia finishing her answer, Norah breezes into the store with Ben in a stroller. "Morning."

Maia and I greet her in unison. Ben waves his chubby little hand at us.

"Are you here for Reese's order?" Norah asks me.

"Jordan didn't mention it, but I'll take it with me."

Norah tilts her head in interest. "Jordan? Not Mr. Devereaux?"

"Mr. Devereaux prefers I call him Jordan."

"Not buying it, Alex. Can't blame you though. He's gorgeous and, from what I can tell, an amazing father."

"True," Maia chimes in.

"Girls' night soon, so the bonds of secrecy apply, yes?" Norah asks.

"Yes," we reply at once.

"I need to get going. I need to run a few errands before picking up Reese," I inform them.

"Think about what I said," Maia states.

"Same, girl, same." I hug her tight, then Norah, and pinch Ben's cheeks before leaving the store with Reese's stack of new books.

I hurry through the department store and grab a few new items I need for the upcoming events Jordan wants to attend. Leggings and graphic tees aren't going to work for a football game or a fancy dinner out. I assume the dinner is fancy and the suits I have aren't going to work.

I park at the school and wait for thirty minutes rather than drive home for ten. While I wait, my phone rings. The caller ID concerns me. *Jordan.*

"Hello. Is everything okay?"

"Yes. I have a short break, and I wanted to talk to you."

"About?" A video chat request pops up on the screen, and I accept.

"Hi."

"Hi."

"Nothing specific. I wanted to see your face."

Holy hell! This is what being courted feels like. I like it... a lot. I can't contain my smile and unconsciously look away from him.

"Alejandra, where did your thoughts go?"

I love the way my name sounds when he says it. "It isn't important right now. We can talk about it later."

Jordan smiles before he says, "Every thought you have is important, and I want to hear them all."

"I'll share with you tonight or tomorrow. I picked up Reese's books this morning."

"Okay. Thanks. Don't you need to go in to get her?"

I glance at the clock. "I have two more minutes. Principal Platt isn't keen on extra people loitering in the building."

"Okay. I'll be home at regular time."

"We'll see you later." I end the call and take the remaining minute to settle the butterflies in my stomach. Jordan Devereaux is a force of nature. Also, he isn't playing a part. He's being himself. I really like who he is and how he makes me feel. Honestly, no man has merely wanted to say hello without an agenda. I suppose Jordan has an agenda, namely a date or fifty, but I'm coming around to his page quickly. Maia's advice is sound. I can separate protecting Reese and my feelings for Jordan. I hope.

CHAPTER TWELVE

JORDAN

I pull along the curb in front of a nondescript concrete building on the outskirts of Crescent Bay. We decided it made the most sense for me to drop Alex off after bringing Reese to school. I didn't want to skip it, and taking two vehicles didn't make sense either. "I'll be back in a little over an hour to pick you up."

"Okay," she replies, her voice shaky and uncertain.

I curl my hand around her wrist and immediately pull it back. I won't hurt her, but I'm still learning what actions might trigger responses from her. Pinning her to a door is definitely a no-go option. "What are you worried about?"

"I'm not used to being able to rely on others, especially men."

I lift her hand to my mouth. "Consider this morning my first test. Have a good class."

She leans closer and presses a chaste kiss to my lips and slides out of the SUV. "Thank you."

"For what?"

"Being exactly who you said you were."

"I'll prove it every day. Go teach others your brave ways."

She smiles and closes the passenger door.

I drive a short distance to a grocery store and pick up a few things for our… date. I'm not sure Alex would consider today a date. I would like to, but pushing my luck isn't a solid plan. Although dinner after the game will be a public outing for the three of us, not exactly a date. I don't care what she calls it. If she wants to call it hanging out or whatever is fine as long as I learn more about her.

I make my way back to the gym, park across the street, and wait for her class to finish. She exits the building slightly more than an hour later with two other women. After a quick chat, she crosses the street. I hustle around the SUV to open her door.

"Thanks."

I round the front of the truck and grin at her. I notice the two women she was chatting with are watching us. I reach into the back seat, produce a single red-tipped rose, and give it to Alex.

"Thank you." She lifts the flower to her nose.

"You're welcome. How was class?"

She doesn't answer. I wait a few moments in the uncomfortable silence.

Instead of pulling away from the curb, I twist to face her. "Did I overstep?"

Alex turns in my direction. "No. I'm reconciling how we feel with how I thought a relationship should feel."

I cover her hand with mine and curl my fingers between hers. "How do you feel right now?"

A fierce blush overtakes her flawless skin. "I'm not sure… a mixture of happy and cared for, I guess."

"I do care about you."

Her head drops. "I know. You've been showing me. You have been since I moved in by ordering chocolate dessert before you could've known it's my favorite or making me breakfast. It's just…."

"You can say anything. I'll take it at face value."

She exhales sharply. "Ramon was like this in the beginning too." She shifts her gaze out the window.

I squash the urge to defend myself. Mistreating women, any woman, but especially her considering the trust she gave me sharing her story, will never happen. She just needs time to trust her gut again.

"I'm sorry. I've ruined your sweet gesture."

"Alejandra, please look at me." She meets my gaze. "You didn't ruin anything. I have the desire and means to give you anything and everything you could ever want. This"—I point to the single rose—"is significantly pared down from what I wanted to give you. I will never do anything to break your trust in me. You're going to have to stick around and allow me to show you my word is unwavering."

"I've never met anyone like you. I care about you. Reese too. Thank you for being patient with me."

"You're welcome." I press a light kiss to the tip of her nose. "Ready to have some fun?"

She raises an eyebrow but doesn't object. I pull away from the curb and drive home.

"What are we going to do here?"

I smirk at her. "You sound skeptical."

"No, not exactly."

"We're going to have a little competition, and I won't go easy on you. Although I thought of a flaw in my plan."

"Which is?"

"Do you have a swimsuit here and do you know how to swim?"

She wrinkles her nose. "Yes, I can swim quite well actually."

"Good. Any other hidden talents I should know about?"

"A girl needs to keep an air of mystery."

"I want to learn all your secrets, Alejandra. Competition starts in fifteen minutes."

She laughs and hurries down the hall. I make my way outside and toss ten colored rings into the pool randomly for our first game. My intention was to have fun, not for the opportunity to see Alex in a bathing suit. I'm considering it a bonus. It's a plum-colored two-piece. The top has two ties that cross over her taut belly and tie in the middle of her lower back. Damn! She's gorgeous. It isn't a new observation, but her exposed skin and curves make my mouth as arid as a desert.

"How do I win this competition?" she asks after setting a colorful towel on the chaise.

I laugh and explain the rules. As I do, Alex circles the pool. I'm more mesmerized by her toned legs than what she's doing and why. "Ready to lose?"

"What do I get when I win?" She's awfully confident.

I shrug. "Bragging rights, I guess."

"Okay. Let's do this!" Her excitement leads me to believe I'm about to lose handily. I'm man enough to admit defeat... if necessary.

The smile on her face is worth each loss she handed to me over the three rounds of the game. The first round, she scooped up eight rings in one smooth pass along the bottom of the pool. I got a late start because my focus was on her assets diving beneath the surface rather than the game. Round two, I fared better, but she still won. The third round she won six to four.

With three rings hanging around each wrist, she joins me near the edge of the pool. "You know I only have one person I trust to brag to, maybe two."

"Reese will believe you, mostly because I let her win at this game. You on the other hand, I tried, and you schooled me."

"It can be our little secret if you want." She's in a class all her own. "Do you have more games in mind?"

"Sure, plenty, but I would rather talk instead."

"About?"

"You."

"One for one, like last time. Deal?"

"Deal."

She wades over to the stairs and climbs out of the pool.

I should be respectful and look away, but she's tempting. As mightily as I try, I simply can't avert my eyes. Running the playbook in my mind or the names of my coaches since high school isn't working either.

"Jordan."

My name filters through my brain. "Yes?"

The expression on her face tells me not only did she catch me ogling her, but she isn't offended either. Her hands stretch out in my direction and her stance staggers for balance. I'll take any offered opportunity to touch her. I set one foot on the edge of the pool and assist in pulling myself out. The sliver of space between us is electric with potential. Her head tilts upward, and her mouth opens as she exhales. As much as I want to kiss her breathless, I need to wait for her to initiate.

I take a seat in the corner of the couch with one foot on the stamped patio blocks and the other against the back cushion. I open my arms to her, and she carefully nestles into me. Her sun-warmed skin feels decadent beneath my palms as I skim along her arm.

"You go first," she offers.

"What was your favorite tradition when your parents were alive?"

She shifts in my arms so she can watch my expression before answering, my hand now resting at the nip of her waist. "The bodega never made a ton of money. We had what we needed, but not many extras. On our birthday, we were able to choose any item from the local department store with seemingly no budget. I don't know about Miguel, but I never spent more than thirty dollars. It meant we truly needed or wanted what we selected."

"That's unique."

"My parents were best friends and understood connection is key in every type of relationship."

"I agree with them. I would have liked to meet them. How often do you see your brother?"

"Two questions?"

"Fine, you can have two in a row."

"Miguel is in the army. He's stationed in Texas not far from where we grew up. I saw him at Christmas."

"It was a long time ago."

"Yeah, it was."

"You miss him?"

"Three, going for three?"

I laugh. "Sorry. I want to learn everything, and you're easy to talk to."

"It's a bit complicated. I miss my brother, but when everything happened with Ramon, he was deployed. Things changed between us then. Miguel blames himself for not being there for me, for not protecting me despite the numerous times I reminded him Ramon was at fault and no one else."

"I didn't know you then, but I'm crazy proud of you for fighting your way out of that relationship."

"Thank you. Three questions. Let's see. Have you created any traditions that aren't centered on your job for Reese?"

"We don't have anything unique to us. I am the parent who gets matching pajamas for Christmas morning."

"Really? Seriously cute."

"Yup. Cute, huh? I made boot prints leading up to the tree from the fireplace at our old house."

"This doesn't count as a question, but does she still believe?"

I grin at her. "She hasn't come out and told me she doesn't believe any longer. I'm grateful she plays along though. What else you got for me, Alejandra?"

She shifts onto her heels between my legs. I'm nervous I said something inappropriate. I race through the last few sentences and come up empty.

"Will you repeat that?"

Her full name is an aphrodisiac for her, at least when I say it. "Alejandra."

She sets her hands on my chest, eliminates the space between us, and wets my lips with her tongue.

Holy hell! She's sexy as... The air around us is charged, and the temperature rises to a thousand degrees. If the move wasn't enough, she tugs my lower lip between her teeth before melding her lips to mine. My fingers dig into the flare of her luscious hips, and I'll happily respond to whatever she wants to do. While my instinct is to cage her beneath me and travel down her body, my brain is slowing me down exponentially.

She pulls back quickly. Trepidation mars her beautiful face.

A sight I don't like at all.

"Did I misread you?" she asks quietly.

"No, not at all."

"But...?"

I look skyward for a few seconds and slide my hands away from her. "A few things in no particular order. I haven't kissed anyone in a long time. I'm nervous how you might respond to me if I were to act instinctively. Also, I'm attempting to avoid any more missteps today."

She presses a kiss to my forehead, then takes my hands and places them on her hips before stealing nearly all the space between us. "I refuse to utter his name in this moment. Though I will share the violent aspects of my previous relationship didn't impact my sex life. I trust you. Kiss me, Jordan, as if I were a normal woman."

"You're exceptional, Alejandra." I flatten one hand on her back and slowly move to hover over her. The initial press of my lips on hers is tentative but warm and still explosive. She was placed in my path to set my soul on fire.

A soft moan spills from her mouth before my tongue tangles with hers. Her hands drift down my chest and around my sides before marking my back with crescent marks from her fingernails. With one hand, I tilt her head to allow me to travel along her jaw and over the slope of her neck.

Alex attempts to squirm away, but she's trapped by my hips. The friction is more than I'm prepared to handle.

I see you. I continue along the strap of her top and mark the curve of her breast with kisses. When she tenses beneath me, I retreat and look at her. "Please share."

Her hand presses on my chest.

I bend my knees and push to kneeling in front of her. The warmth of her momentarily short-circuits my brain.

"I have scars."

"So do I."

Her head moves left to right slowly. "I mean physical ones in addition to the emotional ones."

"So do I."

She pauses again.

"You mean from him."

"Yes."

"Do you need me to stop?" I ask, willing to do whatever she needs.

"No."

"Alejandra, do you want me to stop?"

"No. I wanted you to be aware."

I kiss her lips tenderly and draw her onto my lap. The heat of her core is evident through the damp swim trunks, which do absolutely nothing to mask her effect on me. I draw the strap of her top down her arm and follow with my tongue. I squash the anger I feel toward Ramon when I see scars of what appear to be cigarette burn marks along the outside of her breast. I press a kiss to each one and circle her aroused nipple with my tongue. Her fingers bruise my sides.

"You good?"

She nods.

"I need words, sweetheart."

"I'm more than good."

I smile against her skin and continue my quest to explore her from head to toe. Each kiss and nibble I bestow on her otherwise flawless skin feels like progress. Each whimper of pleasure allows me deeper in this relationship with her. The valley between her perfect breasts is a sweet spot, as well as the point of her hip. As I drag my tongue along the seam of her bikini bottoms, an alarm blares from the table.

Whispered and laced with desire, my name falls from her lips. "Jordan. We need to go."

I hastily trace a path upward to her lips with my tongue. "I'm not done exploring you."

She tugs her lower lip between her teeth. "I don't want you to be, but we need to pick up Reese from school."

I groan and reluctantly dress, which ends our alone time together for the near future.

CHAPTER THIRTEEN

ALEJANDRA

After school drop-off, I make my way to Millie's for chocolates for Reese. Her birthday is tomorrow. Her other gift arrived a few days ago. I scan the cases and select a few options. I would get her books, but Jordan already did.

Jordan.

The man is beyond words. He's sexy as hell, smart, an amazing father, and incredibly patient with me. Jordan has committed to mastering each spot and curve on my body that will make me moan with pleasure. I'm completely on board. Unfortunately, we only had so much time yesterday. Also, we haven't discussed how, when, or if we're sharing anything with Reese. I haven't given many men the opportunity to know me. In fairness, only one since Ramon went to jail, but Jordan is different.

With Reese's gift in hand, I stop next door at the small market for the ingredients to make a cake for her as well as candles. With the necessities in hand, I settle into the driver's seat and head toward home.

On the way, I get a call from Jake. "Where are you?"

Panic courses through me. "What's wrong?"

"It isn't Reese."

A pit grows in my stomach. He was never worried about himself.

Jake continues, "Team security alerted me about a package sent to Jordan at the facility. Christoph and Cruz are on the way there. Jill has eyes on Reese, but I need you to go back to the school and monitor the building. Platt knows you're on your way. Please do your best not to alarm Reese."

"Does Jordan know any of this yet?"

"Security plans to alert him when Christoph and Cruz arrive."

I take a sharp U-turn before answering. "Okay. Is it Trey, Christie, or something else?"

"Undetermined at this time."

"Got it."

"Thanks, Alex."

I end the call and focus on the road. As much as I don't want to scare Reese, if she sees me during the day, the outcome will be exactly the same. I consider my options, pull into the spot closest to the main entrance, and make a measured trip around the exterior of the building. I'm more concerned about people attempting to get into the building than Reese leaving. Additionally, it's comforting Jill is inside and has seen her since this incident started. My level of worry hasn't decreased, so I slow my speed and pace the grounds of the school. My phone rings as I round the last corner with a call from Jordan.

"Are you back at the school?" he asks.

"Yes. I'm making a second perimeter sweep."

"You didn't go inside first?" His tone sounds accusatory.

"No, Jill talked to her within two minutes of the call from the facility. I don't want to scare her unnecessarily. She's perfectly safe in the building."

"I'm sorry."

"No apologies necessary. Your fears are legitimate, especially today. She's the center of your world and this location terrifies you."

"Thank you. I need to go. Please...." His words are strangled and pleading. It's heartbreaking and haunting to hear.

"I've got her, Jordan." Protecting Reese is as important to me as it is to him. I shouldn't be surprised; she's amazing. I finish my second trip around the building and lean against the SUV for a little while.

Christoph: There's no immediate threat to Reese.

Me: Understood.

Christoph: The package was from her mother. Please bring Reese to the house immediately after school.

Me: Will do.

Christoph: Ideally, I'll be able to keep Jordan away from the school.

Me: Good luck! He's crazy protective.

Christoph: I understand how he feels, and Liz is an infant. We'll need to meet either at the office or his house later today.

Me: Got it. Thanks for the update.

I exhale and make my way inside the building. Her schedule indicates she should be in the cafeteria. I scan the room for Reese and come up empty. A second and third pass yield the same results. Fear grips me. Did

I miss something? I can't fail them. *Her*. *Them*. I scan the room assignments and make my way to where her next class meets. As suspected, the room is empty. My worry ratchets up another notch or two. I orient myself in the building again and make my way to Jill's classroom. After a light knock on the door, Jill waves me in.

Reese greets me first. "Hi, Alex. What are you doing here?" It takes her only one breath. "Is Dad okay?"

"Yup. Your dad is fine. I'm just sweeping the building."

Jill nods behind Reese, partly reassurance and partly kudos for my diplomatic answer.

"'Kay." She cleans up her trash and zips her lunchbox closed. A faint bell rings. "Time for me to go. Thank you, Mrs. Cruz."

"You're welcome, Reese."

Reese throws her arms around me, and I hug her tight. Then she rushes out the door.

Jill verifies the door is closed before speaking. "Do you have an update?"

"There was a package from Reese's mom. The guys are handling it. Thank you for checking on her."

Jill waves off my praise. "No problem. She's great."

"She is."

"Falling for her already, huh?"

I smile. "How could I not? She's smart, precocious, has a deep love of books, and her take on life is refreshing."

"True. What about her father?"

I consider my response too long.

"You don't have to answer. With the amount of information I have, Jordan seems to have had a rough early life. He's an amazing father. There's something about him. I can't pinpoint what it is, but—"

The door to her classroom flies open. Her aide and students file in.

"That's my cue. Thanks again."

"Bye, Alex."

I'm grateful for the reprieve—aside from being unsure how I feel about Jordan. *Not true.* I care about both. How we handle it is another matter. Also, I refuse to share information I know because Jordan told me or I read it in his file. It was hard enough sharing my hunch with Jake.

I stroll the hallways and check the emergency exits. Afterward, I exit through the main entrance and sweep the perimeter again. My phone vibrates in my hand as I lean against the stone pillar near the base of the main stairs.

Jordan: I'm sorry.

Oh, my heart. This man feels deeply. He hides it from those around him extremely well. Except Reese... and me.

Me: Nothing to be sorry for.

Jordan: I need you to know that I trust you.

Me: I know.

Jordan: I'm at the office. I'll be home as soon as possible. Ideally with a plan to handle Christie.

Me: We'll be there when you arrive. I'll hold off dinner as long as I can.

Jordan: You're... thank you.

Part of me wonders what he wanted to say. The rest knows he isn't alone.

Me: You're welcome.

Nearly thirty minutes later, the bell rings. Reese greets me with another hug at the main entrance.

"How was the rest of your day?"

"Fine."

We round the SUV, and she climbs into the back seat. The ride home is unusually quiet. Reese typically spills her school day in painstaking detail.

"Are you okay, Reese?" I should've known from her response. Fine is never fine no matter how old a woman is.

She shakes her head. "Did you lie to me?"

I consider pulling over, but I know it's not the best plan. Also, doing so is against protocol. "No. I will never lie to you." I hand my phone back to her. "Call your dad."

I wait patiently until he answers.

"Dad?" A pause while he answers her. "Yes, she's driving me home." Pause. "I just wanted to say hi. Love you to the moon."

I hear him reply in my head. *I love you to the moon and back.* She hands my phone back to me. "Feel better?"

"Yes, I'm sorry for accusing you."

My heart constricts. Both of them feel deeply. "I understand. You were worried. I promise I will never lie to you."

"Why is Dad worried about this area? It has to be more than it's where he's from."

Damn! "You're the most important person in the world to your father. He should answer your question, not me."

"Fine." She crosses her arms over her chest and is silent the remainder of the ride.

I consider my options: press her more or wait her out. I decide to wait for Jordan to get home. He needs to explain his fears and reasoning for them to his daughter. It isn't my place. Pulling into the garage, I close the door behind us. Reese hops out, chucks her shoes near the door, and disappears down the hall to her room.

I rummage through the fridge and set some turkey burgers to defrost. Slightly more than an hour later, I hear the garage door open. Expeditiously, I step into the garage, hoping to talk to Jordan before Reese.

He slides to the floor and stops at the foot of the small staircase. His arms curl around my waist and draw me close. His kiss is possessive and hot. He's letting his emotion pour from his mouth.

Hesitantly, I add some space between us. His hands rest at my waist. "As much as I would like to kiss you indefinitely, we need to talk about Reese."

"Is she okay?"

I cup his face with my hands and press a sweet kiss to his lips. "She's physically fine, but she was asking questions."

"About?"

"She asked why you were worried about this area."

Jordan shudders with fear.

"I didn't break my agreement with you. I told her she needed to talk to you."

The door between the house and the garage whips open. *Crap!* With smooth ease, Jordan shifts around me and climbs the steps. Ideally, Reese didn't see his hands on me—a topic it appears he and I need to talk about and soon.

"Hey, peanut."

Reese squeezes him tight before he can step into the house. After a solid minute, Reese releases him and allows us into the house. "Is everything okay, Dad?"

"It will be," Jordan offers in response.

"What do you mean?"

Jordan pauses for a few moments. "Why don't you wash up so we can get started on dinner? I'll answer you and share about today's issue with you."

Without a word, she takes off down the hall.

He turns to face me fully. "I'll share with her and give you more details later. We also need to talk about how we're going to work."

I nod and attempt to push away the gnawing feeling in my gut. My feelings must be written on my face. Jordan takes my hand and leads me into his office to decrease the chance we'll be overheard. "You're walking a thin tightrope. I want to set up some boundaries. Although I think you unknowingly set some today by asking Reese to talk to me first. I appreciate you and your discretion. Talking about how we're going to work is not a fancy way to say I want to stop exploring what we could have. You and me and the three of us."

My eyes flutter closed, and I exhale slowly. I don't need to open my eyes to feel Jordan without touching him. I can feel his proximity, and I'm not ready to give it up.

"Alejandra, open your eyes."

I comply.

"I care about you. We'll figure out how to make this work. If we need to come clean to Jake and Connor, we will."

I attempt to defend my reasons for not sharing yet, but then again Jill saw right through me today despite holding her tongue. "I agree to talking for now."

"Okay. Let's go cook and talk to Reese. Then later you and I will talk more in depth about Christie and about us." He presses a light kiss to my lips and leaves me in his office.

CHAPTER FOURTEEN

JORDAN

I leave my office and join Reese in the kitchen. How much of the truth do I plan to share with my daughter? I knew this day would come, but I didn't think it would be so soon. I suppose Christie is pushing the revelation with her package.

"What can I do, Dad?"

I scan the ingredients we have in the fridge and the defrosting turkey burgers. "Think you can cut the sweet potatoes into fries?"

Other than her hair being darker and curly, Reese is a carbon copy of me right down to her sparkling blue eyes. "Piece of cake."

Alex joins us in the kitchen a few minutes later. I watch her until she acknowledges me. "How can I help?"

"The only thing left is the fixins for the burgers, the rolls, and setting the table," I share.

"On it."

Reese laughs as she finishes peeling the sweet potatoes.

I start the conversation with my daughter and steel myself for her answers. "What do you remember about your mother?"

Reese pauses her cutting and looks over at me. "I don't remember her at all. I recall you told me she wasn't ready to be a mom."

"Okay. When you were five, my statement was accurate and palatable. You're older now and can handle more information. On the advice of Mr.

G and Coach Apple, I asked her to allow me to be a single parent. She agreed. Do you know what a surrogate mom is?"

Reese furiously shakes her head.

"When a woman can't carry a baby on her own or a couple with two men want to have a baby, a surrogate agrees to carry a child for them."

Alex acknowledges this mode of explanation and continues preparing the burger toppings.

"My mom carried me and left me with you."

"Exactly." Despite my disdain for Christie, she gave me Reese and I'll be forever grateful. My niceties toward her end there. I won't trash her, if possible, regardless of my personal feelings. I don't intend on sharing the payout if I can avoid it. Knowing her mother took money may cause Reese to harbor ill feelings toward Christie despite her choosing to allow me to raise her alone.

"She gave me up to you."

"Yes, and she terminated her parental rights."

This conversation might be over the head of most nearly ten-year-olds, but in the interest of bridging to today's events, Reese needs to know that detail.

Reese ponders this information. "She gave me up and doesn't have to take care of me at all."

"Yes."

"Okay."

I don't think Reese realizes the legal implications, but it may become clearer when I share the rest of the day's events. Alex rounds the island and grabs the silverware in the drawer beside me. She discreetly offers her support by squeezing my hand out of Reese's view. I glance at her and acknowledge the gesture.

Reese finishes cutting the potatoes and brings the board and knife to the sink. "What happened today? Does it have anything to do with why joining this team and moving here worried you?"

Alex knows the delicate nature of this conversation and offers, "I can finish dinner if you want to sit and talk, Jordan."

I explained this choice to Alex already, but she needs to be aware of how I frame it with Reese. "Thank you. I'll stay here though."

Alex nods and prepares the air fryer for the fries.

"Today was about your mother, but it's separate from why this area concerns me."

Reese looks up at me, expecting an explanation.

I've tried my hardest to avoid having this conversation, but I suppose it was inevitable. "Your mother sent a letter to the facility demanding to see you tonight for your birthday."

My daughter's head tilts to the side. "My birthday is tomorrow."

Her response guts me. "I know, peanut."

"Do I have to see her?"

Hell no! I won't allow it. "No."

"Good."

"There's another facet of this. Your mother intends to go to the press about our arrangement if I refuse to let her see you, among other things."

"Are you going to let her?"

"Legally, she can't go public with our arrangement."

Reese frowns. "Why not?"

"Your mother signed an agreement that states she promises to keep our arrangement private."

"What happens if she breaks it?"

"There are penalties." As I work on the rest of my response, Alex interrupts.

"Time to eat. Can you fill the drinks, Reese?"

"Sure. Iced tea, Alex?"

Alex freezes momentarily and crinkles her nose. I'm beside her before I realize I shouldn't be with Reese in the same room. Regardless of her presence, I sidle closer to Alex and whisper, "I'm insanely proud of you." Goose bumps erupt on her skin. "I want to kiss you deeply right now."

Her head turns to the side, our lips a mere inch apart, and she inhales sharply. "Thank you. I'm proud of you too. You handled the explanation well. I would welcome a kiss or ten if we were able."

With a wink, I lift the serving plate and bring it to the table. We gather around the table and dig into the food.

"What are the penalties?" Reese asks.

"Boring adult stuff." My reply is intended to end this line of questions from my inquisitive daughter.

Reese shrugs and keeps eating. Either my daughter is starving or truly forgot her second question. I imagine hearing more truth about Christie is going to take some time to process. Ideally, Reese won't press me on the reason this area troubles me. It's enough to share about Christie, but how much of my dysfunctional and troubled youth to share with her is not something I want to determine today or anytime soon. Never would be preferrable.

Reese heads to her room to complete her homework once the kitchen is clean.

"Office?" I suggest to Alex.

"Sure." Although unnecessary, she checks the front door, garage door, and French doors before we return to my office.

Once she's inside, I close and lock the door then sweep her into my arms. I take two long strides and lean against my desk. Her curves melt against me as her tongue explores my mouth. My hands dip beneath the hem of her tee and climb upward. Her skin is soft and supple. I set her atop my desk and move between her thighs as she tugs my shirt off.

A muffled groan passes her lips before she marks my chest with her mouth. She travels down my midline out to the left and back. My hands slide up her legs, my thumbs skimming the seam of her leggings. The heat is unmistakable.

"What were you thinking about, Alejandra?"

"You."

"More specifically?"

I feel her smile against my abs before she looks up. "It's going to sound weird."

"Doubtful."

"You're an amazing father. Handling today's events and sharing them with Reese carefully and purposefully. It's hot as—"

I interrupt with my mouth on hers and glide my thumbs over her clothed core. Her fingernails skim up the front of my quads, and then she deftly opens the button of my jeans. She dips her hands into my boxer briefs and jeans, pushing them to the floor before circling my shaft. Containing a groan is impossible. I attempt to recall the last time a woman touched me and fail. It's been so long. I also forgot how fantastic it is when your partner has no agenda. Her hands glide up and down in the same rhythm as my thumbs.

"Holy hell!" My words are louder than they should be.

"Shhh!" Her admonishment lowers my next statement.

"Don't stop," I manage as the base of my spine tightens.

"You either."

My thumbs press harder and move faster. She matches my pace as the waves of her release crest. Her hands deftly glide over me until I explode. We didn't think this through at all. Although, I don't think when I'm with her; I feel—an action I haven't done in far too long, at least for myself.

"Any chance there's a box of tissues in here?"

"No," I reply, running potential ways out of our current predicament in my mind.

"Do you still have a load of clothes in the dryer?"

I tilt my head in question. She notices everything. "Yes, why?"

"I have a plan. I'm going to clean up using your shirt. Slip out of here, grab a cloth for you and a fresh shirt, all without Reese having any clue we like one another."

Laughter bubbles up. Alex laughs too.

"Good luck."

"I might need it. My ninja skills are a bit rusty. Most of my clients are adults. To date, none have been as observant as Reese."

She cleans her hands with my tee and slips out the office door. I'm a grown man in my own home, and I'm sneaking around like a teenager again. I love it and hate it at the same time. The newness of exploring Alex is fun and exciting. However, hiding it from her bosses and Reese isn't the best plan. I understand her reasoning and even support it a bit, but I want to tell the world about us, but with Christie and Trey, I know it isn't the right choice. Plus, I would prefer to keep our life as private as possible, for me, for Alex, and especially for Reese.

"Success," she smirks when she returns.

I clean up, pull on my clean shirt, and take a seat on the comfy leather couch in my office. Alex sits at the far end of the couch, eliminating any chance I can touch her without moving. "Why are you over there?"

She smiles. "You know why. If I'm close to you, you'll kiss me, and you won't share your conversation with Connor."

"Why would kissing be a problem?"

She shakes her head. "What did you tell Connor?"

"I told him to let her go public. It was the right choice. I protected both of us from her. At least I thought I did."

She covers my hands with hers. "You did."

"You may change your mind after I share the rest of the content of her letter. She intends to trash me by disparaging Trudie, Kirsten, and you."

"Let her. I can handle it."

"Are you sure? She plans to say I bring random women around my daughter."

She frowns, then rebounds. "Let her. It isn't remotely true. She also doesn't have any way to prove her statements. How many caregivers has Reese had in her life?"

"I wouldn't categorize all of you equally. The answer to your question is three. Trudie was with her during the early years and in New England. She was an older woman with grown children. I needed help, and she was willing to teach me what I needed to know to raise Reese properly. Grandmother and nanny would be an accurate way to describe her. She was with us round the clock, but I took care of Reese in the evenings when I was home. She guided me with care when I needed it. Kirsten replaced her simply for drop-off, pickup, and away games when Reese was six. Kirsten didn't live in. She only stayed overnight when I was travelling to an away game. Now, we have you."

"My position is the same. Let Christie say what she wants. Then sue her for the inaccuracies of her statements."

I shrug. It's an option, but I don't want to put Reese or her through a lawsuit if possible. "Plus, the NDA has a penalty clause that states she forfeits the money if she goes public. She probably doesn't have it, but there's a penalty nonetheless."

"Honestly, I don't think you can stop her. If she wants to disparage you to make herself look good, she's going to fail miserably."

"You're right. I can't. The NDA protects Christie too, but she's seeing dollars signs again. I won't allow her to see Reese. I won't pay her more money. Nor will I sit idly by while she disparages the exceptional women I chose to help me care for and protect Reese."

She takes my face in her hands. "Your decisions have been on point since Reese was born. Trust your instincts; they haven't steered you wrong yet."

"Thank you." My instincts are screaming about her. Hopefully, I'm correct there as well. I close the small space between us and kiss her sweetly. Before I can increase the intensity, there's a knock on the door. I drop a kiss on the top of Alex's head and answer the door.

"What's up?"

"I need some help with my math homework."

"Okay. Bring your stuff to the dining room. I'll meet you there."

"'Kay. Where's Alex?"

Jordan points in my direction. "We were talking. She's right here."

Reese pokes her head into my office. "Hey. I set the books on your bed."

"Thanks."

"Still up for reading before I go to bed?" Reese asks Alex.

"Sure, if you and your dad can pull off your math homework."

Reese giggles. "Are you any good at math, Alex?"

"Depends. Geometry, yes. Fractions, not so much."

"Perfect. Can you help too? Then we'll have time to read, the three of us."

"Yes."

Reese runs back to her room. Less than ten minutes later, the three of us are working on fifth-grade math. I don't recall doing geometry until high school. It doesn't take long for us to figure out where Reese goes wrong. A few changes and explanations later, the three of us are curled up in the living room reading. I purposely positioned myself across from Alex so I could see her fully and thwart my ability to touch her. Each encounter between us brings us closer to sharing our budding relationship with her bosses and fully with each other, physically at least.

Every few pages, I glance over at Alex who is intently reading the fourth Harry Potter novel. The second or third time, I notice she's twirling her hair around her finger repeatedly. A deep part of me wonders why and resolves to ask her about it later. Alex fits with us, and I can't imagine how I'll feel when her job is over.

"Dad?" Reese filters into my head.

"Hmm. Yeah?"

"You good?" my daughter asks.

Alex looks up from her book and stops curling her hair with her finger.

"Yeah. Thinking about this passage." *Lie.* I certainly can't tell my daughter I'm falling for her security detail, at least not yet. *Can I? Should I?* "What's up?"

"I'm going to bed."

"Good night for the last time, nine-year-old Reese."

Reese shakes her head before hugging me. Then Reese moves across to Alex and hugs her too.

Alex hugs her with equal tension. "Good night, Reese."

For a short while, I remain in my seat. The longer I wait, the more the ache in my chest increases to be near her. Silently, I relocate to the corner of the couch. Within seconds, Alex sets down her book and snuggles against me. My fingers brush the exposed skin of her lower back.

"I like noticing new things about you. In addition to the cute nose wrinkling, you have a cluster of freckles on your shoulder blade, but I want to know why you twist your hair around your finger."

She inhales deeply.

"You don't have to share, but I'd like you to."

Alex tilts her chin upward, and her eyes meet mine. "It's unconscious. I do it when I'm comfortable."

"Isn't that a good thing?"

"Yes and no."

"Please explain." I shift her higher so I can fully see her face.

"I'm here for Reese, not us."

"I truly love tiny, meaningful words."

"Me too. It's scary though. I don't like having a split focus. Except here in these walls, I know she's safe. No one who has access here will harm her. Here I'm unguarded for her and for me."

"I like you unguarded. It's the real you. It's that Alejandra I refuse to let go."

"I will choose Reese over us if it comes to it."

I shouldn't be surprised by her statement. Truthfully, I'm more surprised I understand her position. "I know. I would too."

"I know." Rather than push away, she cuddles deeper against me. She's beside me with her head on my chest and my arms clasped at her waist. It doesn't take long before her breathing shallows and she's fast asleep.

I take the time afforded me and memorize her. I commit the slope of her nose, the curve of her cheek, and the single beauty mark in the hollow of her collarbone to memory before deciding what to do.

The right thing for me to do as her quasi boss is to wake her and escort her to her room. What I want to do as the man who desires a solid, stable relationship with her is to wake up in my bed tomorrow morning in the same position as we are right now. Despite the clear, correct choice, I opt for the middle ground, set an alarm on my phone, and allow sleep to overtake me.

CHAPTER FIFTEEN

ALEJANDRA

"Alex?"

I hear my name in a soft, sweet voice. Cataloging how I feel though is another matter. I'm warm, secure, and in Jordan's arms. *Jordan.* Before I can answer Reese, he does.

"Morning. Happy birthday, peanut."

"Morning. Thank you. Is Alex okay?"

Oh, Reese. I'm amazing, but not sure how I should handle the opposing emotions swirling inside me. I shift slightly. "Morning. I'm fine. Thank you for asking. We were talking and fell asleep. Happy birthday, Reese."

"Thanks." She looks between Jordan and me, then asks, "Are we training this morning?"

"Of course. I'll meet you back here in ten minutes."

"Sweet. I'm going to change into training clothes." Reese hustles down the hall.

Jordan cranes his neck over the back of the couch. "Morning. Couldn't have given me more than five minutes, huh?"

I attempt to speak but fail.

"I'm kidding. Though I slept quite well with you in my arms last night, even here on the couch."

"I did too. A little too well."

He checks for Reese again, then leans forward and skims his lips across mine. "No such thing as feeling too secure in your home wrapped in your man's arms."

I set my hand in the center of his chest and push onto my heels around his thigh. *My home? My man?* "Mine?"

"I want to be, if you'll have us."

"It isn't about want Jordan. I *want* deeply. My self-control slips daily, but…." My response is cut off as I hear Reese move into the bathroom. "I need to get moving."

"We need to talk more," Jordan insists.

I nod and rise to my feet. As I pass, Jordan grabs my hand and presses a kiss to it.

With nearly no time to spare, I return to the kitchen and find Reese stretching just inside the slider doors. "Ready to get started?"

"Yes. I like training with you every day."

"Can I share a secret?"

Her eyes widen, and she nods furiously.

"Me too."

We giggle and head outside. It's a bit chillier this morning than I expected, but we ignore the temperature. Thirty minutes later, which is shorter than normal, we step back inside. My heart constricts at the sight I see. Not only did Jordan shower and get dressed for work, but he's busy preparing breakfast.

"Think you can get ready, including a shower, in the next fifteen minutes?" Jordan asks Reese.

"Piece of cake," Reese scoffs.

"What about you, Alex?"

"I love challenges, though this one, like she said, piece of cake."

"Ready, set…."

Reese is gone before he finishes.

"Better hurry, Alejandra. Reese won't hesitate to eat your plate too." Jordan steals a quick peck and winks at me as I round the corner to my room.

Reese beats me back to the kitchen, but both of us are ready before Jordan is done cooking. I watch him, completely enthralled by his movements and the tension in his forearms as he finishes preparing breakfast for the three of us.

"Alex?"

"Yeah, Reese?"

"I asked if you were ready for the birthday dinner tonight."

I shake my head. "Nope, please share your birthday traditions, Reese."

"First, Dad makes my favorite breakfast. He sets up cupcake delivery to my class because he can't come himself, which I understand because it's during the season. When he gets home, we make dinner together and have cake."

"Sounds perfect. I think you're forgetting something though."

Reese frowns at me. Jordan cranes his neck in interest to what I may say.

"I mean, I get presents on my birthday. Don't you?"

"Oh yes! Dad is awesome at giving gifts. In addition to books, he always finds something special each year. When is your birthday, Alex?"

"November 4th."

"Sweet, I have plenty of time to find the perfect gift with Dad," Reese shares.

"Thank you, Reese." Jordan's is May 10th.

Jordan sets a plate with pancakes with a face made with M & M eyes, a strawberry nose, and hair as well as a smile with whipped cream in front of Reese.

"Pancake man is on point, Dad."

Jordan smiles at his daughter.

Their bond is unlike anything I've ever seen. It's endearing how he cares for her but works on himself and his profession as well. Being taken care of is a foreign feeling for me. I take care of me, no one else. The conundrum is... I like Jordan taking care of me.

Then he sets a plate in front of me and one beside me for himself. Mine doesn't have a face but strawberries and whipped cream in the shape of a heart. I look at him sideways as he sits beside me. With his right hand, he digs into his food while his left links with mine beneath the granite island out of Reese's view.

About fifteen minutes later, two distinct alarms sound at the same time.

"We need to go," I announce. "Set the dishes in the sink, and I'll take care of them when I get back from drop-off."

Reese slides off her stool and makes her way to the sink with her dirty plate and glass. Then she disappears down the hall, presumably for her bag and shoes. I grab my dish and coffee cup and follow suit.

Jordan traps me against the sink as he sets his dishes atop mine. His left hand brackets my hip, his face near the shell of my ear, and the length of him holding me against the dark wood cabinetry.

A memory trips my brain, and I grab his wrist to ground myself. *Jordan won't hurt me.* Instead of letting the memory turn this sweet, sexy moment sour, I refocus on how fantastic he feels pressed against me. How can I decrease my immediate fear response and take the pleasure for what it is?

"Breathe, Alejandra. It's me and no one else."

I heed his request.

"Again." He hears Reese approach first. His hand falls away with a glacial pace. Then, obscured from her view, he drops a kiss on the curve of my neck and whispers, "I'll see you later," before stepping away.

"We'll be here. Could you call me if you have a chance?"

"I will."

We exit the garage at the same time. At the school, I park and escort Reese inside with less than a minute to spare. I take a trip around the school building and scan the perimeter. An inescapable instinct urged me to check. As I round the north side of the building, I see a tall male at the edge of the grounds. I quicken my pace in his direction, but he slides into a parked car before I get a good look at him. I scan the plate and commit it to memory before taking an extra sweep around the building and texting Connor.

Me: Morning. There was a guy who appeared out of place at the
  school.

Me: Tall, black hoodie. Got into a black sedan, VA plate TJW-1274.

Connor: On it.

I make my way out of the lot and turn toward the house. Before I get far, I think better of it and change course toward the office.

Connor: Where are you heading?

Me: Toward the office now.

Connor: Good plan. I'm sending Cruz to the school for a double check
  and an impromptu coffee drop-off for his wife.

Me: Much appreciated.

I drive directly to the office because there's no reason for me not to. I pull into the lot and use the rear entrance.

Connor is on the phone. "Don't care. Pull whatever you need to as soon as you can." He addresses me after he ends the call. "Thanks for the heads-up."

"Reese is amazing, and it's my job to notice."

Jake and Christoph join us in the conference room.

"Morning."

"Did we have a meeting scheduled?" Jake asks.

"No. There was a suspicious guy near the edge of the school parking lot at drop-off," I inform him.

"Have you told Jordan yet?" Christoph inquires.

I shake my head. "No, I wanted more information first. Ruining Reese's birthday is not an option."

"Understood."

Connor's phone rings again, and he steps into the hall for quiet. A few minutes later, he returns. "Blaine was able to run the plate and pull video footage from the area around the school this morning. The plate is for a rental. It's registered to a Corey Mikel. Overall, the description you gave me matches the one on the license he provided to the rental car company."

I'm waiting not so patiently for the rest of Blaine's findings. I hate Reese needs me to bring her to school. What I mean is me as in a bodyguard, not me as in her... father's other half and her future mother figure. I haven't seen myself as either of those two things in a remarkably long time because of my history. Separately, Jordan and Reese are amazing people with unique perspectives to add to the world. Together, they are a dynamic little family and I'm grateful I get to watch from the outside looking in. For now anyway. Oh how I wish it could be true. Maybe it can, but we need to deal with Christie and Trey first... if there's a way to eliminate them as threats anyway.

Connor continues. "His preliminary search doesn't raise any concerns."

"Okay. Then I need to get back to the house and handle a few things before pickup. Please let me know if anything changes."

"I will," Connor responds.

Expeditiously, I make my way back to the house. Instead of tackling the dishes first, I get the cake in the oven. I'll have enough time to finish it when I return from pickup. Midway through the dishes, my phone rings. Warmth cascades through me when I see the name.

"Hi."

"Hey. I only have five minutes. What do you need to talk about?"

"Did you order a cake for Reese?"

"No, I'm going to make it when I get home."

"Oh, I didn't know baking was part of your tradition."

I get a video request. His gorgeous, chiseled face appears on my screen. How does he look so good in the middle of practice? I wonder. "It isn't. I should've made it last night, but we were talking, and you know the rest."

"It just so happens, there's a cake in the oven as we speak." The expression on his face is difficult to read. "We don't have to use it," I immediately add.

"Why wouldn't we?"

"I didn't mean to do something for her you normally would."

"Alejandra, I'm not upset. Reese will love you made her a cake."

"Okay. But I took it away from you."

"Not the important aspect of our conversation. I love how you care for her, and me, if I'm being transparent."

I tilt my head in question.

"Yes, you may not realize it, but you take care of me too."

"I think you have that backward."

"I love taking care of you. Has anyone ever done it before?"

"A man, no."

A sexy grin appears on his face. "Good."

"How do I take care of you?"

"By caring for Reese and taking my worries away while I'm here. You and I both know I would prefer to do everything for my daughter. Reality is a slap in the face. I can't do it all. More importantly, by hearing my story and sticking by me despite it."

"You're much more than your history."

"As are you. As much as I want to keep talking, I need to return to the field. I'm hoping to get home a little early today. See you later."

"Bye, Jordan." I pull the cake from the oven, set it on a wire rack near the rear of the counter, and verify we have enough milk before I need to leave.

When I meet Reese at the main entrance, she has a huge smile on her face. Over the course of the school day, her teachers and classmates have added to her outfit. She now has a birthday girl sash, a hat with sparkly sprite ears, and a button. She hugs me and loops her arms around mine. "Hey!"

"How was your birthday at school?"

Glee is plastered on her face. "The kids are nice here."

I open the rear door for her, and she climbs in. Before I ask my next question, I settle into the driver's seat. "Were they mean at your last school?"

She shakes her head. "They were all normal at my last school. Here there are kids like me."

Fear grips me momentarily. I worry where the answer to my next question may go. "What do you mean like you?"

"Some of my schoolmates have dads who are like my dad."

I relax almost instantly. She means play professional sports.

"They get wanting to be normal, though most of us, especially me, don't really have to worry about getting the things we need."

"You were worried about other students finding out who your dad is?"

"Yes. When they learn who my dad is, I'll have an insta-friend. They aren't really my friend though."

"No?"

"No. They want to see where we live, meet my dad, and probably get his autograph or free stuff. It isn't about me at all."

"Was making friends really hard at your last school?"

"Sort of. I don't tell anyone what my dad does for work. Here though, Carter came right out and asked me. I answered his question truthfully. His dad plays offensive tackle with mine."

"Good. What is Carter's last name?"

"Luther."

"Sweet. How were the cupcakes?"

Happy and smiling Reese is the goal every day. "They were delicious. Way better than the ones from the last few years in New England."

"Glad to hear it." I pull through the gate and then into the garage.

"Can I ask you something?"

Cautiously, I reply, "Sure."

"Do you like working with me?"

"Of course. You're smart, a great helper in the kitchen, and this weekend my football teacher."

"Good. I can't wait. The plays in the yard were just the beginning. I like you a lot. My dad does too." After she drops her loaded statement, she takes off to her room.

Part of me wants to press her, but instead I'll share with Jordan after she goes to bed tonight. I tug my phone from my back pocket, google the team roster, and text Connor.

Me: Could you check out a Christopher Luther and his immediate family?

Connor: Sure. Everything okay?

Me: His son Carter is Reese's classmate. Just want to make sure he's solid.

Connor: I'll get back to you.

Me: Thanks.

I end the conversation and move into the kitchen. With the ingredients set up, I search for a mixer. When I do, I find Reese hovering.

"What are you making?"

"Whipped cream frosting. Want to help?"

"Absolutely!" She scurries to the sink and washes her hands.

I grab the chilled bowl and beaters from the fridge and set them out. "Have you ever made frosting before?"

"Nope."

"No worries. This recipe is simple. Your cake is chocolate. Do you want chocolate frosting as well or something else?"

"Is mocha flavored possible?"

"Um, yes!" I turn and brew a cup of espresso and put it in the freezer to cool it as quickly as possible, then pull out the cocoa powder. "First, we need to beat the heavy cream in this bowl." I snap in the beaters.

Reese pours the cream into the bowl and gets to work.

"Slow and steady," I instruct and let Reese mix the ingredients.

"Alex, I think this part is done." Reese pulls the beaters up, and the cream is whipped into perfect peaks.

"Great job! Next, we sift the sugar and cocoa into the mixture and fold it in with a wooden spoon."

Reese grabs the sifter, and I fold as she sifts. About midway, I hear the garage door open. Jordan comes in quietly and winks at me behind Reese's back. I wrinkle my nose and smile. I want to greet him properly.

"What's next?" Her voice is laced with sheer joy.

"We add vanilla and espresso." I add the chilled coffee, and Reese adds the vanilla and folds it into the frosting. With spoons at the ready, we taste test our creation.

"It's yummy, Alex! Thank you for letting me help. I like spending time with you."

"Thanks. I love—"

"Hey, hey. Did my girls start the party without me?" Jordan interrupts.

My girls. I love his words.

"Dad!" She sets down her testing spoon and throws her arms around him. "Today has been awesome so far, and I can't wait to make dinner with you and Alex."

His eyes meet mine over his daughter's head. Reading him right now isn't difficult. He wants the same thing I do—a proper "I just got home from not seeing you all day kiss."

"We need to frost your cake, Reese, or do you want your dad to do it?"

"Perfect idea, Alex. Dad can do it."

Jordan hesitates, though I'm unsure why.

"Dad, what are you waiting for?"

He smiles at Reese and makes his way to the sink to wash up. With freshly washed hands, he grabs a frosting knife I didn't see in the drawer and gets to work. I shouldn't be surprised. Jordan seems to live by the mantra of everything worth doing is worth doing well. I'm so engrossed I don't notice Reese is taking photos.

She directs us soon after I notice. "Move in closer, Alex."

Jordan turns his gaze toward me. Holy hell! His eyes are smoldering with lust. I shouldn't be surprised. He told me himself. More importantly though, I want him. I want them. The bigger question is do I need to come clean to Jake?

I sidle closer to Jordan and smile for Reese. After she takes a few photos, I urge her to switch with me. They goof around for a dozen more photos and set the cake in the fridge until after dinner.

Dinner is a group event, much like the other meals we've eaten together. We settle at the table with Reese's meal choice—chicken with asparagus and pesto ziti.

As we dig in, Jordan's hand settles at midthigh beneath the heavy wood table.

I glance in his direction but say nothing. "This is delish, Reese," I offer.

She laughs. "All we did was warm it up basically."

"Either way, it's tasty."

"Thank you."

Jordan squeezes my leg. Containing a sigh is harder than I anticipate. He covers for me expertly. "Reese, how was your day at school?"

I take the reprieve to sort through my opposing feelings. Not true. My feelings aren't opposed. How to handle them is. I tamp down my thoughts and focus on Reese. After all, it is her birthday.

"Can we go hang outside a while before having cake?" Reese asks.

"Sounds good to me," Jordan replies.

"Alex?"

"Yes."

"I meant both of you."

"Thanks. I would like to join you. I'm going to get a hoodie first. I'll meet you both out there."

"'Kay," Reese replies.

They rise from the table. Then Reese loops her arm around Jordan's, and I watch them step outside. Their bond is special.

I take my time searching for a hoodie, despite knowing exactly where it is. I resolve to tell the boss men about my growing interest in a personal relationship with Jordan next week. I grab Reese's gifts and set it on the island for later. As I make my way toward them, I overhear their conversation.

"Can I ask you something?" Reese asks.

"Anything."

"Do you like Alex?

Half of me wants to push the screen open to give him an out. However, the deepest parts of my heart he has touched like no one ever has before wants to hear his answer.

"Of course I do. Don't you?"

I imagine Reese shaking her head. "No, Dad. I mean like a girlfriend like her."

"Why do you ask?"

"You're different since she moved in with us, in a good way. You smile more. Basically, you're happier when Alex is around."

"The truth is… yes, I do, and she does make me happy."

"Ask her on a date."

"It's complicated, peanut."

"Why?"

"Alex is here to take care of you for me. Her bosses won't be happy about her and I dating."

"So don't tell them. The way you two look at each other is super cute and sweet."

With Reese's seal of approval, I slide the door open. Jordan is sitting on the couch, and his observant daughter is across from him. "Alex, you should sit next to Dad," she directs me.

Containing my joy is nearly impossible, but I pull it off. I take a seat next to Jordan but purposefully leave appropriate space between us. I look between her and Jordan after taking a seat. "Why are you staring at me?"

"No reason." She looks expectantly at Jordan.

However, he doesn't take the hint. It also isn't wise to share we've already been sneaking around, sort of, for a while. Thankfully, I'm saved by my phone ringing with a call from Connor. "Excuse me."

I press the green button and step away. "Shouldn't you be home by now?"

"I am, but I wanted to share the update from Blaine. The Luther family is clear. It's fine for Reese to hang out with Carter at school or otherwise. Nothing else popped up on Corey Mikel either."

"Great! Anything else? I'm sure you didn't call only to share the Luther family is clear."

"Perceptive as always. There are some rumblings of Christie putting out feelers for sharing her story with the press. Nothing is definitive yet, but we felt you and Jordan should be aware."

"Thanks. I'll speak with him after cake and gifts for Reese."

"Good night, Alex." He ends the call.

I turn to retake my seat, but they're on their way inside. "Time for cake and presents?"

Sheer glee is plastered on Reese's face. "I couldn't wait any longer."

"I think waiting until now is more than most girls your age could handle," I offer.

"Thanks, Alex."

Jordan pulls the cake from the fridge and plunges the candles into the frosting. Once the wicks are ablaze, Jordan and I sing to Reese.

"Make a wish, Reese."

Reese taps her lips with her finger and blows out her candles. After the good luck cut, she passes the serving duties to Jordan. He plates three pieces of cake, and Reese takes the first bite.

"This cake is amazing. When did you bake it, Dad?"

Jordan looks me square in the eye. "Alex made your cake this year."

Her mouth drops open as she rounds the island and hugs me close. "You're the only adult other than Dad to make me feel important and special, like I matter. Thank you, Alex."

Tears well in my eyes, but I silently implore them not to fall. As I tighten my hold on Reese, Jordan's arms surround both of us. "You do matter. I always will, Reese."

His right hand slides up my arm, and he cups my face, swiping away the few fallen tears. "Thank you for seeing both of us," Jordan whispers for only me to hear.

My eyelids flutter closed, and a few more tears fall. Jordan wipes them away with the pad of his thumb and presses a kiss to my forehead. I settle my emotions with a deep breath, draw back, and look at him. A flood of emotions cross between us. I want to look at him each day.

"Who wants to finish the cake?" I ask.

A muffled, "Me! Me!" vibrates between us.

Jordan chuckles and releases us. I compose myself more while preparing two cups of decaf coffee.

Reese asks for her gifts when I return to the island.

"Here you go." Jordan sets a glittery pink and purple bag in front of her.

She throws the tissue paper left and right until she gets to the bottom of the bag. Reese pulls out a boxed set of the Harry Potter series. Confusion overtakes her features.

"Open the first book," Jordan directs her.

"Ohmigod! How did you get this?"

I lean over and notice the book has been signed by J.K. Rowling with a note to Reese.

"Keep going. There's one more thing in there."

Reese reaches into the bag again and pulls out an ivory card with a wax seal. "What's inside? I don't want to open it. The seal is for the House of Gryffindor."

"May I?" I extend my hand to Reese. She obliges, and I use a sharp knife to slice across the top and not break the decorative seal.

She reads the card more than once before jumping up and down. "Really? Really! When?"

"As soon as school ends."

She hugs Jordan. "I'm already excited, and the school year just started. We're really going to the Wizarding World of Harry Potter at Disneyworld?"

"Yes."

I gather this gift has been a long-term request. "Ready for mine?"

A surprised look casts on Jordan's face, but Reese smiles. "Yes, please." I slide the bag across to her. She follows the same manner as she did with the other bag. A colorful pile of tissue paper litters the island. She pulls out the box from Millie's first. "Thank you, Alex. Did you get my favorite?"

I shrug. "Maybe." I know I did, but I like to keep her guessing.

Instead of opening the chocolates, Reese digs back into the bag. The white box is nondescript, so she tugs off the lid and pulls out a replica of Hermione's time turner from the Harry Potter Series. "This is aahhh-mazing! I always wondered if I could get one. Thank you, Alex."

"You're welcome."

"Can I borrow your phone?" she asks me.

"For?"

"I want to take a picture and email it to myself so I can share my gifts with Carter."

"Sure." I pull my phone from my back pocket and slide it across the island.

Reese takes a photo and types away on my phone.

"Who's Carter?" Jordan asks.

"Can you share with him? I want to go send this right away." Reese states.

"As long as your dad is okay with it."

"Sure," Jordan replies.

"Good night, Dad and Alex. Thank you for an awesome birthday. I'm going to message Carter."

"Night. I'll be there later to say good night again." Jordan shares.

"'Kay" echoes down the hall after her.

CHAPTER SIXTEEN

JORDAN

"Who is Carter?"

She sets her hand on my chest and walks me back a few steps into the hall leading to the laundry room. Fisting my shirt, she tugs downward until her lips are a whisper from mine.

"I've wanted to kiss you deeply since I got home," I admit.

"Me too. After we do, we need to talk about a few things."

"As long as I can kiss you first, I'm good."

Keeping in mind her history, I back myself against the wall, stealing the space between us, and kiss her with abandon. The speed and intensity of our kisses ratchet up to near inferno levels. I reach out to my right and open the laundry room door. I lift her into my arms, then set her on the folding table while closing the door with my foot.

Without hesitation, she lifts my shirt overhead and lets it float to the floor.

"Nope, my turn tonight." I sweep my hands beneath her shirt and tug it over her head. Her long tresses fall around her shoulders in waves. "You're gorgeous." I ignore the slight flash of disbelief in her eyes. "I'll remind you each day, not only because it's true but because you deserve to hear it."

Her head drops slightly. I lift her chin back up and press a tender kiss to her lips, willing her to believe my words. Surrounding her back with my arms, I unclasp her pink bra and draw it away. I lower her to the table and mark her skin, savoring her taut nipples with my mouth and teeth. As I delve my tongue into her navel, I shimmy her leggings and lacy panties down her thighs to the floor beside my shirt. The barest touch of my fingers up her legs makes her shiver.

"If you need me to stop, tell me."

"I need you to touch me." Her words emerge breathless and filled with yearning.

I repeat the same path with my fingers before skimming her core from bottom to top and back again. Her skin turns a light shade of pink. I dip a finger into her core and draw circles on her swollen clit with my other hand. The closer she gets to her release, the more I decrease the speed of my fingers. She squirms and attempts to slide downward.

"Jordan." My name falling from her lips is a stern warning and a needy plea at the same time.

"Alejandra, let me learn how to make you shudder with pleasure."

A whimper falls from her mouth, which tells me light touches and slow movements keep her on the edge of bliss. Adding a second finger while continuing with my other hand, I increase my speed slightly. Her hands curl around the edge of the table as her back bows, putting her breasts on full display. Now her skin is flushed red. She moves in time with me, hoping to speed me up.

"Trust me, sweetheart. It'll be worth the wait."

A groan followed by a sharp intake of breath is her only response. With measured increases, my fingers plunge faster. Her inner muscles tighten until she splinters into a million tiny shards of her former self. Alejandra, who was afraid to trust and afraid to be completely vulnerable with a man, is slipping away. She's being replaced by a stunning, self-assured, confident woman inside the border of our relationship to match her outside of the house. I move within her pulsing walls and over her clit until her body is ready to shatter again. Then I bring her back up beyond the height of her last release twice more before allowing her to fully recover against me.

A possessive, hard kiss later, I add a small space between us. "You okay?"

"Okay doesn't come close to how I am. Will we…?"

"Face value. Just say it."

"Will we keep getting more adept at this?"

"I certainly plan to steal each moment with you I can."

A sinful smile graces her flawless face—one I could look upon daily for the rest of my life. "Can I share a secret?"

"Always."

"I want that too."

"But?"

"No but, just time and boss issues."

"Say the word and I'll fix the boss issue."

"How would it work?"

"Easy. 'Jake, I need to add another team member because I want to openly date Alex without any risk to Reese.'"

"Well, I see you've thought it through, except that isn't how it would work though."

"No?"

She shakes her head. "He could replace me altogether or have someone with me and Reese, as if my feelings will in some way impact how I protect negatively. The irony is my feelings make me more vigilant regarding her, not less."

"I hadn't thought of it that way. Then we won't worry about it for now. Okay?"

"Yes."

"I want an *us*, Alejandra. I want to wake with you in my bed each morning on purpose."

"Me too. I need time to do right by Reese."

"I understand."

"Really?"

"As I stated before, I'm a patient man. When you're ready, I will be too." Hell, I'm already there.

"I have no words to adequately describe how well you care for me."

"None are necessary. I care about you. I want you to be mine, however long it takes to get there." I take her mouth in another soul-baring kiss before tugging on my shirt and checking on Reese. I find her fast asleep with a huge grin on her face.

When I return, I find Alex has made her way to the living room. "Want to talk here?" she asks.

"Here is fine unless privacy is required."

She shrugs. "I don't see Reese getting up anytime soon, do you?"

"No, but what do we need to talk about?"

"Reese is fine. I have some information."

"Who's Carter?"

She laughs. "Carter is a classmate of Reese's. He's also the son of one of your teammates. She's happy there are kids like her at school."

A flick of sadness passes through me. "She had trouble at her other school?"

Alex links her hand with mine. "Not exactly. She learned early on people only wanted to be her friend because of you. Carter is obviously different because his dad is in the league too."

"Oh. She never mentioned the kids were shallow and deceitful to me."

Alex lifts her shoulder in acknowledgment. "Maybe she did to Kirsten. Anyway, I had Connor check out the family as a precaution. One of the things he mentioned on his call was the Luther family has no red flags."

"Good. You said one of the things."

"Caught that, huh? This morning there was a suspicious man outside the school. I did an extra sweep and called it in to Connor. He ran the plate and deemed the guy a nonthreat. Everything matches—his description, the names on the receipt and credit card, and his license."

"Does Reese know?"

"No. I didn't want to ruin her birthday."

"Anything else?"

"The team is aware Christie is currently shopping her story as an exclusive into the life of a blue-chip football player. So far, the story hasn't been picked up yet."

I lift her into my arms and hold her against me. "I'm sorry. I know you wouldn't keep anything urgent to yourself."

"No apology necessary. I didn't want to ruin Reese's evening."

"I appreciate that." I take a moment before adding, "I'm going to miss you."

Increasing the space between us, she raises an eyebrow. "What?"

"My game is away. I leave on Saturday in the morning and return late on Sunday."

"I know. We'll be fine."

"You're more than capable of caring for Reese. I'm going to miss you."

"I'm going to miss you too, Jordan."

"Is there anything else we need to talk about?"

"No, I want to enjoy the quiet with you."

I snuggle back into the cushions of the couch and tighten my hold on her. Her admission she would choose her job—Reese—over us is enough for me to trust her word. Alex will protect my daughter as if she were her own, perhaps because some part of her loves her as if she were.

The last few days have flown by preparing with the team and at home for our first away game of the season. I'm not worried about Reese per se. She's fine with Alex. My current concern on the home front is Christie. Despite the safeguards in place, I see her breaking our agreement and thrusting my daughter into a place I never wanted her to be. A place where I'm no longer an amazing dad but a man who made two youthful indiscretions. One which cost a year of my life and made a mortal enemy of Trey. While the other cost money but has been my greatest joy since the day she was born.

"Dude, Little Miss will be just fine." Cam's voice pulls me from my worries as he takes the seat next to me on the plane.

"I know, except Christie is making rumblings about going public."

Cam shakes his head. "I thought you took care of her."

"I did—at least my attorney assured me I did. The package I received a few days ago was from her. She demanded to see Reese, or she would go public."

"You would never allow her near Reese."

"Correct. Now I'm waiting like a fiend for my next hit for her to go public and destroy the safe cocoon my family has been living in for the last ten years."

"Sorry, man. That sucks. I'm sure she's fine with... what is her caregiver's name?"

"Alex." The mere thought of her makes me smile.

Cam has known me for years and calls me out. "Dude, did you sleep with her?"

"N—"

Ty interrupts as he takes his seat across the aisle. "Did he sleep with who?"

"Reese's caregiver," Cam answers.

"We're not having this conversation right now, if ever," I declare firmly.

"I'll drop this after I state a few things. First, you deserve to be happy. If you care about Alex, you should tell her and court her properly."

Working on it, Cam.

"Second, the smile on your face hasn't faded since you reminded me of her name. I may not want to settle down and have a family right now, but I know you do. Also, your content smile is the same as my father's for nearly thirty years with my mother."

He isn't wrong. Does Alex want a family?

"Then why are you a player, Cam?" Ty interjects.

"If a woman crosses my path who wants me for me not my bank account, I'll change my ways. Until then, I'm going to stick with the never-ending buffet that is my adventurous sex life."

His words described Alex perfectly. "Thanks, guys. I appreciate your support."

Cam replies, "Anytime, brother."

"Are we reinstating our competition from college?" Ty asks. When we were in college, we each set out our goals for the game the day before.

"I'm in."

Cam adds, "Me too."

Ty sets his as one interception and three pressures.

"Taking it easy for the first game?" I suggest.

"I don't want to lose because I'm overconfident," he replies.

"Twelve receptions for 206 yards with two touchdowns." I set as my goal.

Cam adds, "Six receptions for 87 yards."

"All right, game on!"

We relax the remainder of our flight to Pittsburgh. When we land, we're whisked to the field for an easy walkthrough. We check into our hotel, and I lock myself into my room.

Near six, my phone vibrates in my hand. The caller ID says it's Alex, but I suspect it's Reese. I answer the video call. "Hey, Reese. How was your day with Alex?"

"It was great!"

There's a knock at my door. "Hold on a second. My food is here."

I answer the door and find Ty and Cam on the other side instead of my dinner. "We came to chill with you while we wait for our dinner reservations."

"Is that Uncle Ty?" Reese's voice surrounds me through my phone.

I lift my phone and turn it toward Ty, and he takes it from my hand. "Hi, Little Miss."

"Uncle Ty!"

Cam all but pushes Ty out of the screen view. "What about me?"

"Uncle Cam!"

"What have you been up to today?"

"After training, we went to the farm. I fed and brushed Trix. Then we walked to the point with Amara, Myers, and Sutton. After lunch we read by the pool. Now I'm going to watch a movie with Alex."

"Training? Aren't you a little young for training?"

Reese giggles. "Alex is teaching me martial arts. We train every morning."

"Cool," Ty replies.

"How are the field conditions?" she inquires, making the three of us laugh. Not many daughters know the answer is important for the game.

"The turf was in great condition. It's only week one," Cam shares.

"Duh, silly question," Reese replies.

There's another knock on my door. This time it's my dinner. I sign the slip and wheel my food over near the window.

"Almost ready, Reese?" I hear Alex's sultry voice through the phone. Warmth cascades through me.

"Yup. Can you give the phone back to Dad please?"

"Of course. See you next week," Ty replies to her.

"See you then."

Ty hands me my phone.

"I want to hear everything about the babies when I get home."

Cam looks over at me when I say "babies."

"Okay, Dad. Love you to the moon."

"Love you to the moon and back."

Reese hands the phone off to Alex. "Hey. I assume you heard her rendition of her day."

"Yes."

"You should eat before it's cold. I'll call back when our movie is over."

"Okay." I end the call and lift the cover of my food.

Cam and Ty are looking at each other, then to me. Each shrug once and shakes their head. Cam speaks first. "No way, bro. You aren't getting out of discussing what just happened."

"What just happened?" I ask.

"Your face lit up when her—sexy-as-fuck, if I do say so myself—voice came through the phone. Then when you saw her face, you relaxed one thousand percent."

"I don't know what you're talking about, Cam."

Ty adds, "Let him stay in denial. It gives her more time to run away."

"Funny. She won't run. Alex is amazing with Reese. I respect her too much to destroy my agreement with her. I will share she had a rough past like me. A relationship with her needs to be approached with slow and measured steps."

"So you are courting her?" Cam questions me.

"It's a bit more complicated but yes."

"I can't wait to meet her in person. The only woman able to set the mighty Jordan Devereaux off kilter. We won't press more—"

Ty interjects, "For now."

I throw my hands up in mock surrender. "Thank you." We bro hug, and they leave for their dinner reservation. I look out over the lush courtyard and eat my balanced dinner. Near nine, I answer a video call from Alex.

"Hey."

"Hi. How was the walkthrough?"

"Good. Movie over?"

"Yeah. Hiking tired her out. She fell asleep about halfway through. I stopped the movie and guided her to bed."

"How did it go with three babies today? I'm sure Reese was ecstatic."

Alex laughs softly. "Surprisingly well. Amara and the twins were chill the entire hike. We fed them at the point and then walked back. Reese was insanely happy. She always kept at least one busy while Callie was feeding the others."

"I'm glad it was smooth. How are you?"

She tilts her head in question. "I'm fine. Reese is on her best behavior."

"I'm sure she is. I asked about you."

"I'm not worried about us, Jordan." The concern mirrored on her face is evident.

"Why are you worried about me?"

Her eyes close briefly and reopen to look at me again. "Call it a gut feeling, instinct, whatever. I don't trust…. I don't want to see you and Reese go through any more upheaval."

"Sometimes things need to get harder before they level out. My only hope was to protect Reese. The steps I took were for her, not me. I would prefer it never be public. However, I knew the agreement was only as good as the lesser of me and Christie."

"Admirable and exceptional considering Reese wasn't born yet. In my opinion, you did everything right. The lesser in this situation is absolutely Christie."

"Thank you. I certainly tried. Can you do two things for me?"

"Of course."

"Could you walk to her room for me? The first away game has always been tough for me. Less now than when she was an infant."

She rises from the couch and turns down the hall. Alex silently slips into Reese's room and turns the camera toward my daughter. Reese is sleeping peacefully. I take a few moments before thanking Alex again.

"What's the second thing?"

I smile at her. "Please go into my bedroom."

She raises an eyebrow and stops walking. I understand where she's coming from. She hasn't been in my bedroom since we assembled my bed on moving day.

"It'll be worth it. I promise."

Reluctantly, she pushes open the door and steps into my bedroom—alone.

"In my closet, please." I set flowers for both my ladies there before I left yesterday, as well as *Football for Dummies, Football A Beginner's Guide*, and *The Complete Idiot's Guide to Football* tied with a bow.

"Jordan, you shouldn't have."

"Those will help you keep up with Reese."

She leans forward and smells the flowers. I opted for a mixed bouquet this time instead of straight roses. The roses in Alex's are red, while Reese's are pink. Her head moves slowly from left to right before she adds, "Thank you."

"Our circumstances are unusual. I respect the line you've drawn between us and your job with Reese, but I wanted to show you I meant what I said after picking you up from class. Like then, this is pared down, but the sentiment is the same. Without a doubt, our family is stronger with you as a part of it. Hell, so am I."

I have stunned Alex momentarily speechless.

"Please share, sweetheart."

"I...."

"Take your time. I'm not going anywhere."

"I'm still working out how I feel." She shakes her head. "I'm not explaining this well."

I don't interrupt. She'll find the words she needs to say.

"How I feel with you and for you—both of you—is new, exciting, and all-consuming. I'm learning to be comfortable but not fearful of it. I'm working on reconciling how I feel with what you want to do for me with believing it's all real. Am I making any sense at all?"

I grin at her. "It makes sense to me. You're trying to reconcile how you felt in the past with how you feel now. How now is different in a scary, amazing way and makes you question what you thought you felt before."

"Exactly."

"I was where you are a few weeks ago."

"Really?"

"Yes, really."

"Thank you for thinking of me."

I can't stop if I try, nor do I want to. "You're welcome. I should get some sleep. Good night, Alejandra."

"Good luck tomorrow. Night, Jordan."

I end the call and stare at the ceiling. Alex isn't a normal woman. She's been emotionally scarred by men—one man—and is skeptical of my genuine gestures. I don't blame her. All I can do is keep being myself and proving my intentions as often as possible.

CHAPTER SEVENTEEN

ALEJANDRA

"Alex, it's time," Reese calls from the living room.

"Coming." Instead of sleeping last night, I read the books from Jordan after setting Reese's flowers on her bureau so she would see them first thing this morning. Not all the books, but most of the first one. When I join her, she's curled up wearing a jersey from Jordan's old team.

"Ready for this?" she asks me.

"Not sure. Your dad gave me some books, so I've been studying."

"Cool. Did you get flowers too?"

My stomach knots. The truth is the only way to go. Right? *Right?* "Yes. Why do you ask?"

"My dad likes you. He never involved Kirsten in anything. The only other time I see him smile for real is when he's proud of me. I guess it's a little different because of the security part. Either way, he wants to spend time with you too."

I don't know how to address her statement. "How do you feel about that?" She doesn't know I overheard their conversation a few days ago.

"I like you, and I like you and my dad together too."

"Thanks, Reese. I like both of you. It's a little complicated because I work for your dad."

She frowns at my response. Thankfully, I'm saved by kickoff. "How do you want to learn more?"

"Can I ask questions as needed?"

"Yes."

"Will you explain the plays?"

"Easy-peasy. I'll make you a football expert by midseason."

"Thanks, Reese."

The teams are locked in a defensive struggle through the first quarter. My attention is riveted to the screen. I would like to say I'm focused on the game, but I'm more intently watching Jordan run his routes down field. As the second quarter starts, I ask, "Post route, right?"

"Yup. Way to go, Alex." Reese high-fives me and returns her attention to the television.

I wrinkle my nose and smile. The next play, Jameson throws a deep slant to Jordan who evades a tackle and scampers into the end zone.

"Woo-hoo! Go, Dad! First touchdown of the season." At the same time as Jordan on screen, Reese bends at the waist in a bow.

"How long have you two been bowing?" I ask as I notice he bows a second time before handing the ball back to the referee.

"Oooh! I was right. I knew my dad liked you a lot. You got a bow too! You better practice for the next one."

Now Jordan's card with the flowers makes more sense. In the postscript, he told me to watch for a secret hello during the game. My heart nearly explodes with emotion. Is this how a real, stable relationship feels? I certainly hope so. It's fantastic.

We watch the rest of the first half, and I learn tons of little things from Reese. She pointed out how Jordan clenches his fist when he knows the ball is coming to him and how Jameson throws off the defense with his head fakes. My entire body tenses when Jordan takes a hard hit from the opposing safety.

Reese must see the worry on my face. "Don't worry, Alex. Dad is fine. He wears as much padding as possible. The only rule is it can't interfere with his catching ability or slow him down."

"Good to know." The team has a three and out, which thankfully Reese explained. When the team is unable to convert a first down, it's called a three and out—three downs and off the field. The score at halftime is seven to three with Jordan's team on top.

While we wait for the second half to start, we prepare nachos and a few other salty snacks. We take our seats just in time. The opposing team starts with the ball and charges down the field but only scores another field goal. Jordan's team responds with a touchdown reception by Cameron Beau. The possession changes again. This time Tyson Beck picks off the pass and runs it back to the forty-yard line. Two plays later, the team is up fourteen to six on a second touchdown pass to Jordan, his celebration complete with two bows, one for each of us. *Oh, Jordan.* Reese and I high-five again after we both bow in the living room.

The third quarter winds down and the fourth starts with a long drive by the opposing team. However, our defense thwarts their drive and pulls off a fourth-down stop. Now we have the ball near midfield.

My phone lights up on the ottoman with Connor's name. "I'll be right back, Reese." Into the phone, I say, "Hold on a moment, Connor."

Reese warns, "Be quick. We can't miss another touchdown."

I smile at her. "I'll do my best." I step into Jordan's office. "Go ahead, Connor."

"I wanted to give you a heads-up. Christie went public. Cruz is on his way to you. Christoph and I will meet Jordan at the airport."

"What do you suggest I do aside from stay here?"

"Prevent Reese from watching the postgame coverage and interviews," he replies.

"Okay. What is the plan for damage control?"

"Don't have one yet. I expect Jordan will be asked about it during his postgame interview. He'll attempt to decline to answer. If he gets my voice mail first, he'll likely skip it and pay the fine because the interviews are required by his new contract."

My heart drops to my toes. I recover from the hit to my heart and attempt to settle my thoughts. As I end the call with Connor, Reese shouts from the living room, "Alex!"

I hurry beside her. Before she says anything, her arms are tightly around my waist. I see the scroll at the bottom of the screen: Star wide receiver Jordan Devereaux paid for child. It's terse, click bait, and wholly inaccurate—well, not wholly inaccurate, but the spin certainly is.

"What's going on? Did my dad pay the surrogate?" Reese's words are muffled and strangled as her tears soak my shirt.

The last thing I want to do is say the wrong thing. "I don't have all the facts, so I can't answer your questions."

As Reese considers my response, the doorbell rings. She recovers and asks, "Who's here?"

"Cruz. I'll be right back."

"This is really bad, isn't it?"

I exhale sharply. The truth. *You promised her you would never lie to her.* "Things are going to get harder, yes." Leaving Reese in the living room, I answer the door.

"Hey, Alex. How is she doing?"

"Not great. She read the scroll while I was talking to Connor."

He nods and makes his way inside. "Hey, Reese. How's the game?"

She lifts her hand in a weak wave, shrugs, and plops down on the couch. Cruz shoots a look in my direction and takes a seat to Reese's right. I point to my phone and escape down the hall into my room.

Me: I'm so sorry. I didn't catch it in time.

Me: I'll put off answering her as long as I can.

Me: I...

I've let them both down significantly. I catch a glimpse of my flowers on the bureau in my room. Reese deserves better than my split attention, right? No. No one will care for her better than I am. Because I've fallen for her without reservation as deeply and unapologetically as I have her father. To hide my feelings, I wait longer than usual before returning to the living room.

Somehow, Cruz has managed to get Reese talking about the latest Nancy Drew book she's reading. I nod in appreciation when I catch his attention before busying myself figuring out a plan for dinner. With ingredients ready to go, I ask, "Hungry, Reese?"

"No."

"Cruz?" I hope a positive response from him will get a reversal from Reese.

"I could eat," he replies.

"What are you making, Alex?" Reese asks.

"One of my mom's specialties, pork risotto, or in Spanish, *arroz atollado Colombiano*."

"How did I not know you can cook Columbian food?" Cruz asks.

"Same as I didn't know you have a Spanish food recipe book in your head until Jill shared at girls' night."

Reese moseys into the kitchen and washes her hands. "How can I help?"

I set the tomatoes and scallions in front of her, and she starts to chop in silence. Cruz also offers to help, and I have him set the table.

"What does all of this mean?" Reese asks.

"As I said before, I don't know all the details. We have to wait for your dad to get home to talk more in depth."

"Fine. Can I go to my room?"

"Sure. I'll come with you. I need your tablet and your laptop for now."

"Fine." She sets down the knife and leaves with her head cast downward.

Less than a minute later, I return to the kitchen with her devices that could connect to the internet.

"This situation sucks," Cruz states when I return.

"Yeah, it does. Unfortunately, I can't offer anything more. Jordan needs to handle this with her."

CHAPTER EIGHTEEN

JORDAN

"Mr. Devereaux. Jordan." The throng of reporters clamor for my attention. Today's game was decent. A great performance for the first game with a new team. The press liaison points to a younger reporter in the front row.

"Mr. Devereaux, do you have a comment on the story that dropped an hour ago pertaining to allegedly paying a woman to carry your child?"

Reese. Anger pulses through my veins. Christie went public. I need to get to my phone. I consider my answer carefully. Madeleine is in my head, reminding me I only have to be present for these pressers, not necessarily participate. "No. I won't comment on my personal life. Next question, Stu?" I engage Stu from a reputable sports publication and website.

"Good game today, Jordan," Stu offers.

"Thank you. I'm here to help this team realize its full potential. With Jameson's arm and my hands, I think we have a decent shot to make the playoffs."

"Any comment on a report you have hired personal security for your family?"

I shake my head. "No comment. Does anyone have a question about today's game?"

Silence blankets the room. "Have a lovely evening." I make my way out of the room and bolt to the team bus. When I tug my phone out of my bag, I have numerous voice mails and texts.

The ones from Alex make my chest tighten. I take a deep breath and reply to her before handling anything else.

Me: None of this is your fault. None. It's a result of my choices.

Me: Thank you for trying to hold off until I get there.

Me: I'll be there as soon as I can. I...

I listen to the voice mails from Connor and Madeleine. I reply to Madeleine via text with a simple yes and push down the rage in my body. I know when Cam and Ty board the bus because they each pile into the row with me but remain silent.

It isn't until the bus pulls away from the stadium that I look at them.

Ty speaks first. "How can we help?"

"You can't, but I appreciate the offer. Madeleine is working on a press release with my newly retained media relations manager. It appears I'll have an escort home this evening. Now Reese not only has Alex with her but Cruz too."

Always the voice of reason, Cam adds, "You know you did the right thing a little over a decade ago. Do you know why she's coming forward now?"

"I only see one reason—"

"Money," Ty supplies.

"What do you plan on doing?" Cam asks.

I'm not giving her anything, money or otherwise. She's absolutely not seeing my daughter. "I'm still mulling my options in my head. I'm sure Madeleine will provide more I haven't thought of as soon as we land."

"This sucks, man," Ty adds.

"Yup. I tried to put Reese first, and it still backfired on me."

They both drop the discussion. We exit the bus on the tarmac and board the plane for the flight home. Whether purposeful or not, I'm the only person to move when the plane lands. The usher escorts me to a small anteroom at the airport. When I step inside, I'm greeted by Madeleine, Christoph, Connor, and a curvy blonde I've never met before.

"Hey, Jordan. Great game," Madeleine offers.

"Thanks."

"Jordan, please meet Celeste Bronstein."

I take her extended hand. "Thank you for coming on short notice."

"It's the job. With some basic information from Madeleine, I have taken the liberty of drafting a press release. Please review it and let me know what changes you would like, and we can discuss them."

I lower to the chair and review her words. "Can we change this to child instead of daughter? Protecting her is my priority."

"We can, but—"

Madeleine intercedes on my behalf. "As I explained, Miss Wingate signed a nondisclosure agreement concerning Mr. Devereaux's daughter. She has broken it. Sharing as little as possible is the right way to go."

I acknowledge Madeleine's words and my gratitude for the same. "I'm willing to say I had a consensual relationship with Christie in college and she became pregnant. I would prefer not to mention the payoff she requested, which I paid, or the fact she threatened to abort my daughter. She took my money in exchange for carrying the child and terminating her parental rights." I pause a moment. "I need to balance my actions with the repercussions for me and my daughter. Do you have a copy handy, Madeleine?"

Madeleine produces a copy of the termination, the agreement, and the amount I paid Christie to carry Reese for me.

"I understand. In my expertise, sharing as much of the truth from the start is the best way to go in situations like this," Celeste pushes back.

"I appreciate your position, but under no circumstances will Miss Wingate see my daughter, nor will I pay her another dime. I followed through on my end of the agreement. My daughter is thriving, and I haven't, nor will I, opt to disparage Miss Wingate in the press despite my option to do exactly that in this moment. She's coming forward now because my new contract is lucrative and widely known."

"Putting your child first is admirable, but it won't make Miss Wingate go away quietly."

"Either way, I stand by my position. Please make those changes," I instruct her.

She nods and takes a seat at the small table near a laptop.

I scrub my hand down my face. "Do I have time to talk to Reese?" My question is directed at Madeleine.

"Yes, of course."

I pull out my phone and walk away from the group.

Alex answers before the first ring completes. "Hi."

"Hey. I'm at the airport with my new media relations person, Madeleine, and the guys. How are things there?"

"Not great. She's been in her room for nearly an hour. I've checked on her, but she doesn't intend to leave until you get here."

"Can you share what she knows?"

"She saw the limited scroll at the bottom of the screen. She asked if it was true you paid your surrogate."

"How did you answer her?"

"I didn't. I think she's in her room because I don't have answers. More accurately, it isn't my place to share them."

"Okay. Can you bring your phone to her and stay while we talk?"

"Yes, to the first part and only if she wants me there for the second part."

"I understand." I hear Alex knock on Reese's door.

"Reese, your dad is on the phone."

Silence passes over the line. Alex knocks again. After a minute passes, she opens the door. "Reese!"

I push the request for a video call. "Alex, what's going on?" Fear bubbles through me.

"She isn't in her room anymore."

Remaining calm is getting more difficult by the second. "How long since you checked on her?" My intention isn't to accuse her of failing. It's more for reference.

"Fifteen minutes max. Cruz, do you have eyes on Reese?"

I overhear Cruz checking rooms of the house and calling them off through the phone. The angst in my body is leveling up with each passing moment.

She checks the closet, under the bed, the office, her room, and then she approaches my room. Sobs and harsh breaths hit my ears.

"Reese?" She kneels before her in my closet.

My daughter has my tablet in her lap.

Alex's voice is laced with concern. "Oh, Reese. Why didn't you listen? I took your tablet and laptop for a reason."

"I wanted to know the truth." Her sobs ramp up to full-on wails and tears.

"Reese," I call her.

"Dad?"

"Peanut, I tried my best to protect you, and I failed. I'll share the entire truth when I get home. Please stop scrolling through the internet. Those words are only partially true and skewed to your biological mother's benefit."

"Okay. How long will you be?" Reese asks.

"Let me talk to Madeleine for a moment." I mute my phone and inquire about the time frame for completion. A minute or two later, I return to my ladies. The video shows Alex with Reese curled up in her lap. She loves Reese as much as I do. My heart squeezes. "Reese," I call out after unmuting my phone.

"Yeah." Her voice is strained and muffled.

"I should be there in less than an hour. Please leave my closet and eat the food Alex prepared."

Reese nods and pushes to her feet.

"Why don't you wash up, and I'll be there in a minute?" Alex suggests.

"Okay," my daughter replies and leaves my closet.

"Thank you, Alex."

"You're welcome."

"Alex, don't blame yourself at all. I did this for her. You thought to take her electronics. I wouldn't have."

Emotions I can't categorize cross her face. "I'll do my best. You did what you needed to do. She will understand."

"I certainly hope so. I'll be there as soon as I can." Reluctantly, I end the call and review the final draft of the press release. Celeste has me acknowledge the press release leaves out information she feels pertinent to stifle Christie. Once Celeste feels free from blame, she provides the press release as an exclusive to the press office for my team and leaves the meeting. It reads:

I would like to address the statements made by Christie Wingate earlier today. She and I were in a consensual sexual relationship about a decade ago. Near the end of our relationship, Miss Wingate indicated she was pregnant. After some discussion, she carried my child to term and then voluntarily terminated her parental rights. Miss Wingate does not have a relationship with my child, nor will one be established going forward. I ask for privacy at this time to handle the fallout from Miss Wingate's choice to renege on her assurances to keep our agreement confidential. Thank you, Jordan Devereaux.

I likely have enough time to get home before my statement is national news. I scrub my hand down my face and join Madeleine and the team. "What happens now?"

Connor replies, "We escort you home and you take care of Reese."

"And tomorrow and every day after?"

"The most important facet of this situation is to get you back to your daughter," Christoph states, his hand linked with Madeleine's. The four of us make our way through a private exit to a waiting Blackthorne SUV.

"Can I have your keys, Jordan?"

I look at him puzzled.

"Your car keys. I'm going to pick up your car at the facility and meet you at the house."

"Oh, I appreciate the offer, but it's unnecessary. I can take an uber there tomorrow. The lot is locked and secure overnight."

"No problem," Christoph replies and climbs into the passenger seat.

Once we're all in the vehicle, Connor pulls away from the terminal and drives toward Reese.

"Can I request another deeper look at Christie? Something doesn't add up. Going public doesn't get her what she wants." I request.

"What do you think she wants?" Connor asks.

"At first, I thought it was more money, but why go public straight away? Why not contact me first and request more to remain silent? It can't really be about Reese. She didn't want a child in the first place unless it would tie her to me and my bank account. What's her real angle? I realize my rage clouds my judgment. However, I don't see it, at least not yet."

"I'll have our investigator dig deeper," Connor assures me.

"Thank you." The rest of the ride passes with minimal talking. My phone vibrates in my hand a few times before I check.

Cam: Call if you need anything.

Ty: I can be at your place in under fifteen minutes, just ask.

I answer them both with thanks and then tackle the last one.

Alejandra: I won't be able to ask this right away, so I'm asking now. Truly, how are you?

Me: I did everything I could to protect her, and I failed. I need to reconcile that before anything else, after I delicately share with my daughter how I screwed up before she gave me a chance at a real family.

Alejandra: She'll understand, Jordan.

Me: I hope you're right.

Connor pulls to the front door. I rush out of the car and twist the knob at the same time as Cruz. It seems someone gave him a heads-up.

"They're in her bedroom," he informs me.

I thank him and keep moving. The sight of Reese wrapped in Alex's arms on the floor at the foot of her bed drops me to my knees beside them. Until her, no one has loved Reese as well or as strongly as I do.

Reese shifts into my arms. "Did you lie to me?"

With five words, my daughter guts me. "No. I tried to balance your feelings and mine."

"I'll let you two talk," Alex rises to her feet and attempts to leave.

"Please stay, Alex," Reese pleads and blindly reaches for her hand.

"I need to talk to Connor and Cruz for a few minutes. I don't want them to stay if they don't need to. Can you hold off until I get back?"

Reese nods against my shoulder. Alex slips out of her bedroom to talk to the team. If I had to guess, at least one of the guys will be back in the morning to escort me to work. Reese may have more than one escort to school as well. We remain in the same position until Alex returns an undetermined amount of time later. It feels like an eternity, but likely wasn't more than a few minutes.

Carefully with measured words, words that don't reflect my anger toward Christie and her actions, I share the unvarnished truth of how she became the center of my world.

"She didn't want me?" My daughter's voice emerges trembling and soft.

"No, she didn't."

"She isn't any better than my insta-friends at my old school."

"It's a good analogy."

"She took money from you though?"

"Yes. I agreed to pay her a certain amount of money and her medical bills for carrying you."

"Why now?"

"I don't know."

Reese inhales and exhales deeply a few times. "Do I have to meet her?"

"Not as far as I'm concerned."

"Good. I may say not nice things to her."

Alex stifles a laugh and turns her face away.

"You're entitled to feel however you feel about her."

"'Kay. Can we talk about this more later? I'm tired."

"Of course." I set Reese on her feet and join her. We each grab one of Alex's hands and help her stand.

"Thanks. Do you want to train in the morning?" Alex's question is directed at Reese.

"Yes, definitely."

"It's okay to take a day off every now and then."

She shakes her head furiously. "No. It helps me start the day with a calm mind."

"I see Alex is rubbing off on you," I suggest.

"Yup. She's awesome." Reese throws her arms around Alex and squeezes tightly.

A fierce blush creeps into Alex's cheeks. I resist the urge to agree with my daughter's sentiments out loud. After saying good night, we leave her room. Once we're out of sight, I thread my fingers through hers and lead her into my bedroom. She tenses but doesn't say anything.

CHAPTER NINETEEN

ALEJANDRA

A bit of fear slithers through me as Jordan leads me into his bedroom after we leave Reese in hers.

"Why did you tense up?"

No one has ever been as attuned to me as Jordan. "We haven't come in here together since moving day."

"Oh. Would you prefer to talk somewhere else?"

"No. Here is fine."

He leads me to the sitting area on his private balcony. We take seats on the couch facing one another. "There are no words for me to express how grateful I am for you."

"None are necessary. While initially being here was a job, and it sort of still is, I… I care about Reese. I'll do whatever it takes to protect her for you." I've fallen for both of them, but I can't bring myself to say it out loud. The emotions coursing through me are terrifying and unlike anything I've ever felt before.

"Thank you. My daughter loves you. You have been there for her each time I couldn't, and you refuse to let her down."

"I meant what I said. I will always be here for Reese, even if she doesn't need me to escort her to school anymore."

"I'm convinced knowing how you feel will make her burst with happiness."

I smile at him as he sidles closer to me. "Can you share the plan for the near future?"

I explain the plan, which includes Cruz temporarily escorting Reese to school with me and Christoph tailing Jordan to work as a precaution.

"Okay. Can we move onto a different topic?"

I arch an eyebrow at him. "Such as?"

"How was watching your first game with Reese?"

A huge grin grows on my face. "It was pretty awesome. The books were helpful, and Reese is a great teacher."

"It'll be better in person at the stadium next week."

"You should know, she picked up on the extra bow."

"Good. I don't want to hide our relationship from Reese anymore. Hell, I don't want to hide my feelings for you from anyone."

I lean forward and brush my lips across his. It was a mistake because we're no longer talking about us. I wasn't considering the untamed desire flowing through my veins whenever he's near me. Within a second, he pulls me onto his lap so I'm straddling his thighs. Wetness pools between my legs as I settle against him.

"What do you mean, not hiding from Reese?"

"She told me to ask you on a date. I told her it was complicated."

"Interesting."

Jordan tilts his head. "What?"

"She told me the same thing, and my response was the same."

"What does complicated mean to you? What are your limits?"

"Right now, in this moment with you, I don't have any."

It takes Jordan an extra half second to seize my mouth in a hard, possessive kiss. I tug at his shirt until it's untucked. He breaks our kiss only long enough for me to cast his shirt to the floor. My shirt and bra join his in a pile. I twist my fingers into his soft hair and lean forward. The warmth of his skin on mine and the contrast between his hard body and my curves is mind-blowing.

He rises from sitting with me in his arms and sets me on the bed. My hands work open his pants and slide them, along with the boxer briefs, down his muscular thighs. After a mad dash for the bedroom door, he closes it quietly and locks it.

I set my feet on the mattress and glide my leggings off before he gets back to me.

"In a hurry?"

"No, just helping."

"Good. I plan to take my time with you."

A thrill courses through me. Jordan curls his arm around my waist and lifts me to the center of his luxurious bed.

"At the risk of destroying the mood, I have to confess it's been a long time since I've been with a woman. I need you to be patient with me in here."

"Same. A steady pace is fine with me too." She shakes her head. "Not a woman."

He smiles down at me. "I understood." Being trapped between the silky duvet and Jordan's absurdly sculpted body is heavenly.

When I think it can't get any better, he proves me wrong. Jordan twines our fingers together and lifts my arm overhead. He repeats the action with my other arm and traps my wrists in one hand. The sweet kisses he places along my jaw, over my collarbone, and down the valley between my breasts has me squirming against his hold. His hand slides down the rest of my torso and between my legs. Without any wasted movements, he plunges two fingers into my soaked core.

"What were you thinking about?"

"Us. Us moving forward."

"The thought of us arouses you this much?"

"Yes, and then some."

He rotates his wrist at the same time as he withdraws from me and immediately returns. Containing the whimper of pleasure is impossible.

"You like that?"

He repeats the same movements, and a shudder overtakes me. My inner muscles pulse around him, and I ride out the waves of my first orgasm of the night.

"Yes?" He grins down at me.

"Hell yes!" The grip of another climax claws its way up my spine. It doesn't take long until I succumb to the pull of carnal bliss. While I would like to say I relax completely, I don't. Jordan intends to keep me on the edge of ecstasy as long as possible.

"I need to touch you."

He releases one hand but holds the other in the same position. I drag the tip of my fingernail down his chest and encircle him in my hand. A few languid strokes later, he lengthens and hardens more. Reaching for the strip of condoms he set on the bed, I tear one open with my teeth.

Jordan takes the packet, sheaths himself, and gazes directly into my eyes, his emotions playing out on his face. He's all in.

I am too, but I need to muster the courage to say the words again. I know my emotions are real this time. "I need to feel you. Like you and I are one. Where I don't know where you begin and I end."

A strangled groan falls from his lips. With one hand linked overhead with mine and the other bruising my hip, Jordan aligns himself with my center. Inch by glorious inch, he moves into me. I lift my hips slightly and wrap my leg around his lower back, causing him to settle deeper. The fullness is like nothing I've ever felt before. My eyes flutter closed.

"Alejandra, look at me."

I comply and tilt my hips upward, urging him to move. He withdraws and thrusts forward with a measured rhythm.

"Jordan," I call out as my next peak rises within me.

Each time he slides deeper, the sensations in my body demand attention. Spikes of pleasure radiate through me as Jordan bursts forward. He lowers himself to the bed and gathers me against him with his lips pressed against the curve of my neck. Together we skate along until the aftershocks of us decrease to a lingering ache to chase our high again.

Not once before him did I feel like I do right now. I don't want to move from the cocoon of his arms. Yet I should. Even more, I'm wondering if having Cruz with me on outings with Reese is wise either way. *No.* Protecting Reese is of equal priority as building a relationship with her and Jordan.

"Stop thinking so hard."

"I can't. I'm trying to force myself to move."

"Do you want to move?"

I crane my neck to look at him. "No, I want to stay."

"But… you're worried about Reese?" he suggests.

"Yes."

"I want to wake up with you in my arms tomorrow morning. Not true. I want to wake up with you beside me every morning. Should it be insanely early so we're awake before Reese? Probably until we are ready to tell her about us."

"Are you sure?"

"About you, about us? Absolutely. I'm crazy about you, and so is my daughter."

"Good. I'm crazy about both of you too." After cleaning up, we slide beneath his ultra-soft sheets and set an alarm for the crack of dawn. Successfully, after a night filled with two encores, I slip out of Jordan's arms and tiptoe across the hall.

The week has passed with minimal disruptions since Christie shared her story. So far, Christie hasn't made any more rumblings. Either Jordan's statement struck a nerve, or she went back to planning and plotting something else. The only issue was the same car I saw at the school was parked down the block when I escorted Reese home on Thursday. Cruz informed Connor immediately after we secured Reese inside. I was concerned the revelation would have Connor rethinking allowing Reese to attend the home game tomorrow. Surprisingly, the plan to attend is still a go.

We sit around the dinner table, and they discuss the plan for tomorrow.

"I need to be at the stadium much earlier than the two of you. Cruz will meet you here and bring you to the family entrance. Madeleine and Christoph will also be attending the first home game.

"Cool!" Reese exclaims. "You're forgetting something, Dad."

"I am?"

"I can't wear my old gear to your first home game with a new team."

A naughty smile graces Jordan's gorgeous face. Thankfully, I'm sure only I see the underlying mischief. "You should go check out the huge box in my office as soon as you're done eating."

"I'm done," she announces. Then she sets her plate in the sink and rushes to his office.

Oohs and aahs filter from her cheers. "Alex. You should come in here too."

I cast a glance at Jordan who gifts me a devilish wink. After adding my plate to the sink, I step into Jordan's office. Reese hasn't made it to the bottom of the enormous box, yet I can easily determine there are two of each item, from hoodies to hats and jerseys.

Reese tosses me a hoodie. "Try it on," she demands.

I tug on the hoodie while she tries hers. I'm sure Jordan knows her sizes, but mine? I mentally shake my head. Of course he knows. He has skillfully explored every dip and curve nightly since the first time we were together last week, each one more intimate and fulfilling than the last. Awareness jolts through me when I feel him approach me from behind. He sets one hand on the middle of my back away from Reese's view.

"I can't wait to see you wearing my name emblazoned on the back of a jersey to a game like Reese." His words alone warm me from the inside out. His breath near my ear combined with the underpinnings of his meaning has me clenching my legs together. Jordan doesn't miss a thing. "I'll take care of the ache between your thighs later, Alejandra."

I turn with my lower lip caught between my teeth and lift my eyes to meet his.

"Work for you?"

I release my lip and whisper, "Hell yes."

"Is this enough gear, Reese?" Jordan asks his daughter.

"It's a great start," she quips.

"Seriously, I got both of you one of everything."

"I'm messing with you. I love Alex has the same clothes too. Kirsten only took me to one game. She said it was too crowded. The rest I had to watch on television. We need to make sure we match tomorrow, Alex."

"No problem. I'm thinking jeans with a tank top, the jersey, and the hoodie in case we get cold."

Reese replies, "Sounds perfect. On a scale of one to ten, how excited are you about going to your first game?"

"Ten. Watching it here with you was fun. In person will be amazing! Plus, I have the best guide when I have questions." I raise my hand to high-five Reese.

She meets my hand and says, "Yeah, you do!"

"Hey, what about me?" Jordan asks. "I helped teach you the plays for the first time ever."

"He's right, you know?" My statement is directed at Reese.

"He did help a little with the route running practice and the books," she reminds me.

"True. You get a high five too!" I raise my hand in Jordan's direction, and he smashes his against mine. Then he winks at me.

Reese and I take our DC gear into our rooms. Then the three of us reconvene to discuss the defense for tomorrow's game and how Jordan can exploit their weaknesses until Reese goes to bed. Mostly I listen to the two of them banter, and I learn a lot. Hopefully, one day I'll be able to join in and offer something of use.

I attempt to sleep alone in my room to give Jordan more appropriate rest. Instead, he follows me into my room and sets an alarm for himself.

In the morning, he gets up before the team breakfast and Reese. After getting ready, he slips back into my room and presses a kiss to my forehead and then my lips. "I'll meet you in the tunnel after the game."

"Have a great game."

"You have fun too."

I kiss him again a bit more thoroughly, despite not having brushed my teeth, before releasing him. I curl up, inhale him on my pillow, and sleep for a little longer before Reese wakes me to train.

Reese buzzes around the house until Cruz arrives for the game. "Hey, Cruz! Have you ever been to a game before?"

"Yeah, but it was a long time ago, and it wasn't in the luxury suites."

"It's awesome!"

"A bit excited, Reese?" Cruz asks her.

"I always am."

I join them in the kitchen and give Cruz a jersey to match us. "Any issues?"

"No."

I nod, and we leave for the stadium. Jordan directed us to the players' entrance and to speak with a guy named Bill.

"Good afternoon," he greets Cruz. "Credentials, please?"

Cruz provides the tickets and the family passes.

"Excellent. Is Miss Devereaux back there? I have a gift for her from her father."

At the word "gift," Reese unbuckles and leans forward. "Hi! I'm Miss Devereaux."

"Pleasure to meet you. Here you go."

Cruz takes the bag and sifts through it as a precaution. No reason to be concerned but just in case. He hands the bag to Reese and listens to Bill's instructions.

Reese tears into the bag and pulls out a small box. "He didn't forget." She smiles and pulls out another box.

"What is it, Reese?" I ask her.

"For each team, my dad adds a charm to my bracelet." She lifts her left wrist. There's a lighthouse dangling from the bracelet, presumably symbolizing New England, and an alligator for Florida. "It isn't usually the logo for the team, but something to describe the area."

"How sweet. What did he pick for this team?"

"You should see for yourself. There's a box in here for you too."

My heart leaps out of my chest. Believing he and I could pull off a solid relationship is a lot for me to handle. However, this gift took thought, time, and effort. His patience astounds me. I take the box from her and open it. Inside I find a platinum charm bracelet exactly like Reese's with a blue crab charm.

"Let me help," Reese offers.

She secures the bracelet on my wrist. It's then I catch Cruz's reaction in the mirror as he parks the SUV. He won't say anything, but it's something I need to address with Jordan so he's aware. Reese adds the new charm to her bracelet. Then we make our way to the luxury suites.

Madeleine and Christoph are already there, and Reese rushes over to share her new charm with Madeleine.

"Hey. Nice jersey. How was the ride over?" Christoph asks Cruz.

"Thanks. Reese thought the three of us should match. The ride was clear."

Christoph nods and turns his attention to the field. Reese bends Madeleine's ear until the teams take the field.

"Come on, Alex! We have to get closer." Reese grabs my hand and leads me down to the seats overlooking the field. She plops down into the seat and watches the game intently like at home. It hits me like a freight train. They are home for me.

The first quarter is all Cam. He pulls down four receptions and a touchdown. Ty follows it up with a pick six. The team is winning fourteen to zero going into the second. Even in the luxury suites, the game is miles better than at home, which was great. The roar of the crowd and the rush of being here is more thrilling and heart pounding.

In between the quarters, I gather a snack for Reese and a few waters. I also send a quick text to Jordan.

Me: I know you won't see this until after the game but… thank you.

I chat with Madeleine while I wait. "How are things going?" she asks.

"Good. Reese is a superstar. She listens well and does what I ask."

Madeleine nods. "Jordan?"

I can't stifle the smile his name brings to my face.

"I thought you two might get along well."

I notably stumble over my words. "I…. He's handling it as best he can."

Madeleine's face lights up. "I've worked with Jordan a long time. Not once before he met you have I seen a sincere smile on his face, except when Reese was involved. You're good for him."

He's amazing for me.

Our conversation ends when Christoph approaches, slides his arm around her back, and kisses the top of her head. I roll my wrist, and the charm hits the bottom of my palm. I smile inwardly and return to Reese.

She's talking Cruz's ear off about the formation but falls silent when Jameson drops back.

Jordan leaps and plucks the ball out of the air. Reese grabs my arm. She must have seen one of his tells. He crosses into the endzone and bows twice. Reese and I join in the celebration, then share high fives all around. The team continues marching up and down the field until the final whistle, earning a decisive win at the first home game of the season.

"Did you love it, Alex?"

"Ummm, yes!"

Reese is beaming from ear to ear. It could be because of my answer, or it could be because Jordan played amazing today. Either way, she's giddy and ready to meet up with her dad. Thirty minutes after the game ends, we walk down to the entrance we used to arrive. The locker room is located down a perpendicular hallway. We wait with Cruz, Christoph, and Madeleine for the mandatory postgame press conferences to end.

CHAPTER TWENTY

JORDAN

I take a seat at the table to Preston's right and wait for the inevitable question about Christie. It doesn't matter I nearly broke two records today or how my team handed our opponents, the Super Bowl runner-up from last season, a thirty-point defeat.

Melanie from media relations points to a newer reporter in the third row.

She's tall and thin, but her nerves are evident. "Great game today!"

"Thank you. Jameson makes my job easy." I extend my fist to him, and he bumps it.

She follows up with, "Have you been made aware of claims you fathered additional children with Miss Wingate?"

"What's your name again?"

"Anna."

"As previously stated numerous times, Anna, I won't comment on my personal life or my family aside from the statement I released last week. Next question."

Melanie points to Stu.

"How did you focus on today's game with the turmoil of last week?" Stu asks.

"One has nothing to do with the other. When I'm between the lines, my focus is work. The team brought me here to help them win. Today Jameson and I left it all on the field. Are there any more questions about today's game?"

No one raises their hand, and I leave the press room. Once outside I take a deep breath and head into the locker room.

"Dude! You blew away your prediction." Cam slaps my back as I sit in front of my locker.

"I'm shocked myself. Pres was on fire today. Hell, you and Ty got one too."

"Ty's was thrown by our opponent though."

I laugh. "True. Still counts just the same. Hurry up and get ready. We can't keep your dinner date waiting."

"Your daughter or her caregiver?" Cam chides.

"You set up a date with my daughter. Alex's presence is for my piece of mind, but she's off-limits to you and Ty." *She's mine.*

Cam raises an eyebrow. "Did you…?"

I'm not answering his question any time soon. "None of your business."

"Unfortunately, I can't tell if you're lying because you never shared your personal relationships."

"Exactly. Get moving," I urge him. I hustle through the shower. When I return to my locker, Ty is dressed and ready for dinner.

"How did you dress so fast?"

"I didn't take any questions. Melanie only had me in the wings."

"A pick six is a big deal, Ty."

"Maybe in a regular game when you pull down only two scores. Was this your highest yard and scores in a game in your career?"

"Yeah." Today I had three hundred and sixteen receiving yards and four touchdowns. Shy of Flipper Anderson's record by twenty yards and one shy of the record for touchdowns, which is five, held by three players including Jerry Rice.

"What's the secret?"

Alejandra. I shrug, and he accepts it as my answer. Alex is the answer. It isn't one specific thing. She makes me happy. She brings joy into our home. I actually relax in my downtime with her and Reese. Together we can handle anything. With a grin on my face, I finish dressing for dinner. Then I check my phone. Since I started in the league, I've learned not to check it as soon as the game ends whether we win or lose. I need time to settle.

> *Alejandra: I know you won't see this until after the game but... thank you.*

I type, *You're welcome. I'll be out soon.*

Alejandra: We're here with Madeleine and the guys.

Me: Okay.

I signal the guys and make my way down the hall to my ladies.

Reese's smile grows bigger when she sees me. Alex on the other hand is discreetly watching me, considering the others in the group. I don't blame her. I'm doing the same thing. She looks hot as hell wearing a jersey with my name on the back. I know it's soon, but I want her name to be Devereaux too.

"Hey, Dad! Great game! It was so fun! Where are Uncle Cam and Uncle Ty?"

Leave it to my daughter to put my huge game into perspective. I'm quite certain she knows those record-setting stats. "They're coming. They'll meet us at the restaurant."

"Okay."

"Thank you for coming, Madeleine. Christoph."

"Great game, Jordan," Madeleine states. "Garnet and gold suits you."

"Thanks. I appreciate your hard work."

"You're welcome. Have a great dinner. It was great to see you."

"You too, Miss Madeleine. Bye, Mr. Christoph."

"Don't forget about my invitation, Reese," Christoph reminds her.

My daughter tilts her head skyward to look at him. She frowns and then recalls what he means. "Dad, are you playing on Thanksgiving?"

"Not this year."

"Can we go? Please, pretty please. Now Alex knows some plays, she can join the game too."

Cruz immediately looks to Alex in question. He clearly knew she had no idea who I was and nothing about football before taking this assignment.

Alex replies to his unasked question. "Reese is an awesome teacher."

Cruz's expression is priceless. His disbelief evident.

Reese informs him, "I taught her the difference between a post, slant, and go route. The list is long. Can we go to dinner now?"

"Let me guess, you're hungry?" Alex questions.

"Yes!" Reese and I answer at once.

Everyone laughs. As a group, we make our way to the exit. Cruz veers off after a few rows.

"See you later," Reese calls after him.

"Night, Reese."

Madeleine and Christoph are chatting with Melanie from the media office right near the exit. When I turn back, Madeleine waves us on. I open the rear door for Reese and then the passenger door for Alex. I move closer and murmur so only she can hear me, "Are you okay?"

"Yes. Too many people. We can talk later."

I nod as she sits and latches her seat belt. I thank Bill for his assistance with Reese's gift as we exit the lot.

"Happy to help, Mr. Devereaux. Great game tonight."

"Thanks again." I pull into traffic and drive toward the restaurant.

Despite not being alone, I set my hand on top of Alex's and squeeze. Her gaze lifts to mine. I catch a huge smile on Reese's face when she notices. I pull up to the valet and get out. A second valet opens the passenger door for Alex. Unnecessary jealousy sprints through me. It isn't as if he offered her his hand. I shake off the thought. Reese takes my arm and Alex's hand as we enter the restaurant.

"Good evening. How can I help you?" the concierge asks.

"We have a reservation under Beau," I reply.

"Right this way. Mr. Beau hasn't arrived yet."

"Thank you."

He leads us to a small private room near the rear of the restaurant. Your server will be right with you.

"Excuse me," Alex asks.

"How can I help you, miss?"

"Is there an exit closer to this dining room than the front one?"

He nods. "Yes. There's a secondary exit at the end of this hall." He indicates the hall to her right.

"Thank you." Alex takes a seat beside me at the table, and Reese is on the other side. We peruse the menu while we wait for Cam and Ty.

When they arrive, Reese is on them something fierce. "About time you got here." She stands and hugs Cam as best she can.

"Little Miss, you're so big!" Cam states the obvious.

"Duh, Uncle Cam. It's been a while since I saw you in person. You're still big though!"

He laughs and passes Reese to Ty. "Hey there! How's my favorite miss?"

"Awesome! Great touchdown dance today. Anyway, my new school is great. Alex is the best ever, and I love our new house."

"How does she do that?" Ty questions me.

"Do what?"

"Say so many words so fast."

"No idea. It astonishes me sometimes too. Cam and Ty, please meet Alex."

Cam extends his hand first and Alex takes it. "Pleasure to meet the person caring for Reese."

"You as well. Good game today."

"Thank you."

Ty attempts to shove him out of the way. Instead, Cam steps aside and Ty trips over the chair, nearly falling to the floor. I completely understand. She knocks me off my feet every time I look at her. He recovers and takes her hand in his. "Nice to meet you, Alex. I have to ask, what are your intentions with my brother here?" He points in my direction.

"Ty." My tone is a warning and a reminder. I'm sure my phone will receive a barrage of text messages after our meal ends. The topic of those texts will focus on one thing—Alex.

Her face turns a light shade of pink before Reese rescues her. "Can we order please?"

"Of course, Little Miss. What were we thinking?"

"Don't know, but if I'm hungry, you must be starving."

Cam replies, "You know it." He fist-bumps her before taking the seat beside her. Then he calls over our server.

We place our order and chat more about the game. Then Ty asks Alex about her job. I casually link our fingers beneath the table. I don't think Ty will press her, but just in case.

"How did you start in your job?"

Reese saves Alex from answering by doing it herself. "She's awesome, Uncle Ty. She was a marine. Then she started working with people like me."

Cam's interest is piqued, and Ty is stunned silent. Her prior service reminds them both messing with Alex isn't a good idea. Not only because I warned them off, but because she has skills Reese doesn't realize she possesses.

"Wow. You just got more interesting, Alex," Cam admits.

"Thank you."

Our server arrives with our drinks and appetizers, and the questions for Alex diminish.

The rest of dinner passes with the guys sharing stories from college before Christie, including the senior prank pulled on the three of us freshman year and the time the cheerleaders painted our lockers pink after we toilet papered their changing room.

"We should share with Alex the time Jordy got stuck in the locker room with Coach's niece," Ty suggests.

Alex squeezes my hand beneath the table before glancing in my direction with an intrigued look on her face.

"Don't share that one." I shake my head.

Cam grins. "Now we need to."

"Fine, but keep it clean."

"I'm sure Alex can handle a little bit of college shenanigans," Ty adds.

I shake my head until he recalls Reese is here too.

Ty reconsiders, "Perhaps we should set up a time for an adults-only dinner."

"Boo, Uncle Ty. I'm great!"

The rest of us laugh.

"You are, Little Miss. But we can't share stories of your dad's exuberant youth with you here."

Reese frowns at him. "Fine." She crosses her arms across her chest and makes a pouty face when Ty doesn't share the story.

"We have plenty of season left. Plus, Reese has school tomorrow," I offer. "Are we skipping dessert?"

"I'm stuffed," Reese announces.

"Same here," Alex adds and leans closer. "I can take her home if you want to stay."

I turn my head so they can't read my lips. "I would rather go home with you."

She exhales slowly. "Whatever you want is fine. I'm offering to let you hang with the guys."

"I will always prefer being alone with you instead of them."

Alex adds enough space to look at my expression. She nods tightly when she sees my sincerity reflecting at her. Ty requests our check and pays the entire tab before Cam and I are able to fight him on it.

The guys say their goodbyes to Reese, complete with their cute handshake they created when she was a toddler. Both wave to Alex and head outside. I barely hand the ticket to the valet before my phone is buzzing with messages. I ignore them until after I open the door for Reese and Alex. As I round the SUV, I scan the preview. I smile and thumb out a response to Cam.

Cam: Dude, she's out of your league. Hold on to her.

Cam: She's the first woman to bring a true smile to your face.

Cam: I know where I would be spending my Tuesdays if I were you.

If he only knew the Alejandra I know, the woman I find more intriguing each day, he would realize the deeper truth of his words.

Me: She absolutely is. She makes us both happy.

Then I check Ty's message.

Ty: She's smoking hot. How do you keep your hands to yourself?

Leave it to Ty to lack tact.

Me: I respect her.

He doesn't need to know the herculean effort it took since I saw her in the tunnel and during this meal not to kiss her senseless. When I pull away from the curb, I notice a few photographers across the street.

"Can you call Connor?" I ask Alex.

"Why?"

I tilt my head toward her window. As I pull away, she checks the side-view mirror. She pulls out her phone and texts Connor. "All set. Don't worry. He'll monitor for them, especially…." She points to the back seat.

I nod, link our fingers, and continue toward home. We escort a groggy Reese to her room.

"Congrats on your huge game, Dad. You were super close to breaking Flipper's record. Love you to the moon."

"Thanks, peanut. Love you to the moon and back."

Without hesitation, I lead Alex to my bedroom and lock the door. With a few long strides, I pin her against the closet door. Her entire body tenses in my arms, and not in a good way. Instead of giving in to the memory of her past, she cups my face and stares me in the eye.

"I'm insanely proud of you right now."

"So am I. Kiss me, Jordan. I've been waiting patiently for hours."

I grin at her and take her mouth in a soul-searing, penetrating kiss. In under a minute, most of our clothes are in a heap on the floor. The only thing between us is my jersey.

"You have no idea what seeing you wearing my jersey does to me," I admit.

She slides her hand down my abs and grips me. "I think I have a pretty good idea. It does things to me too."

"What kind of things?" I lift the hem of the jersey enough to slide my hand between her thighs. "Damn! You're soaked." I plunge two fingers into her and curl the tips.

A whimper falls from her lips before she shares, "I know this is complicated, but I want to be yours. Both of you. I don't know how it looks like work wise, but—"

I cut her off with a hard kiss and move my fingers in time with her strokes on my shaft. Running the playbook in my head, I stave of my fast-approaching climax. Once the pulses from her first orgasm slow, I withdraw my fingers.

The pout on her face is priceless.

"Don't worry, beautiful. I've got you." I lift her and wrap her legs around my waist. I steal a few more kisses and walk to the edge of my bed and lower us to the duvet. Her toned thighs fall to either side of my legs, but she's hovering over me.

"Are you on some type of birth control?"

"Yes." Her gaze catches mine as she slides her thumb along my lower lip. "Are you sure?"

"I trust you, Alejandra." With my daughter and my heart. However, I might scare her away if I share the latter aloud, especially in this moment.

Those four words are all it takes. She lowers onto me inch by torturous inch until I'm deeper than ever before. Her inner muscles tighten and constrict around me. She marks my back with her fingernails and sinks her teeth lightly into my shoulder.

"Baby, I need you to move." My words are strained and pleading.

At my request, Alex rocks forward, lifts, and plunges downward. My fingers dig into her hips, and I meet her with an upward thrust of my own. Each deliberate movement causes pleasure to slither up my spine. I hammer into her until I can't contain the intensifying pressure within me.

Alex shudders around me as I surge forward, emptying into her in hot bursts. When she collapses forward against me, I lean back and tug the jersey over her head. Then I repeat the action with her threadbare cropped tank I find beneath it.

She looks at me with questions in her eyes.

"I need to feel your skin against mine."

Seemingly satisfied with my answer, she melts against me, and I savor the feeling of us while our heart rates decrease incrementally. Pressing a kiss to the cap of her shoulder, I follow her collarbone inward until I reach her mouth.

She pushes off my shoulders, and I guide her to the floor. After we clean up in the bathroom, we curl up in my bed. She falls into a blissful sleep within minutes of her head resting on my chest. Shortly after her breathing shallows, I succumb to sleep as well.

CHAPTER TWENTY-ONE

ALEJANDRA

"Ready to leave?" I call to Reese in her room.

Jordan's arms collapse around me from behind. "Why didn't you say anything, beautiful?" Jordan says against my exposed shoulder.

My giddiness about girls' night must be written on my face. "I didn't realize it until after Connor offered." Last week at the team meeting, Connor realized I haven't had a day off. "Spending time with you two doesn't feel like work."

"You two are so cute together," Reese observes when she joins us in the living room.

"It isn't weird for you?" Jordan asks her.

"No. Alex is awesome, and you're stupidly happy together."

She's absolutely right. "What about you? Are you happy?" I ask her.

"Would I like to be a normal kid? Occasionally, sure. Most of the time, having a superstar dad is amazing. This team, this school, my real friends like Carter and Layla, and you both make it easier to handle." Layla's dad is the kicker for the DC team.

"If it becomes too much, promise you'll tell one of us?" Jordan asks.

"Of course. Can we go hang out with the babies now?"

I laugh. "Yes, let's go."

Twenty minutes later, we pull up to the gate at the farm. I input the code, and Jordan pulls through. We ride up the long driveway and park near the barn. I squeeze Jordan's hand before hopping out of the truck. We're still attempting to keep our personal relationship private. I direct them to Connor's house, and Reese gives me a huge hug. I watch them walk away a little too long.

"Hey, I thought it was you. Are you coming in?" Jill asks as she opens the front door.

"Yeah... actually, can I ask you something? You don't have to answer if it crosses a line between you and your brothers."

Jill steps onto the porch and closes the door. "Go ahead."

"When is the right time to talk to the guys about Jordan?"

Jill smiles. "I don't know your whole story, but I surmise you've been through some painful things in your past. If Jordan makes you happy, you should be with him. If you think your relationship will impact your ability to protect Reese, then you need to tell the guys immediately."

"I appreciate your candid answer."

"You're welcome. On a side note, you two are ridiculously perfect for each other."

The mere mention of him makes me smile. "Thanks. I'm scared it's too perfect."

"If I learned anything waiting too long to share my feelings with Javier, it's scary to believe there's one person for each of us, especially if you've been hurt before. Even though we're still out here, the bonds of girls' night apply."

"Thanks, Jill." I follow her inside, grab a drink, and meet the rest of the ladies outside around a roaring bonfire in the backyard.

Maia sets down her drink and rushes over to me. "I miss you so much!"

I hug her close. "Hey, girl! Me too."

We take seats side by side. Norah, Callie, and Madeleine are discussing feeding options for the babies.

"Before I forget, I brought your mail. It's in my bag. You should take it with you," Maia shares.

"Thanks."

"How did you swing this?" she asks.

"Connor offered on Tuesday. Reese will take any chance to spend more time with the babies. How are you?"

Maia shrugs, and a sadness crosses her face. "He doesn't want to talk about the party or anything that happened between us."

"He just moved to my not-a-fan list. Did he say why?"

Maia's shoulders slump even lower. "He said it can never happen again, and he refuses to talk to me now."

"Have you seen him in person or just on the phone?"

"Just on the phone. He's avoided me when he's in town."

"I'm sorry."

She mumbles, "Me too. I knew what I was doing, and I thought…. I didn't think it would turn out like this."

I set my hand on her forearm and squeeze. "I know."

"Your turn, Alex. How are things going?" Norah asks over the flickering flames.

"Good. Reese is settled into her new school with a few new real friends, and the routine works for her."

Callie laughs out loud. "As someone who fell head over sequined heels when Connor showed up at my door, let's get some real details. We won't share unless Reese's safety is at risk."

"I mean, the man is hot to a preposterous degree, he's a doting father, and oh yeah, he's the best wide receiver in the NFL," Madeleine adds.

The girls laugh. I don't need a mirror to know my face is a bright shade of red. "All of those things are certainly true. I trust all of you. At the risk of revealing more than we discussed, we're taking things slowly."

"Woo-hoo! Pay up, ladies!" Madeleine cheers. A flurry of twenties fall into Madeleine's outstretched hand. "I knew when we escorted Jordan home after the Pittsburgh game you two were together. The seemingly opposed combination of fear, concern, and relief on your face was evident."

"What? You guys are betting on what exactly?"

Jill offers, "You and Jordan would hit it off spectacularly."

"I see. Any other bets I should know about?"

"None I'm aware of," Jill replies. "We want everyone to be happy like we are." Jill's gaze turns toward Maia.

Her defensive walls go up immediately. "Nope, I'm not sharing anything."

"So there is a guy?" Callie asks.

Maia buries her head in her hands. "I can't. Not now. It's too soon. I'm sorry."

Norah replies, "No need to be sorry. We're here when you're ready to share or give Nolan a good, strong kick in the ass."

Maia lifts her head and looks at Norah in disbelief.

"It's impossible to miss how his face lights up when you walk into a room when he thinks no one is looking," Callie offers.

Norah adds, "Look, sometimes guys are blind and make ridiculously stupid choices. Hell, Jake, Christoph, and Cruz had their matches right in front of them long before they figured it out."

"I appreciate the support, but it's raw right now," Maia manages.

I reach over and give her a side hug.

"Thank you though," she says aloud.

"Let's shift to lighter topics. Thanksgiving dinner and flag football game," Norah says, moving away from Maia's love life. "We need to know how many people to cook for."

I answer, "I believe the three of us are in. Let me know what we can bring. Reese is crazy excited about the flag football game."

"Sweet!" Norah replies and notes the other's replies on her phone. Mine vibrates in my pocket.

Jordan: Are you ladies done talking about us?

Me: Lol. For the most part, why?

Jordan: Reese wants to come hangout there since the babies are asleep.

Me: I'll ask.

"Any reason Reese can't switch parties?"

"Not at all," Madeleine answers.

Me: She can come down. Want me to meet you?

Jordan: Sure.

"I'll be right back." I walk through the house and step onto the front porch. Before Reese reaches me, Jill joins me.

"Hey. I'm going to Callie's to keep Javier company. He volunteered to stay with the babies."

"Not surprising at all. How long until you guys have one?"

Jill smiles. "If he had his way, tomorrow."

"We should remind him it takes longer than a few months."

She laughs. "He knows, but being a father is the next thing he wants to achieve."

"Get to work then," I quip.

"We're practicing as often as possible, but not trying yet."

Jordan, Reese, and the rest of the guys are closing in on the porch.

"Mum's the word, Alex."

"No worries. Girls' night bonds are sacred." I hug her, and she walks past the guys.

"Hey, Reese. How are the babies?"

A huge grin grows on her face. "They're awesome! Cruz was feeding two of them at once. It was crazy!"

Jordan laughs as she stands behind Reese. The rest of the guys nod and head into the house.

Reese continues talking about Liz and Ben. "There are five babies…."

Honestly, I stop listening. My gaze is pinned to Jordan's face, and I would give nearly anything to kiss him right now. His expression matches mine. Instead, I guide them into the house and grab waters for them.

We make our way to the bonfire in the backyard. The couples have paired off. Callie is sitting on the arm of Connor's chair, Jake and Norah are kissing near the snack table, and Madeleine is whispering in Christoph's ear as he leans over her chair.

I want to share us outwardly.

Reese plops down beside Maia, and I introduce them as I take my seat again. Jordan leans against the side of my chair. "Reese, this is Maia. She's my bestie and roommate."

"I thought me and Dad were your roommates."

I laugh. "You are." Part of me wants to add "for now," but I can't imagine moving out when Reese doesn't need security anymore. The only move I want to make is across the hall to his room.

Jordan leans down so only I can hear him. "Yes, to every thought passing through your mind."

I turn my head so no one can read my lips. "You have no idea what I thought."

"Doesn't matter. You won't hurt us, and I don't want you to leave...."

"I don't either."

"I know."

"Let me know when you're ready to go home. Your game is later, but you still need to sleep."

"I'm fine for a bit longer. Reese is having a blast."

I nod and return my attention to Reese who is talking her favorite book series with Maia—Harry Potter. Nearly an hour later, Reese asks to go home. We say our goodbyes and head out.

"They're really nice people, Dad," she murmurs in her half-asleep state on the way home.

"Yeah, they are."

"I really like it here."

"Me too, peanut." He lifts my hand to his lips and kisses the back.

After Reese climbs into her bed, we make our way to the living room and curl up on the couch. I'm against the back cushion tucked against his side, my head on his chest.

"How did it go with the guys? Did you get grilled too?"

"The guys were fine. Cruz asked some pointed questions, but they amounted to big-brother statements, like 'don't hurt her,' rather than warning me off. He's protective of you."

"He was a cop before working here, and he has two sisters. He can read people extremely well. He doesn't know any of my story, but he was able to discern I had a rough go for a while."

"Fair enough. What did you share with the girls?"

I shake my head against his chest. "I tried not to share anything, but Madeleine... Madeleine wagered with the girls we would get together. I swear it was the craziest thing I've ever seen." I recap the information I shared and how the ladies forked over their cash.

"Wow! I'm not surprised though. Madeleine has known me for years. She would be one of the few people who could accurately assess whether a person would be a good fit for me and Reese. She does it for coaches and teams, why not my better half?"

I crane my neck and gaze at his face. He's completely serious.

"Can we talk about Reese's statement earlier?" His voice is soft and barely audible.

"What about it? She didn't say anything inaccurate or inappropriate. She didn't out us."

"No, but I kind of wanted her to. I don't want to hide anymore. I want to greet you properly, sit close to you, or hold your hand wherever we are regardless of the people around."

"Me too. The wives and Maia saw right through me. I didn't share much, but they're rooting for us. What about Reese?"

"What about her?"

"My job is to protect her and care for her. I don't want to hide us anymore either, but we don't have a choice, do we?"

He pinches the bridge of his nose. "I don't know, but I want a choice. You make me happy. I refuse to give up on what we're building because of how you came into our life."

"Perhaps it's time to talk to Connor and ask for Maia to join me or replace me?" I suggest.

"No solution that includes you not being here with us is sufficient."

"I don't want to leave either Jordan, but…."

He waits for me to continue. Jordan knows there's more than sharing our relationship on my mind right now. "What else?"

"How adept you've become at reading me is astounding."

"Not any more than you seeing me."

We can handle this. Right? Right! "Maia brought me my mail. There was a letter from the Texas Department of Corrections."

Jordan shifts onto his side so we're looking at each other, his thumb gliding along my cheek. Then he waits for me to continue.

"Ramon is getting released early due to good behavior and overcrowding."

"What worries you about his release? I assume he's going to be on parole and can't leave the state. Right?"

"Arguably true."

"Can you get a restraining order, just to be sure?"

I shake my head. "It won't be granted because he isn't supposed to leave Texas, and I'm not close enough to warrant one."

"I'll call Connor tomorrow myself and ask to add another team member when you leave the house with Reese."

"Why?" I manage.

"I need to protect your job and your heart at the same time."

My eyes flutter closed, and I suck in a lungful of air.

As if those words weren't enough, Jordan isn't done. "I let you in and you stole my heart, but it isn't enough to give me yours."

"That isn't true. You don't understand. I'm terrified he'll ruin what we have. I love you. Madly, truly, and more deeply than I've loved anyone ever before. I love Reese the same, but I can't risk either of you. He will come for me again, and I can't—no, I won't allow either of you to take a risk on me."

"It isn't for you to decide alone, not anymore, and it isn't a risk. I love you to the stars, Alejandra. Whatever you need to face, we'll do it together."

"But... the risk."

"There is no but. I love you. I like our family better when we're with you."

I grin at him. "Did you just paraphrase lyrics from a pop song?"

"Not intentionally. How did Jake handle it when Connor fell in love with Callie? He was her bodyguard, right?"

"Yeah, he sent Christoph to be there as well."

"Okay. Having Cruz or Maia here wouldn't be so bad, would it?"

"Fine, I'll talk to Connor at our meeting on Monday."

"What upsets you most about my request?"

"I'm not."

"Alejandra, please look at me."

I comply. The pain on his face is heart-wrenching.

"Asking for an extra set of eyes isn't a slight. I know without question or hesitation you will protect Reese as if she were your own. I want the world to know you're mine. If we share our relationship, you become a target of Christie and Trey too."

"Your statement is true now because I'm with Reese every time she leaves this house."

He starts to reply but pauses to consider my last statement more thoroughly. "I suppose you're right. However, we don't act like a couple outside these walls. My selfish need to claim you as ours puts a target on your back to hurt me, not to get to Reese."

"Would you like me to call first thing tomorrow?"

"Monday is fine. You and Reese aren't leaving the house tomorrow, right?"

I pout. "No, we're watching from here because it's too late on a school night for her."

"You're sad about staying home?"

"Yes, at the stadium is miles better."

"You and Reese should travel to the playoff games with us."

Yes please! "I'll add travel to the list of things I need to talk to Connor about. There's no chance we should travel alone."

"I understand."

CHAPTER TWENTY-TWO

JORDAN

The season is moving along at a decent pace. We've played nine games and lost only once. I'm looking forward to our bye week, which falls on Thanksgiving weekend. First though, it's time to celebrate Alex and get through an away game. Reese and I have been scheming how to pull off a celebration she'll accept. It's more difficult than I anticipated, especially now.

Alex came clean to her bosses about our personal relationship. At first, they intended to pull her, citing her inability to protect Reese adequately. Once she explained her increased vigilance with Reese, we only have another staff member when the three of us leave the house together. It's not horrible, but I'm more comfortable knowing there's a layer for security for Alex too. Reminding her it's about me and not her inability to protect herself or Reese was torturous.

I know her birthday isn't until tomorrow, but Reese and I planned an entire day for Alex while she's at school.

"Good morning, Jordan," Maia greets me when I answer the door.

"Hi, Maia. Thank you so much for doing this."

"No thanks are necessary. Alex is my bestie. You make her happier than I've ever seen before. She deserves today and as many others as she'll accept from you."

I completely agree. Alex and Reese enter the kitchen, ready to tackle the day.

"Maia, is everything okay?" The concern in Alex's tone is evident.

Reese grins at me, and I nod, giving her permission to spill the beans. "After you drop me off at school and teach your class, you're spending the day with Maia doing fun stuff for your birthday."

"I am?" Alex's voice cracks.

"You are," I confirm.

Sensing her unease, Reese asks Maia to hang with her in the garage. Alex has been silent since I answered her question.

"Talk to me, Alejandra," I urge her.

"You don't have to do all this for me."

"I know. You deserve today and much more. Plus, I can and want to spoil you. Please let me."

Her posture softens, and her arms circle around me. I kiss the top of her head.

"How big are we talking?" she mumbles against my chest.

"During the day today, not so big. Your time with Maia is only the beginning."

"I can't accept whatever it is you planned."

"You can. I set things up with Connor. Your bosses are aware of my plans and added coverage where necessary. Right now, Maia is here as your bestie and my coconspirator."

"I don't know what to say."

"You don't have to say anything. Remember when I gave you the first rose and then the bouquet and books?"

"Of course."

"Birthdays are a big deal to me. I never thought I would get to adulthood. Foster care was abysmal. Also, I didn't have cake and presents once on my birthday until college. Those first weeks in juvie before I met Mr. G and Coach were excruciating. Each year is worth celebrating and celebrating well. The step up from those gifts to today is big. Please have a great time. You're important to me, not the cost."

She exhales sharply. "I'll do my best."

"Thank you. Now go or Reese will be late for school."

Her smile grows against my chest. She lifts her gaze to mine and kisses me deep and hard. The emotion in her lips is about me, not about the gift. No man has ever put her first. No other man will ever get the chance if I have my way.

"I love you to the stars, Jordan."

"I love you to the stars and back, Alejandra. Have an amazing day."

She grabs her bag and heads toward the garage. I follow immediately thereafter. I greet Bill at the gate and hurry into the locker room.

"Hey, Cam!"

"Good morning to you too. What has you all hyped up?"

Ty chuckles. "Haven't you been paying attention, Cammie poo? Not only is our boy ass over tea kettle in love, but she also loves him back. What did I miss, bro?"

I slap my hand down on Ty's shoulder. "Her birthday is tomorrow, and the sheer number of surprises I have in store for her are going to make her blissfully happy or piss her off."

"She doesn't like surprises?" Cam asks.

"She doesn't hate them, but she isn't used to being taken care of."

"Doesn't she know how much your contract is worth?" Ty asks without tact yet again.

I shake my head. "She does, but it isn't about money. No one has taken care of Alex except her since she was a teenager."

"Alex isn't used to it, and your net worth isn't helping," Cam offers.

"Keen observations, Cam."

"How over the top did you go?" Ty asks.

"Not over the top as far as cost, but the sentiment is stratospheric."

"Did you buy her a ring already?"

"Not yet. She needs small steps forward. If I push too hard, we'll move backward. It isn't a bad thing. Steady is the way to move with Alex."

"Understood. We're happy for both of you, man," Cam admits.

"What he said," Ty agrees.

"Thanks, guys." I glance at the clock. "We need to move, or we'll be here doing extra physical fitness on our easy day."

We hurry to the field and narrowly avoid penalty laps for lateness. As expected, practice ends before lunch. I pull out my phone and check my messages.

Maia: As promised.

Attached is an image of Alex covered in a sheet from the waist down, her arm obscuring her breast with a gorgeous smile on her face. She's relaxed and glowing, which was my goal for today.

Me: Thank you.

Maia: You're welcome. Everything else set?

Me: Yes.

Maia knows every detail of my plans. She tempered my plans a bit and suggested I tone down the tangible gift from me and Reese.

Alejandra: I have no words. Thank you so much. How much more is there?

Me: Just enough. I love you to the stars.

Alejandra: I love you to the stars and back.

Once I clear my messages, I hustle to the airport to pick up Alex's next gift. I patiently wait near the luggage carousel. Normally, I would simply have a driver handle this to avoid being seen. However, this arrival needs to be handled personally.

A tall, fit guy approaches me with a tiny woman beside him. I wouldn't say Alex looks like her brother at all. "Jordan?"

"Miguel?" I extend my hand to him. When I reached out the first time, he was skeptical of my intentions. For a few weeks, we talked nearly daily before I requested he come visit for Alex's birthday.

He nods and takes my hand. "Pleasure to meet you in person. This is my fiancée, Naomi."

I extend my hand to her. "Nice to meet you, Naomi. Do you have more luggage?"

"No, we only have carry-ons," she shares.

"Great. I parked in short-term. The ride is about thirty minutes."

"No problem," Miguel replies.

Before long, I pull up to the house and into the garage.

"Alex lives with you?" Miguel asks.

"Not exactly. She has a condo she shares with her bestie."

"Maia, right?" Naomi asks.

"Yes. She lives here right now because she's working as security for my daughter. However, if I'm being completely honest, I don't want her to leave… ever."

"Does my sister know your plans yet?"

I shrug. "I haven't said those words exactly. Your sister is cautious. Given her history, I understand."

Miguel nods.

"Let me show you to the guest suite. The girls should be back in a little less than an hour."

"Thank you," Naomi graciously replies.

I pace the length of the house more times than I can count, waiting for Maia's text. This surprise could go very well or horribly wrong. I'm hoping for the former. When Alex talks about Miguel, I can tell she misses him but doesn't want to go to Texas. More so now with Ramon out on parole. It would shock me if Alex steps foot in her home state again.

Maia: We're headed your way. ETA fifteen minutes.

Me: Thanks.

I send a text to Miguel. He and Naomi join me in the kitchen to wait. Excitement and a tiny sliver of fear slice through me when I hear the garage door. As soon as they park, I'm in the garage opening her door.

She throws her arms around me tighter than ever before, and I hold her against me. Her lips press high on my jaw before she whispers, "Thank you doesn't begin to cover how I feel right now."

"At the risk of angering you, earlier today barely scratches the surface of the things I want and will do for you. There's another moderately bigger surprise in the kitchen. Please know, there are still more tomorrow on your actual birthday. I love you to the stars, Alejandra."

"I love you to the stars and back, Jordan." She presses another sweet kiss to my cheek, and I lower her to the floor.

It's only then do I see the enormous smile on my daughter's face. Maia insisted Alex would know something was up if she didn't need to pick up Reese. After pickup, Reese convinced Alex she desperately needed more books and chocolates from Millie's. I had no doubt Alex would yield to Reese's wishes, or Maia could persuade her if necessary.

"Come on, Dad! You can kiss her more later. Her surprise is inside, not out here!" Reese scolds me.

Alex lowers her arm and turns toward her. "Do you know my surprise, Reese?"

My daughter nods her head vehemently.

"You're excellent at surprise keeping."

Reese smiles. "It's because I love you to the moon."

The only person she's ever said those words to is me. She'll say she loves Cam and Ty to me, but not to them.

Alex inhales sharply before replying in kind, "I love you to the moon and back, Reese."

She hugs Alex tight for a moment, releases her grip, and leads her inside. I'm right behind Alex when she turns the corner and sees her brother.

"Oh my God!" She turns back to look at me and then back to make sure he's actually standing there. "Come here so I can pinch you to see if you're real."

Miguel laughs and hugs Alex. Tears roll over the balls of her cheeks. She squeezes Naomi's hand despite Miguel not releasing her.

"It's wonderful see you again, Naomi."

"You too, Alex," she replies.

Alex leaves her arm around her brother's waist and asks, "How long have you been working on this?

"The first time he reached out was five weeks ago or so, I guess," Miguel replies. "I was skeptical at first. It took about three or four calls and a photo of you frosting a cake together before I believed him completely."

"Understandable. How long are you here?"

"We're flying home after the game on Sunday."

A huge grin takes flight on Alex's face. "You're coming to the game with us?"

"I actually liked football before Jordan shared he was your boyfriend. You on the other hand—"

I interject, "Had absolutely no clue who I was when we met."

Everyone laughs. The smile on my woman's face is priceless, and I can't believe I pulled this off.

"He's right. Miguel and Naomi, please meet Reese and my roommate, Maia." They exchange handshakes.

"I've heard tons about both of you," Maia addresses them.

"Can I get anyone a drink?" Alex offers.

"No, you can sit. I'll get the drinks and dinner started." I pull out one of the stools and wait for her to sit. After catching her gaze for a few long seconds, which aren't enough, I kiss her lightly on the temple and move to the fridge.

The shock on Miguel's face when Alex heeds my request is nothing short of comical. I think it's more surprising Alex allows me to take care of her at all.

Hours later after a delicious meal complete with chicken marsala, a few veggie sides, and some childhood stories, our guests turn in the for the evening. Maia heads home, and Reese excused herself to her room about fifteen minutes ago.

"Are you ready to go to bed?" I ask Alex who is looking out the doors toward the backyard.

"Sure. Can I ask one thing first?"

I tilt my head in concern. "Go ahead."

"Are there any more big surprises?"

Maybe? "I wouldn't categorize them as surprises."

"What would you categorize them as?"

"Gifts," I reply earnestly.

"Plural?" she mumbles.

"Yes, one from me and one from Reese." Technically both from me, but only because of the cost. The gift from Reese was completely her idea to continue the matching theme.

"Okay." Her face falls more.

I take her hand and lead her to the tufted bench along the wall. "What's wrong, beautiful?"

"Nothing's wrong. I'm not used to all of this." She motions around her and to me. "I'm not used to how I feel."

"How do you feel?"

Her gaze lifts to mine. "Loved, cared for… happier than ever before."

"As you should because I do too. You belong with us." I spoke too soon. She wasn't done. "But?"

"I'm terrified something will happen to you or Reese or both if I allow myself to believe we're a real family, something we can't control or prevent."

Like her parents. "We are a real family. Family isn't necessarily blood. Family is shared bonds. Family is what you make it. You consider Maia and your other team members as family, right?"

"Yes."

"Nothing is going to happen to us. We have you watching out for us every single day. Plus, you have backup when the three of us go out as well. The guys will manage Christie and continue to keep tabs on Trey. We're going to be fine."

She tucks into my side and links her fingers around my waist. "I trust you. I believe you."

"Let's get some sleep. You have a big day of hanging out with your brother tomorrow until dinner out after work."

"Did you plan the day or…? Who is joining us?"

"I didn't plan the day. Miguel did with input from Reese. Maia and Cruz are joining us for dinner."

She wrinkles her nose, which is still adorable. "Why two?"

"Maia is coming as your bestie, not working."

"Thank you."

"I know you miss her even though you see her weekly and talk all the time."

She smiles at me. "You're right. I do."

"Let's go to bed." I lead her down the hall after she rechecks the doors and the alarm. Piece by piece, I strip off her clothes and worship each square inch of her soft skin until she's barreling toward an orgasm with my hand over her mouth.

CHAPTER TWENTY-THREE

ALEJANDRA

Earlier than normal, Jordan attempts to sneak out of bed.

"Babe, don't go. Come back."

"Babe, huh?"

I bury my face into my pillow. "Don't like it?"

"Not used to it."

I raise my arms, beckoning him closer.

He complies only enough for me to skim my fingers down his bare chest. "Happy birthday, Alejandra."

"Thank you. Come back to bed."

"No can do. Your birthday breakfast calls."

"I could get used to being yours."

"You absolutely should because I don't plan on giving you up." He leans forward and presses a kiss to my forehead.

His statement would've made me shudder in fear soon after Ramon. Now though, I take Jordan's words for what they mean. We're in this together—long-term. We should probably discuss what that looks like.

"Alejandra, where did your thoughts just go?"

"I have some questions."

"You can ask me anything, sweetheart."

"Are you sure you want me to ask right now? I mean, birthday breakfast and all."

He grins at me. "Maybe narrow it down to a broad topic."

"What does our future look like to you?"

He sits beside me and takes my hands into his before replying, "Whoa! Okay. Why don't you tell me some of the actual questions so I can relax a bit?"

"Do you want more kids? Do you want a wife? What about my job?"

"Yes. I want a bigger family. A blue-eyed girl with dark hair and olive skin like her mother and then a boy, to start if that works for you. The job question isn't easily answered. Honestly, you need to decide for yourself, and we can work with what you want to do. I want to talk about each concern and desire in your head. Please know without question, I want you beside us as long as you'll have us. Give me twenty minutes, then your breakfast will be ready." With another soft kiss, he's out the door with a cheeky smile on his face.

I roll out of bed, fix it, and grab some appropriate clothes for our company. When I make my way to the kitchen, the smell of bacon and something sweet greets my nose.

"Happy birthday, Alex!" Reese says as I turn the corner.

"Thanks, Reese."

Jordan kisses my temple and hands me a cup of coffee.

"You two are super cute." She smiles and grabs the stool beside me.

As much as I love having Miguel and Naomi here, I'm glad they're still sleeping. Just the three of us is perfect. Jordan sets a plate with chocolate waffles, fruit, and bacon in front of me and Reese, then sits on the other side of me.

"This looks amazing!"

"Dad's birthday breakfasts rock!" Reese states before she digs into her plate.

I lean into Jordan and whisper, "Thank you."

"My pleasure. Eat up. You have a big day ahead of you."

"I do?"

"Training after breakfast," Reese states.

"Wouldn't miss it."

Jordan flashes a signature smile in my direction. "Miguel planned your day today. Then tonight we're going to Chez Michel for dinner and cake here afterward."

With her mouth full, Reese adds, "And presents, Dad. Don't forget the presents."

"And presents."

Jordan hurries out the door to work sooner than I would like. He kisses Reese's head, an all too quick kiss to my lips, then he grabs his bag and he's gone. Before I hear the garage door close, I get a text.

Jordan: I love you to the moon, Reese. I love you to the stars, Alex.

I laugh, show Reese, and reply in kind. "Do you know what time we're leaving?"

Reese shrugs. "As long as our training is done, I'm good."

"Sounds like a good idea." With a clean kitchen, I change to train.

Miguel and Naomi emerge fully dressed when Reese and I finish our cooldown.

"Morning, Alex," Miguel mumbles.

"Morning. Coffee is set to brew. How long until your plans for me start?"

"We can be ready in an hour, right, Naomi?"

Naomi lifts her head from her phone. "Sure, sounds good." She certainly didn't hear my brother.

"Are we racing today, Reese?"

She shakes her head no and pads to her room to dress, and I do the same.

Miguel opts to check out Crescent Bay to make sure the area is good enough for me. The idea is laughable but cute at the same time. The little brother checking things out. I wonder what he asked Jordan when they spoke. When I visited for the holidays, we didn't hang out much. I met him for dinner, and we opened a few gifts, but otherwise he was occupied with Naomi's parents and brother, as he should be.

We're at the Nook. It seems to be the only store, aside from Millie's, Reese wants to visit. Norah, Madeleine, and their children are here too.

I've been waiting for the inquisition all day long, so while Reese is enthralled in her surroundings, I finally prompt the inevitable conversation. "Ask what you need to ask, Mikey."

"You haven't called me Mikey in years."

I shrug. "I know. I needed to remind you which one of us is older."

"Hilarious, sis. I was shocked when he called. At first, I didn't believe he was who he claimed to be. Why on earth would the best receiver in the NFL be calling me out of the blue? Not only that, he wanted me to take leave and come to Maryland to spend your birthday with you. Even more, it's a surprise. Then he followed through. Each time he said he would call or email, he did. The clincher was the photo though."

"Which one did he send you?"

My brother pulls out his phone and scrolls through his gallery before turning it toward me. It's one of the first ones Reese took. I was unaware and unequivocally unguarded. The love in my eyes is palpable and unmistakable.

"The last time a genuine smile was on your face was before Mami and Papi were killed. Not even when Ramon went to prison did you look as happy as you do with him."

"Thanks, Mikey. I've never been happier than I am with them. Reese is amazing, and Jordan...." *He's everything I could need in a stupidly handsome package.* "His life wasn't easy either. Much like us, he came out on the other side."

"Younger brother or not, less skillful fighter or not, lesser marksman is a toss-up now, I need to do my thing as the only male Mejia in your life."

"*Te amo por eso.*"

"I heard about Ramon. How are you handling that?"

I explain the additional security when the three of us go out, but otherwise don't share anything more. "I can't let him control my life again. Knowing he's out early sucks. I'll continue to look over my shoulder daily despite the small security of knowing he can't leave the state. The only blessing is, if he crosses state lines, he's violating his parole."

"No trips home anytime soon?"

I shake my head. I'm sure he already knew my answer.

"I don't blame you."

Reese's curls are bouncing around her face as she pushes Liz in my direction. "Alex, Miss Madeleine let me push Liz around the store. I found three more books. I had Jessa add them to Dad's account."

I laugh, crouch down, and greet Liz. Her hand grips my pinkie finger tightly.

"Hi, Alex. You must be Miguel. Reese has been talking about you since she arrived," Madeleine greets us.

He takes her extended hand. "Yes. Pleasure to meet you…."

"Sorry. I'm Madeleine, Jordan's agent, and my fiancé is one of Alex's bosses."

My brother nods.

"I see the birthday surprise was a success. Happy birthday, Alex."

"Thanks, Madeleine. We'll see you tomorrow."

A puzzled look crosses her face. Then she replies, "At the game, of course. See you then."

Madeleine leaves with Liz, and Reese hurries to the front of the store to grab her new books.

"I'm ready now, Alex."

I shake my head left to right. "I think we're forgetting one thing."

Reese frowns. "What?"

"Naomi."

Reese laughs. "There were four of us, huh?"

"I'll go find her," Miguel offers.

We make our way back to the house and arrive after Jordan. By the time we get there, he's had enough time to bake me a cake, which is cooling on the island.

"How was your day, ladies?" He high-fives Reese and kisses me lightly.

In under three minutes and as few breaths, Reese spills our entire day to Jordan. Both my brother and Naomi are stunned.

"Sounds amazing. Why don't you get ready for dinner? We need to leave in about an hour."

"Okay." My daughter takes off down the hall toward her room.

"We're going to freshen up too. See you later." Miguel and Naomi head for the guest suite.

As we make our way to the bedroom, I ask how his day was.

"Today was pretty light. We played this team away earlier in the season. Having film of the previous game assists in planning."

I disappear into the bathroom, apply some makeup, and slip into my dress for dinner. When I emerge, Jordan is nearly dressed in a navy suit and crisp white shirt. He's fussing with his cuff links. *Hot damn!* It is unfair to other men how hot he is.

"Stop looking at me like that, Alejandra."

"Like what?"

"Like you want to ravage me."

"I do with my eyes, mouth, and body. You look…."

"I look?"

I take three strides, stopping a mere inch of touching him, and take his hand in mine. "Hot as hell. I can look at you whenever, however, and as long as I want."

He raises an eyebrow. "I see."

I fix the cuff link and shift to his other arm. "Glad we agree." I turn on my heel to leave, but before I can, he pulls me to him, his hard body flush against my back and his crisp scent surrounds me.

With his free hand, he swipes my hair over to my left shoulder and brings his lips near the shell of my ear. "You know what that means, right?"

The heat from his body and the shivers from his words are a distinctly delicious contrast of sensations. "What does it mean?"

He turns me away and draws me in again facing him. "It means I can devour you with my eyes, mouth, hands, and body as I wish as well."

"Yes, please."

"You're torturing me, gorgeous, with your sexy dress and the look in your eyes."

I chose my emerald sheath dress with a super low back. "This old thing." I wink at him. "Do we have enough time before dinner?"

"Not enough to worship you properly. However, I will devour you when we get home. I intend to give you an orgasm for each and every hour I need to wait until I can strip this dress off your curves."

Sweet mercy! "Yes, please."

"No need to beg, sweetheart. I'll willingly give you everything you could ever need or want."

A shudder courses through me. I believe him, and as much as I value my hard-fought independence, I want him. I want a life with them. We need to figure out what it looks like.

Maia and Cruz arrive to escort us to dinner.

"Where did this dress come from? You look hot!" Maia states as soon as she arrives.

"Thanks." I introduce them to my brother and Naomi. Despite joining us as my bestie, Maia is sitting up front with Cruz. The rest of us are in the back of a large company SUV.

I'm accustomed to being led into a rear door because of my clients' celebrity status. It's intriguing when it's my boyfriend's status causing it instead. We take our seats and chat while dinner is served. Cruz relaxes a smidge since we're in a private room and there's only one way in or out.

The chef prepared an exceptional meal at Jordan's request. The entire time we're seated, his hand is linked with mine or resting on my thigh beneath the table. Until him, I not only shied away from sharing my story but allowing a man physically close to me. Now, when he isn't touching me, I feel as if a part of me is missing.

Jordan leans closer after the entrée dishes are cleared. "Ready to go home, gorgeous?"

"I think we should stay a little longer."

"Why would you want to stay?"

I turn my head so no one can read my lips. "Another fifteen minutes would up the number of orgasms to three."

"We still have cake and presents. I'm thinking five is a good number for tonight, what do you think?"

My jaw drops open, and I gasp.

"I'll take that as a yes. Let's go home for birthday cake and presents." He sets a sweet kiss below my ear. "Then I'll fulfill my other promise to you." Jordan rises and extends his hand to me.

I take it and stand impossibly close to him.

"How wet are you, my love?" he whispers.

Only he has brought my carnal needs to the surface so readily. "Dripping. Good thing I skipped panties." My response might be the first time I've shocked Jordan. After my answer, we hastily make our way to the car.

Everyone gathers around the island for cake and sings horribly for me. I think about my wish and blow out the candles. I make a second wish with the first cut of my cake and start serving. Within a few minutes, silence blankets the kitchen.

"Where did you get this cake, Jordan?" Maia asks.

"I made it."

"Do you have a brother?" Her question is surprising since I know she's hung up on Nolan.

Jordan laughs. "Don't think so."

"Is it time, Dad?" Reese questions after polishing off her slice of delicious chocolate cake with chocolate filling and whipped icing.

"Sure. They're on my desk."

Reese is off her stool before he finishes speaking.

Miguel and Naomi laugh. "She's a great young lady, Jordan. You should be proud," Miguel offers.

"Thanks."

Reese is back almost instantly. "Can I go first?"

Jordan motions for her to go ahead. "I wanted you to have some too." She hands me a small, navy bag.

I pull out a little, velvet box. *Breathe. She said some.* Nestled inside is a stunning pair of diamond stud earrings.

"These are…."

Reese leans close to me and points to her ears and then her wrist. "See, now we have matching sets. We both have a charm bracelet and classy earrings from Dad."

I can feel Jordan's gaze on me. Maia's too. Yet my eyes stayed trained on Reese. "These are perfect, Reese."

"Put them in. I never take mine out." I noticed her earrings but didn't think anything of them.

Maia must see my hands trembling because she slips between Reese and me to help. "You good?" she mouths.

I nod almost imperceptibly. By the look on his face, I know Jordan is keenly aware of the inner turmoil within me at this moment.

Miguel must be too because he breaks the silence with "The cake was delicious, Jordan. We're going to turn in. Have a great game if we don't see you before you leave." He bro hugs Jordan then leaves with Naomi.

Cruz and Maia take my reaction as their cue to leave as well.

Maia hugs me close and puts my feelings into perspective. "You deserve everything they want to give you, Alex. It isn't about the value; it's about the sentiment. I'm sure Reese has no idea how much those earrings cost Jordan."

I reply softly, "Love you, girl."

"Love you too. I'll see you Monday at the team meeting." Maia releases me and joins Cruz near the door.

"Thanks, Cruz."

"See you tomorrow for the game. Good night, Jordan. Happy birthday, Alex. Later, Reese."

"Bye, Mr. Cruz."

He laughs and opens the door for Maia.

"It's late, peanut. You should go to bed as well."

"'Kay. Happy birthday, Alex. Night."

I nod, and we reply at once, "Good night, Reese."

Silently, Jordan loads the dishwasher and puts the rest of the cake away. He loops the gift bags around his wrist and extends his other hand to me. I slide my hand into his, and he leads me to the bedroom.

With the door locked behind us, he guides me to the love seat near the fireplace. Without hesitation he gathers me in his arms. "What part of Reese's gift freaked you out?"

I take a deep breath, look up at him, and put my heart completely on the line out loud in words. "It wasn't the gift exactly. I feel like you and Reese are mine... my family. Miguel, Naomi, and Maia... every single person I love was in one room for me, to be with me. The last time... was so long ago it's a tiny shard of a memory."

"We are family. We love you, Alejandra, and we're going to keep you." He slides the pad of his thumb over the ball of my cheek to dry the fallen tears.

"I love our unconventional family."

"I do too. Do you want to wait for my gift?"

"How big is it?"

"Huge. Bigger than bringing Miguel here—sentiment wise."

I drop my head. He leans forward and lifts his gift off the tufted ottoman. Similar to when I opened Reese's gift, my hands are shaking. I push away my worries. Owning how I feel about them is on me. Accepting their statements and actions of love is on me too. The envelope has the same logo as Reese's birthday gift. Where in the world…? I lift the flap and pull out the itinerary for a trip to Colombia.

"Jordan, it's…." Tears prick my eyes, and a few tumble down.

"Perfect?" he suggests.

"Yes. Perfect. I have no other word than perfect."

"If we're lucky, we can take this trip alone."

Surprise and glee rush through me. "How?"

"Our relationship with each other is equally if not more important than ours with Reese. Plus, we are going to visit Harry together."

I laugh heartily.

"Am I forgiven for going over the top with guests and gifts?"

I shake my head. "You didn't do anything wrong. Unless…." I tap my finger on my lips and wrinkle my nose.

"Alejandra, you know how I love when you wrinkle your nose. Unless what?"

"There's still one more part to my birthday celebration."

A devilish twinkle rises in his eyes as he checks his watch. "Why, yes, there is. I believe the required number is six, correct?"

"Hmmmm, six. If your count is six, then six it is. We can wait if it's too late on a game night."

Jordan draws the tip of his finger down my arm, past the hem of my dress, and around the front of my knee. With a flattened palm, he slithers up my inner thighs and dips two fingers into me. "I will never break a promise to you, Alejandra. Nor will I ignore your needs inside or outside of our bedroom for extra sleep." His teeth sink into the cap of my shoulder, and he spears and teases circle after circle on my clit until I scream his name.

"That's one." Jordan starts his countdown until he reaches four.

We fall asleep for a few hours before he wakes me by kissing his way from my toes to my core where he coaxes two more body-shaking orgasms from me. Near seven o'clock I wake to the sight of Jordan emerging from the closet fully dressed.

"Is it time already?"

He takes a seat on the edge of the bed. "Afraid so. Cruz will be here later. See you guys in the tunnel after we win. I love you to the stars."

"I love you to the stars and back." I steal one kiss, and he's gone.

CHAPTER TWENTY-FOUR

JORDAN

It's been almost two weeks since Alex's birthday. My team narrowly defeated our opponent last weekend, and now I'm looking forward to our bye week. First up is a meeting with the Blackthorne guys about whether having security for Reese is necessary any longer. I'm skeptical but willing to listen to them. I hired them for a reason. If they believe we don't need their services anymore, who am I to question them? The outcome of this meeting will impact our family as well.

"Reese, we need to get moving," I state outside her door.

"Coming," she replies.

We make our way into the garage and toward the office before Reese speaks.

"Alex, how is it going to work when you don't have to bring me to school anymore for security reasons?"

"Don't know yet. Your assignment was unique and requires a different solution to ending it."

Reese frowns. "Are you going to leave us?"

"No," Alex answers immediately.

Alex and I haven't discussed her staying, but she did share her desire to stay. "There are a lot of moving parts, peanut," I offer to soothe her.

She huffs and crosses her arms over her chest. I park in the Blackthorne lot, and Alex escorts Reese to read at the Nook. She has already determined Norah is working this morning. We take our seats, and I link our hands under the table.

"Before we get into any planning, we have a more personal issue to discuss," Connor indicates. "Our investigator is extremely thorough. During his search to find connections between Corey Mikel, Christie Wingate, and Trey Edson, he came across other personal information pertaining specifically to you, Jordan. Parts of your early life closely mirrors one of my mother's foster clients."

Shock runs through me. "Joyce is your mother?" I manage.

"Yes."

I look to my right at Alex. "You figured it out early on, didn't you?" Concern and fear cross her face. I tighten my hold on her hand.

"I had a strong hunch, yes."

Connor continues, "If you're interested, she would like to meet with you. I won't share too much, but she has a few clients she's followed into her retirement. You're one of them."

"Yes, I would like to see her again."

"Great!" Connor replies and slides a card across the table to me.

Jake joins the conversation. "I suggest you set it up before the holiday since she'll be there like the rest of our family and close friends. My investigator also determined you have at least two full biological siblings."

My heart and mind race. I have siblings. Before Jake can continue, his phone rings.

"Yeah, Blaine?" Jake pauses to listen. "I understand. When did Miss Wingate land?"

Alex releases my hand and is out the door faster than I run on the field to catch one of Preston's passes, followed closely by Connor. Less than thirty seconds later, Alex's phone on the table blares an offensive sound and has Reese's photo flashing.

Reese! My heart is in my throat. Choosing this football team was a mistake. I attempt to rush next door, but Jake restrains me.

"Let me go!"

"Can't. Alex and Connor will take care of her."

"Jake, she's my daughter!"

He releases me but blocks the exit. "I understand your frustration, but let them do their jobs. Adding you into the mix will only make things harder for Reese and Alex."

I exhale sharply and walk toward the rear of the room and pace back and forth until his phone rings again. It feels like an eternity has passed since Alex ran out of here. In reality, it's been about ten minutes.

"Go ahead, Connor," Jake says into the phone and listens intently.

A police cruiser and ambulance pull in front of the building, and I charge toward the door.

Somehow, Jake prevents me from leaving with one hand. "Understood. We're on our way." Jake hangs up the phone but doesn't move from his position immediately. "Reese is physically fine."

"Thank you," I reply, relief seeping into my veins.

Jake leads me next door through the rear entrance and deposits me in Norah's office. "Stay here. I'll bring Reese to you. I don't want any further issues when you hear what happened. Understood?"

I nod curtly and cross my arms. I circle Norah's office a few times before I hear my daughter.

"Dad!" Reese runs into the office and leaps into my arms. "I used the techniques Alex taught me to defend myself. The woman from the television, my surrogate, she's here. Well, she's in the ambulance now."

"Take a breath, peanut. Are you hurt?"

She complies and continues talking, "No. That's what I'm saying. The woman… Christie, she started talking to me. She said she was my mother and I needed to go with her because something bad happened to you. I asked for the code word."

I can't believe she still remembers. I taught her if a stranger approached her saying I sent them, they would know the word. Only three people know our code word is lighthouse—Cam, Ty, and Kirsten.

"She didn't answer fast enough. Then I pressed the panic button Alex gave me."

"Great job, peanut. I'm so proud of you. How did Christie end up in the ambulance?"

Alex appears in the doorway but says nothing.

"She grabbed my wrist really tight. I yelled for her to let go. She didn't. I tried to squirm away and yelled again. She said the F word a few times.

Alex taught me to escape by pulling my hand toward the opening instead of toward the four fingers."

Her words don't make sense, but I don't interrupt.

"I tried, but it didn't work. Then I amped it up like Alex taught me. I did the same move plus pushed against her arm with my other hand. She stumbled backward and hit her head on one of the shelves."

"I'm so proud of you!"

"It was all Alex. She's the best mom ever!"

"Yeah, she is." I kiss Reese's forehead and hold her closer, but my gaze is locked with Alex's. I mouth, "Thank you."

She replies silently, "You're welcome." Alex knocks on the door to bring Reese's attention to her presence. "Hey, sweet girl. How are you?"

I set her on the floor.

"I'm good. Thank you for teaching me to defend myself." She slides her arms around Alex's waist.

"I hoped you would never need to, but I'm glad you had the skills today."

"Me too. What happens now?"

"If I may"—Jake steps into the doorway—"you need to share what happened one more time with Officer Tim."

Reese shrugs. "Okay. Can they come with me?"

Jake laughs. "It's kind of a requirement for your dad to be present."

"I want both, please."

"You got it. Ready now?"

"Sure," Reese answers him, and we make our way to the Blackthorne conference room.

I'm in awe of my daughter as she reiterates her encounter with Christie for Officer Tim slowly and methodically. He carefully asks for details as he takes her statement.

"Great job, Reese." He praises her. Then he turns to me and Alex. "Your daughter handled herself well today. You should both be proud."

"I'm—" Alex begins.

I cut Alex off. "We are. Thank you, Officer."

"You're welcome. Please let me know if you wish to press charges."

"We will," I assure him. "Thank you again."

Jake escorts him out, leaving the three of us in the conference room alone.

Alex rises and presses a button on the control panel. The glass walls turn opaque.

"Cool," Reese states.

"How are you, Reese?" Alex asks.

"I'm good, except why did she come here?"

I take her hands in mine. "I don't know yet, but I'll find out." More questions filter into my mind. How did she know Reese was off from school today? Is someone following us? Following Reese?

"Does this mean Alex gets to stay with us longer?"

Alex replies, "I was never going to leave. I just wouldn't be working for your dad anymore."

"Oh, so you would be my mom and dating my dad?"

The two of us laugh.

"We should talk about our relationship more in depth at home. I'll share that Alex isn't moving out when you don't need security anymore."

Reese's eyes widen as she pushes up from her chair and throws her arms around Alex. "I'm so happy!"

"Me too."

"Me three," Alex adds.

I lift her hand to my lips and kiss the back. There's a strong knock on the door.

"Come in," Jordan states.

Connor sticks his head into the room. "We're set as far as the incident with Miss Wingate. However, do you want to finish our meeting?"

"Yes, I would prefer to hear the rest today," I answer him.

"I'll take Reese to Millie's to give you some privacy." Alex offers.

"No, I would prefer you stay. Both of you."

If Connor is shocked, it doesn't show on his face. In fact, a small smile curves up at the corner of his mouth as if he knew Alex and I would find peace in one another.

Alex looks at Reese, then to me and back again. "Are you sure?"

"Yes, I'm done hiding. We can hash out a plan about security later this week. Perhaps we need to leave things as they are for the rest of the season and then reconsider. I want—need—to know what Blaine found out about my family."

"I'll grab Jake and be right back in," Connor states.

"Jordan, can you come over here?" Alex whispers, motioning to the corner of the room as far away from Reese as possible. Her words near my ear send sparks of heat southward.

"What's wrong, gorgeous?" I ask as I join her in the relative privacy of the back of the room.

"Nothing. I owe you an apology."

I frown. "For what?"

"I let her get to Reese."

I slide my hand around her jaw and angle her line of sight to match mine. "No, you did nothing wrong. We agreed she could be there. It isn't on you. It's on Christie and only Christie. I will never blame you for something outside of your control. Please don't blame yourself."

She nods, and I press a soft kiss to the tip of her nose. Connor clears his throat when he reenters the room. We take a seat at the table with our hands linked, the three of us.

Jake shares the information the investigator found. "Blaine was able to locate two full biological sisters. One sister, named Julianne, is thirty. She lives locally. We can reach out to her through appropriate channels to see if she's interested in meeting you."

"Yes, please. You said two sisters."

"I did. Your other full sibling is Jillian," Jake shares with us.

"I have two aunts. Miss Jill is your sister?" Reese asks. "She's amazing. So cool!"

I'm speechless. It seems odd to say now, but there was something familiar about her when we first met. Was her experience as terrible as mine? Unlikely, she was adopted. When was she adopted? What about Julianne? My mind is spinning. Do I have brothers-in-law aside from Cruz, Jake, and... Cameron? I think. When I chose this football team, I went from Reese and myself to a slightly larger family with Alex. How large did our family grow? Does Cruz have—

"Jordan." Alex's sultry voice wiggles in between my cascading thoughts.

I turn to look at her. She looks at Jake and Connor and makes a head movement.

"We'll give you some time," Connor states.

"Wait! Thank you. One more question first. Does Jill know?"

"Cruz told her this morning when we were set to share with you," Jake replies.

I nod, and they leave the room.

"Reese, could you go ask Gemma to share the secret snack stash with you?"

"Ummm, yes! I won't leave the office."

"Thanks, peanut," Jordan mumbles. The only sounds I hear is the pounding of my heart in my ears and Alex's breathing. I reach out and draw Alex as close as the chairs will allow and set my forehead on her shoulder.

"I could offer some insight into how Jill is feeling right now, but the bonds of girls' night are sacred."

I grin against her. "I have so many questions."

"I'm sure you do. Honestly, talking to Joyce will help some, but I bet most of your questions are for Jill and Julianne."

I agree against her shoulder. "I had so many reasons to avoid this area. It never crossed my mind... it could be a good thing outside of my career. It led me to you. I love you to the stars, Alejandra."

"I love you to the stars and back. You also gain a couple of sisters," she adds.

"True."

There's a strong knock on the door. Alex kisses me softly and rises from her chair. When she opens the door, Jill and Cruz are on the other side. Her face is red and flushed, probably from crying. I can only hope they're good tears. Without hesitation, I stand and meet her in the middle in a huge hug. I don't know how long we stand there, but when we break, I find we're alone in the conference room.

"I have so many questions for you," she says.

"Same. How much time do you have?"

I laugh, and we take a seat. We trade stories about our childhoods. She shares she was adopted nearly right away. I learn Joyce and the Blackthornes are friends, and she has been Jill's caseworker since the beginning. Jill divulges she was always worried about coming across a sibling the wrong way as in a blind date or meeting a guy at a bar or her father. She asks a few pointed questions about my childhood and how I met Joyce.

"I'm sorry she wasn't assigned to you sooner."

"Me too. Did Cruz tell you everything?"

"About our sister? Yes."

"We should reach out to her," we say at once and laugh.

I consider my schedule for the next week or so. "Are you and Cruz free for dinner on Friday?"

"Yes."

"Good. Please come over. I'll cook."

Jillian tilts her head. "You cook?"

I frown at my newly discovered sister whose blue eyes are exactly the same cerulean color as mine. "Yes, why?"

"It's my passion hobby. I cook all the time."

"Oh. Interesting."

She raises an eyebrow at me.

"My degree is in elementary education with a focus on special needs."

"Wow!"

"Alex had the same reaction. How about we decide on a meal, and we can cook together?"

"Sounds awesome. Give me your phone, please."

I fish my phone from my pocket, unlock it, and hand it to her. Her fingers fly across the keyboard. Nearly instantly, I hear a faint chime.

"How would you feel if I invited Joyce as well?"

"I would like that. Would you mind if I reach out?"

Jill smiles. "No, not at all. She's…. You'll understand as soon as she answers the phone."

We hug and open the door for our better halves, who are suspiciously milling outside the door. I bro hug Cruz, and we make our way home. Reese is shockingly quiet.

"What's wrong, Reese?"

"Our little family just got really big, didn't it?"

"I think so. How do you feel about it?" I ask, watching her expression in the rearview mirror.

"Really, really happy, Dad. Our little family—you, me, and Mom—is awesome, but if Jill is your sister, then Ben is my cousin, right?"

I tighten my fingers on Alex's when Reese calls her mom again, although it's the first time she's said it in her presence. "Yes."

"Any babies Miss Jill and Cruz have are my cousins, right?"

"Yes."

"Awesome! Uncle Cruz loves kids. I bet they'll have a bunch!"

We laugh and make our way home. Today was a split day for me. The fear for Reese and then the sheer joy of learning I have sisters. I can only hope it keeps getting better and Julianne wants to know us as well.

CHAPTER TWENTY-FIVE

ALEJANDRA

A bye week is a little different as far as Jordan's schedule. He'll go to work next Tuesday and be able to have Thanksgiving off. Jordan left about fifteen minutes ago.

"Ready, Reese?"

"Yup, I can't wait. We have only five more days of school until our short break."

I never loved school as much as Reese does. After parking in the lot, I escort her inside mere seconds before the bell rings.

She hugs me tight. "Bye, Mom. See you after school."

"See you then."

My heart has never been bigger or so full of love. These two are it for me, and for the first time, I'm looking forward to the future. With them in mind, I text Connor, asking to schedule a meeting after the holiday. I want to make some changes. They may not be possible, but the first step is to ask.

Maia: Are you free right now?

Me: Where are you?

Maia: Home.

Me: I'll be there in twenty. Do you need anything?

She replies with a shrug and a crying emoji. This can't be good. Instead of grabbing a pint of Ben and Jerry's, which it's excessively early for, I grab a bunch of pastries on my way to our condo. A tug of sadness circles my heart. I'm going to miss living with Maia, but I can't wait to move forward with my newly expanded family. It's weird to think Cruz could end up my brother-in-law. I'm excited for Jordan and hope he and Jill are able to locate their sister.

"Maia," I call out as I step into the condo. She's upset, so there's only two places she could be: her room or the rooftop. I climb the extra set of steps and set the pastries and coffee in front of her. "How badly do I need to hurt Nolan?"

Maia is sitting in the oversized chair with her arms wrapped around herself. When she finally looks up at me, I see her face is puffy and red from crying. "I don't want to hurt him. I want to stop hurting. He's gone anyway."

"Where?"

"Australia for the next three months."

"He took the assignment with Miss Swisher." It's a statement, but she answers anyway.

"More like she requested him."

"It isn't unusual. What did he say before he left?"

"Nothing other than a curt goodbye." She shifts and pulls her legs up into her chest, and her arms close around them.

It's then I notice what she's clutching in her hand—a positive pregnancy test. I kneel before her on the floor and hug her tight.

"How long have you suspected?"

"My periods are erratic. I missed two in a row though and considered it as a potential reason."

I nod. "Otherwise?"

"I'm a little tired is all."

"Does he know?"

"No. He won't even grant me the courtesy of answering my calls. This isn't something I intend to put in an email or text."

"What is your plan?"

"Still working one out."

I hug her tighter and offer, "Whatever you need, I've got you."

"Thanks, Alex. Let's talk about you instead."

"Or we could sit here and savagely attack these pastries."

"Did you get my favorite?" Maia mumbles.

"I got one of everything, just in case."

"You're the bestest bestie eva!"

"I love you too, Maia."

She leans forward and plucks a bear claw from the pink box. "So spill, sister."

"Nothing really to spill. I haven't hidden anything from you. Things are going well. I'm really happy. I'm sorry to say that when you aren't in a good place."

Maia shakes her head because her mouth is overfull. "You deserve it, Alex. Frankly, so do I. Maybe I was wrong and Nolan isn't my person. I'm not upset about the baby. We made a choice, and despite our best efforts, consequences have occurred. His actions are upsetting me more than I thought he ever could."

"I'm squarely on team Maia and baby right now."

She grabs a second pastry, and we chat until it's time for pickup. My instinct is to reach out to Nolan to slap some sense into him, but he needs to figure it out on his own. Hopefully, he'll snap out of his stupidity soon.

I park in the side lot of the school and make a perimeter sweep. I notice the same car in the lot, but the guy isn't near it. After I send a text to Connor, I make my way toward the car and take a seat on one of the nearby benches, pretending to be using my phone.

His response is nearly immediate.

Connor: I sent Cruz for backup. Please wait until he gets there.

Me: We'll go visit Jill.

Connor: Good thinking.

Me: There must be a connection Blaine missed somewhere.

Connor: You're correct. Already asked for a deeper dive on this guy. Please tell Jordan.

Me: Will do.

The same guy approaches the vehicle, and I snap a few photos. Once he pulls away, I wait an extra minute before making my way inside to collect Reese.

"How was your day?" I ask her.

"Pretty good. I didn't share anything with my friends yet. I want to let it settle a bit more."

"Why?"

"Dad needs some more time to process it all. He hasn't told me, but his childhood wasn't easy, was it?"

I consider dodging the question, but I'm not breaking any confidences agreeing with her. "No, it wasn't. Is Miss Jill still here?"

"You mean Aunt Jill? Yup."

"Sweet, let's go say hi."

Reese loops her arm around mine and leads the way. She's none the wiser why I want to stay in the building a bit longer. After knocking on the door, we step into Jill's room.

"Hey there!" She greets us. Considering her connections to Blackthorne, including her husband and brothers, Jill knows something is up given our impromptu visit.

"Alex wanted to stop by and say hi before we left for the day."

"Are you excited for the holiday coming up, Reese?"

"I'm more excited about playing football than the actual holiday itself."

Jill laughs. "It's fun to watch, but I don't normally play."

My phone vibrates in my hand. I lift my hand, indicating it's work. Jill nods, and I take a few steps away from Reese.

Cruz: I'm about five minutes out.

Me: We're in Jill's room.

Even though he won't see it until practice ends and it'll worry him, I send the text anyway.

Me: Same guy at the school. Cruz is joining us as a precaution.

Me: She's fine. He didn't see her or connect me to her.

I snap a pic of her with Jill and send it to him. While I'm working, Jill sets Reese up with a computer game near the side of her room before coming up beside me.

"How long until my husband is here?"

I chuckle softly. "Not long. The same guy was loitering outside. I sent photos to Connor. Maybe Blaine can actually track him this time."

"We're missing a connection somewhere. I'm sure he isn't a parent, or the connection would've come up by now. Any thoughts?"

I shake my head and indicate Reese's presence.

"She can't hear you."

"I doubt Blaine would miss an obvious one. He isn't a parent or family member here, and he isn't connected to Christie or Trey as far as we know. I don't believe there's anyone else of concern for Jordan."

"The guys will figure it out. They always do."

"I just hope it's before another incident."

"Same. Jordan and I just learned about one another."

"I know. Reese is over-the-top happy to have you as her aunt."

Jill smiles. "She's a great girl. Jordan did an exceptional job on his own so far."

"She is and he has."

Jill's smile grows even bigger when Cruz joins us.

"*Cariña*." He kisses her lightly. "Alex."

"Cruz."

Reese turns toward us and pulls down her earphones. "Hey, Uncle Cruz!"

"How was school?"

"Pretty good. I think you forgot something?"

Cruz tilts his head in question. "What did I forget?"

"Coffee for Aunt Jill."

"She prefers her coffee in the morning," Cruz replies.

"Oh. Can we go home?"

I catch both Jill and Cruz smiling. "Sure can."

Cruz hops in our car, and Jill follows us home.

"Thanks, Cruz," I say as we pull up to the house.

"No problem, Alex. Later, Reese."

"Cool. Is Aunt Jill coming to the game too?"

"No. I'll be working."

Reese shrugs, then runs out of the garage to Jill who is rounding her car to the passenger side. She hugs her, waves, and rushes inside.

"I'll reach out to Connor later. I want to give Blaine some time to process the photos." I state.

"Understood."

I wait until they pull through the gate and watch it close before I head inside. Almost immediately my phone pings with an incoming video call. A huge, involuntary smile grows on my face.

"Hi—"

"Alejandra, if this turns out horribly, please promise me you will raise Reese."

"Jordan, you're scaring me. What is going on?"

"Not sure yet. Team security barricaded me in Coach's office. I called Jake already. Christoph and someone named Barrett are on their way here. Alejandra, please promise me."

I know if it isn't written down, there's nearly zero chance I can make his request happen, but I will do whatever I can to pull it off. He isn't worried about us. He's worried about himself. He was never worried about himself. "I promise. I love you to the stars and her to the moon."

"I love you to the stars and back."

Fear grips me. I knew we could end up in this position, but I hoped like hell it wouldn't happen. Casually, I make my way to Reese's room. She lifts her gaze from her book and smiles at me. I nod and retreat to the kitchen.

"Jordan, please don't do…. Please listen to Christoph. We're fine here. Connor just texted. Cruz and Jill are on their way back here now."

"The same goes for you, Alejandra."

I don't confirm his statement. "I need to go. Cruz is back." After ending the call, I admit Cruz and Jill into the house.

"I'm only here in case you need to leave to meet Jordan."

"Okay. I'll get Reese."

I settle myself and walk down the hall. "Aunt Jill and Uncle Cruz decided to hang out for a bit." A necessary lie.

A huge smile graces her face. "Sweet!" She chucks her book and dashes past me. I'm glad she's growing comfortable with them.

CHAPTER TWENTY-SIX

JORDAN

Nearly thirty minutes of pacing and worry after my call with Alex, Christoph notifies me he's coming to release me.

"Hey. Thanks for coming. What's going on?"

"Corey Mikel is the same man who has been seen outside Reese's school."

"He came here?"

"Yes."

"Why?"

"Don't know yet. I'm going to have a chat with him before we make any decisions. Do you want to be present?"

"Yes."

Christoph stops walking and turns to face me. "You will allow me or Barrett question him. You're an observer only. Do you understand?"

"Yes."

He leads me to a small office in the administrative wing of the stadium.

I acknowledge Barrett, then lean against the opposite wall so I can look at Mr. Mikel.

"Why come after Mr. Devereaux?"

"I've been following Ramon's woman. I saw them together outside a gym in town."

No, hell no. Mine.

"What is your connection to Ramon?" Barrett asks.

"He's my boy from back in the day, but she cautious. She has newly acquired skills from the gym in town. Plus, she always has a little girl with her. I ain't 'bout to hurt a kid for nobody."

He must have connected me with Alex when I picked her up from the gym.

"What does Ramon want?" Christoph asks.

"He wants me to give her a message," Mr. Mikel replies.

"You've been stalking her for how long to give her a message? Why not mail her a letter or try to contact her in some other way?" Barrett presses him.

I've never met Barrett before, but he's physically imposing even to me. His question is valid though.

"Ramon was adamant she wouldn't accept anything from him."

"He's right," I admit aloud. My words earn me the side-eye from Christoph—a look I also take to keep my future responses to myself.

"What do you need to tell her?"

"I'm only permitted to share the message with her personally," Mr. Mikel replies.

"If you're unable to speak with her, then what? Did Ramon give you a deadline?" Christoph continues.

"No, but I check in with him through a few intermediaries every few days."

Barrett looks at Christoph. "Can we speak outside for a moment?"

Christoph nods.

"You too." Barrett points at me.

We step outside the small office and close the door.

"I realize my footing isn't the greatest right now, and I completely understand. However, Mr. Mikel hasn't broken any laws. Correct?" Barrett states.

I wonder what he means about his footing, but also realize he's right about Corey Mikel.

"No, I don't think so," Christoph replies. "He didn't breach the school or Jordan's residence. We can't stop him from parking and watching Alex go to the gym and by chance seeing her with Jordan. He also didn't make a fuss when he requested to see Jordan at the visitors' gate this afternoon."

Barrett continues, "We can't keep him here." He turns his attention to me. "What is your opinion of Alex talking to this Mr. Mikel?"

"It isn't up to me. Alex is the strongest person I know. She has a hard line with Ramon. It isn't my place to share why she has drawn the line."

Christoph nods. He likely knows some of Alex's story, but I won't share anything additional with him or Barrett. "We need to let him go. How do you want to handle this with Alex?"

"I'll call her and then talk to her when we get home." I pull out my phone and dial.

"Jordan?" She sounds upset, breathless too and not the good kind.

I push the video button and wait for her to answer. She looks upset and disheveled. "Hey, breathe, gorgeous. I'm fine. How is Reese?"

"She's having a blast with Jill and Cruz."

"Can you go into the bedroom or the office?"

I see her hesitantly walk away from the others toward the bedroom. "Go ahead."

"Christoph and Barrett just finished questioning Corey Mikel. He isn't looking for Reese or me."

A look of realization crosses her face, and her voice cracks when she replies, "Okay. When will you be here?"

"Within the hour. I didn't want you to worry until then. We can talk more when I get there."

She's crumbling right before my eyes.

"I'll be there as fast as I can. We can handle this."

Alex nods and swipes the lone tear falling down her cheek. "I love you to the stars."

"I love you to the stars and back, Alejandra. I'll be there soon." I grab my bag and hustle back to Christoph and Barrett. "I need you to get me home expeditiously."

"You think she's going to run?"

I shrug. "It's a strong possibility. She needs space and time." I hope she won't go far, but I would prefer she isn't alone.

Christoph nods, and we hustle to my car. Barrett follows in the SUV. I've easily exceeded every speed limit and blew a few red lights. I don't care. I rush inside to find Reese and Jill chatting up a storm about a recipe Jill wants to make for Cruz. My SUV is gone.

"Where is she?"

Cruz looks directly at me. "I don't know. She said something about promising to put Reese first, and she took off."

"Fuck!"

"Dad, you owe fifty bucks to the vacation splurge fund."

Jill and Cruz both smile despite the circumstances.

"I'll double it, Reese. Do you know where Alex went?" I have a few ideas but….

"She'll go to the most important spot she shares with only you," Reese opines.

"You're a genius!" I kiss her head and hug her.

"I know. Bring Mom back. Whatever it takes."

The biggest smile grows on Jill's face. Her relationship with Alex precedes hers with me. I'm sure Jill doesn't know all the details about Ramon, but she likely knows enough to know Alex took a risk with me and Reese.

"I didn't do anything wrong, peanut."

"I know. The three of us are happy. Fix whatever she needs fixed. She deserves it."

"I agree, but not everything can be fixed. Not all solutions are easy."

"Even if you can't fix it, bring her back. We need her here."

"I'll do my best. Do you mind hanging out here?" My question is directed at Jill.

"No, as long as you don't have a special use for some of the food in your fridge."

"Have at it and save me a plate please," I request.

"You got it. Let's cook our worries away, Reese."

Reese pumps her arm into the air and shouts, "Yes!"

I turn toward Christoph. "Do you need to come with me, or can I do this alone?"

"You can go alone. We've got Reese."

"Thank you." I look around the room at the four of them.

Cruz responds, "None are necessary. We're family, newly discovered but family nonetheless."

The feelings in my chest are in contrast right now. I'm leaving my daughter, who was the only person in my world until I met Alejandra, with my sister and brother-in-law. If you told me I would be comfortable leaving Reese with anyone other than Ty or Cam, I would've thought you were nuts.

"Go, Dad!" Reese urges.

I grin at my daughter, hurry into the garage, and type out a text to her.

Me: I'm coming to you. Please don't leave.

Alejandra: This is my fault.

Me: No, it isn't. Please wait.

The ride, which took nearly thirty minutes last time, I pare down to twenty minutes. I park and run nearly game speed down the pathway. Rounding the bend in the foliage, I don't see her.

"Where are you?" I call out. I don't get an immediate answer. Then I hear sharp intakes of breath and muffled sobs. I follow the sounds and find my better half curled into a tight ball with her back against the container with the blankets. "Thank you for staying to hear me out."

"How did you know I would be here?"

"Actually, that was Reese. She told me to go to our special place. Here is the only place she hasn't joined us. I had a few other places in mind, but her words led me here first." I take a seat facing her and wrap myself around her.

She burrows close but doesn't unfold her body. "This is my fault."

"No, it isn't. It's mine. It's Jake's and a little bit Blaine as well. We had blinders on. We were only looking for connections to me. No reason for us to suspect Ramon would send someone to find you."

"It's my fault. I let my guard down and started living again. I allowed myself a glimpse into how happiness feels. The only place he could've seen us together is at the gym when you dropped me off on a Tuesday."

"So what? Alejandra, sweetheart, look at me." My tone comes out more demanding than I intend.

Her gaze lifts to mine.

"You choosing to move forward isn't the reason. Reese isn't in any danger, and neither are you."

She shakes her head furiously. "You don't know that! Choosing to learn the skills to protect myself was only the first step. You see the fear I live with each day." Her eyes clamp closed again.

"I did."

At my use of did—past tense—she glances at me, coaxing me to continue. When I don't immediately do so, she asks, "Did?"

"Yes, did. It decreases each day you spend with me, and you get stronger in your belief in our little family. You single-handedly captured my heart and my daughter's. You taught her to defend herself so she wouldn't be in the same position as you were. It paid off with Christie. The only reason she was able to defend herself is because you took steps to protect yourself first. Corey just wants to talk to you. Ramon knew you wouldn't accept or open anything from him.

"Of course not! I don't want anything to do with him ever again. It took too long for me to find my way forward from him. I can't go back."

"You don't have to. The three of us are stronger together than apart."

She unfurls and scoots closer, threading her legs over mine before cupping my face.

"Will he ever leave me alone?"

"Contacting you through a third party is likely not something Ramon is allowed to do. We'll look into it."

"Just like that?"

"Yes. I'll do anything and everything it takes for our family." My words are met with skepticism. "To be clear, I mean scorched earth, no stone unturned."

"You're not angry with me for leaving?"

"I found you easily this time. I would've kept looking until I found you if you weren't here. You're stuck with me."

She shakes her head. "Not stuck at all. I feel free for the first time in quite a long time. Did Corey leave a number?"

I frown at her. "Yes. Why do you want it?"

"If I call him and listen to what he has to say, will it end Ramon trying to reach me?"

"Maybe." I don't like the answer, but it's the best I've got.

She glances over my shoulder at the river and then back to me. "Please keep it handy, but I want to pursue charges against Ramon if possible. I need him to understand I'm not his doormat anymore."

I kiss her forehead. "I'm crazy proud of you."

"Thanks. I'm proud of me too."

We absorb the stillness of the river just the two of us before returning home for an amazing dinner prepared by Jill.

CHAPTER TWENTY-SEVEN

ALEJANDRA

The boss men requested I join them for a meeting at my gym. A little weird… and intriguing. When I asked Connor for a meeting regarding my job after the holiday, he indicated before would be better for them.

"Morning, Alex," Connor greets me on behalf of my bosses and Norah with Ben strapped to her chest sound asleep as well.

"Morning."

Jake opens the front door and ushers me inside. It's early, so there aren't any classes or students milling about. Soon after we enter, Kim and her husband, Daniel, join us. We hug, and Jake gives the floor to Christoph.

"I'm sure you're confused as to why we brought you here. When I learned about Liz, I planned to leave Blackthorne and open a gym. Instead, the guys offered me a partnership that allows me to care for Liz and gives Madeleine the ability to continue to kick ass as an agent and be a mom."

Kim interrupts, "If I may, at the time Christoph was looking to purchase a gym, we had a few cursory meetings from a planning perspective. Now, Dan and I need to relocate to care for our aging parents. When we learned we needed to leave, we reached out to him."

"My plan was to offer self-defense classes to our clients, but we lacked the infrastructure to make it happen. On your own, you taught Reese to protect herself, and those skills proved useful not only for her confidence but to defend herself from an assault." Christoph lets out a deep breath. "This explanation is taking forever. Blackthorne is considering purchasing this gym and putting my plan into action. However, we need you to run it."

Wait, what? "You're offering me the opportunity to run this gym for locals as well as our clients?" It would be a dream come true to help women like me before a domestic violence occurrence, but after as well.

"Yes," Connor replies.

"What about housing?"

Christoph pointedly looks at Jake. "I told you she would see the vision. We're going to update the three guest cottages on the far side of our property and create a separate entrance for clients to use as needed."

My mind is spinning. "What about regular assignments?"

"You wouldn't take any unless we have a dire need of support or a client specifically requests you."

"What about Reese?"

Jake answers, "We are aiming for the first of the year to finish ironing out the details. It'll give you plenty of time to determine which current staff you would retain or if you want to hire someone new. You could run the gym as well as continue to work with Reese."

Containing my glee is difficult, but I rein it in enough to ask for some time. "Can I take a day or two to consider your offer?"

"Of course," Christoph replies.

"Thank you." I shake everyone's hand, kiss Ben's head, and leave the gym. I turn right and make my way to the gazebo before my mind explodes with possibilities. There's no way Christoph could possibly know I don't want to leave Reese. Maybe he could considering how Liz changed his thinking about work. My reasoning wasn't Reese until quite recently. It was more the ability to share my learned knowledge and potentially prevent a woman from suffering like I did. This is a no-brainer, why am I hesitating?

I start dialing before I answer the question in my mind.

"Hey. Is everything okay?"

"Hi. Yes. I didn't mean to worry you, Jordan. Everything is fine. It could be more than fine. Do you have a few minutes? This can wait until you get home, but I'm crazy excited, and the first person I wanted to share with is you."

"I'll make a few minutes. I love you wanted to share with me first. Spill it, sweetheart."

I take about five minutes and explain the job offer.

"Wow! Will there be too much downtime for you?"

"You remember?"

I can hear the smile in his reply. "Yes, I do. It explained your need to always be on the move. You've made strides sitting still with us."

"I'm growing accustomed to the downtime, especially with you and Reese. I'm not out of my mind, right? I can handle it?"

"You can handle anything thrown at you with grace. I'm sure Norah could assist you with the business part if you need it. Although, I foresee you changing from Harry Potter to business books to guide you instead."

I laugh. "You're probably right. It means I can take care of Reese and work on one of my crazy life goals."

"Wait, opening a gym was a life goal?"

"Not exactly. Teaching people to be aware and protect themselves so they don't become victims like me is a life goal. It's why I teach."

"You should do it. We'll make changes if we need to."

"Are you sure?"

"Completely. I want to talk so much more, but I need to get into my meeting. I'll see you at home. We'll celebrate properly. I love you to the stars."

"I love you to the stars and back." As I end the call, I mentally do a happy dance. Before I share my decision, I make my way to the deli and then Millie's where I run into Norah again.

"Hey, Norah." I gently touch Ben's head.

"I didn't really get a chance to congratulate you on the offer."

"Thanks, it's huge for me."

"You're welcome. If you need any assistance with the financials or staffing, let me know. I can offer suggestions and books to guide you."

"Funny, Jordan joked the same thing not two minutes ago."

"Now you rushing out makes complete sense. You wanted to hash it out with Jordan."

I'm momentarily speechless. "Yes. He was the first person I wanted to share with. Neither Maia nor my brother came to mind before Jordan."

"You deserve to be happy, so does he. I'm glad you took the leap to protect Reese."

"Me too."

"After you tell the guys and you're settled in, I would like to talk to you about adding Aikido to your class offerings. It's been a while since I taught, but my credentials are up to date."

"Sweet. I'll keep you in mind. We'll bring a dessert dish or two on Thursday."

"Please coordinate with Jill. She's the menu planner extraordinaire."

"Will do."

"Wait, Jordan cooks too?"

"Yes, and he has his teaching degree like Jill as well."

"Interesting. See you again soon." Norah check outs and leaves.

I purchase some chocolates for me and Reese and a few for Jordan before heading to the school. After parking in the designated spot, I scan the lot for Corey Mikel. I'm relieved he's nowhere to be found. Did I think he would slink away? No, not at all. Am I glad? Yes, very much. I consider how far I've come this year, both personally and professionally, knowing the latter will only get better when I take this new position.

I greet Reese at the exit and ask, "How was your day?"

"Great! You?"

"Same. I know we have a shortened day tomorrow, but I'm looking forward to the extra-long weekend."

"Me too!"

I hand her the box of candy after I settle into the driver's seat.

"Sweet, I won't tell Dad," she vows.

I laugh and lift another box into the air. "That box is for you and me. I got him his own."

"Awesome!" We chat about her day more in depth as we make our way home. Jordan joins us, and we cook up a delicious dinner before we watch the next movie in the Harry Potter series.

CHAPTER TWENTY-EIGHT

JORDAN

The only holiday I've ever look forward to is birthdays, especially after Reese was born. I have a feeling Thanksgiving this year will push it to the top of the list.

"Ladies, we need to leave."

Reese rushes around the corner. "I'm ready!"

I laugh. Her arms are loaded down with cards for Jill, Cruz, and the babies. "You know the babies can't read yet, right?"

"Of course," my daughter scoffs at my statement.

I'm still shaking my head when Alex joins us in the kitchen. We make two trips to the SUV to accommodate our contribution to the food for dinner and head toward the farm. Unfortunately, I was unable to meet Joyce before today. I'm ecstatic and anxious at the same time. I owe her so much, and she doesn't realize it.

The barn is set up for a huge party with seasonal decorations adorning every surface. There are three tables along one wall for food, two for dessert, and at least ten set for eating. Alex mentioned the Blackthornes go big, but I wasn't expecting this big.

Alex ushers us to the dessert table, and we set down our contribution to today's meal before we're greeted by Norah and a guy I haven't met. Hugs around for everyone, then Norah introduces us.

"Cam, you know Alex. This is Reese and Jordan." The average-height, slightly burly guy extends his hand to me. If I recall correctly, either Alex or Jake mentioned he's a firefighter.

"Pleasure to meet you. I'm Jake and Jill's brother." Cameron greets me.

"Interesting, I'm Jill's brother too."

Cam laughs along with me. "I'll share all the childhood secrets as soon as possible."

"Much appreciated."

"Are you my uncle too?" Reese asks Cam.

Not exactly. He glances at me, and I nod.

"Yup. Uncle Cam sounds perfect!"

"Sweet! Now I have two uncle Cams." Reese throws her arms around him. The exponential rate her family has grown is amazing. Mine too.

Cam is rescued by Cruz and another guy who's equally as fit as I am. I surmise he's a coworker.

"Hey, bro!" Cruz greets me. He hugs Alex, and Reese gives him a high five.

"Hey."

"Please meet Lane Hawkins; he's a member of my team."

I see the glimmer of recognition, but it fades almost as quickly.

"Nice to meet you. Are you playing later?"

I grin at him. "I am."

"Awesome!" Lane replies.

"My wife sent me to collect you to meet with Joyce," Cruz confesses. "She's in the house anxiously awaiting your arrival. I can keep an eye on Reese if you and Alex want to meet her."

"Thanks. Much appreciated." I turn to my daughter. "Stay with Cruz. Alex and I will be back soon."

"'Kay. So, Uncle Cruz, where can I find…."

I thread my fingers with Alex's and lead her out the barn door. "You good?"

"Surprisingly, yes. I'm grateful. Today I'll be able to share it with her personally."

Jill greets us at the front door. "Hey, guys." We exchange hugs, and she leads us inside. "Jordan, please meet Joyce."

I'm momentarily speechless. She single-handedly changed my life, and I only met with her once. "Thank you for—"

"It's nice to see you again, Jordan. Hi, Alex. No thanks are necessary. I only wish I met you sooner."

"I appreciate that, but it appears everything turned out as it should have. Mr. Generali and Coach Apple changed my life, and I believe I have you to thank for the introduction."

She nods curtly. "Would you like to sit?"

"Yes, thank you." We each take a seat in the living room.

"Please share more about you and your family. I understand you have a daughter named Reese."

I smile widely and update Joyce about my life from her referral to today. She asks a few pointed questions to clarify some of the information from the news, specifically about Christie and the recent security issues.

"I've followed your career. Mike and Spencer have been keeping me in the loop. Your team is doing well this season."

"We are. I foresee a deep playoff run for the team this year."

She chuckles. "It's why they brought you here, no?"

"I suppose that's accurate. Can I ask a somewhat delicate question?"

"Of course."

"Did you know about Jill and Julianne? Were they your cases as well?"

A sadness crosses her face. "I placed Jill, Jake, and Cameron with Ben and Connie. I wasn't Julianne's caseworker. I knew about Jill, not Julianne. The parameters of my job didn't allow me to connect the two of you."

"I'm not upset. More curious than anything."

"I understand."

Alex's phone pings with an incoming message. She checks and shares the content.

"Jake would like us to join him at Connor's."

"What is he up to, Alejandra?"

She shrugs, but I'm only partially convinced she doesn't know what's going on. Joyce, on the other hand, is grinning like a Cheshire cat. The why is still undetermined.

We make our way to the barn to get Reese so she can join us. Cruz is listening to Reese as she talks his ear off. They join us as we step inside.

Alex asks, "How was your talk?"

"Good. Reese, please meet Joyce. She was my caseworker when I was in foster care. She's also Connor's mom."

"Cool. Nice to meet you."

"You as well."

"We're going for a walk to Connor's. It appears Jake and Joyce have been doing some scheming." Alex adds.

Mischief bubbles in my daughter's eyes, which leads me to believe she's in on it too. "Yes, let's go. Aunt Jill and Uncle Cruz, you should come too."

"That's the plan," Cruz admits.

As we approach Connor's home, I see Jake standing on the front porch. Seated next to him in an Adirondack chair is a thin, blonde woman with the same blue eyes as mine who could easily be Jill's twin. Everyone other than Jill slows as we continue to the foot of the steps.

"When he called, I didn't believe him," she states while rising from the chair.

When I hired Blackthorne to protect Reese, I knew they were the best in the country. Going the extra step to connect me with my sisters is above and beyond my expectations.

Jake introduces us. "Julianne Silva, please meet your younger siblings Jordan and Jillian."

I extend my hand to her. Before she can take it, Jill throws one arm around both of us and squeezes tightly.

"Why don't I introduce all those people to you, and then the three of us can talk?" Jill suggests.

"Thank you."

Jill introduces Cruz, Reese, Alex, and finally Joyce.

"To clarify, he's your husband." Julianne points to Cruz. "She's your daughter and my niece." She points to Reese. "The stunning brunette is your girlfriend." She gestures to Alex. "And you're their social worker," Julianne recaps.

Girlfriend, for now. "Yes. There are more connections, but that's a start," I reply.

Cruz takes a step forward and kisses Jill lightly. "Come on, Reese. Let's go see if Connor needs help with Myers, Sutton, or Amara."

"'Kay. Mom, you should come too. Mr. Jake, what about Ben?"

"Good point, Reese. Perhaps Norah needs some help," Jake answers.

"Nice to meet you, Aunt Julianne. We should talk books soon."

Julianne laughs. "You as well. Yes, we should. Maybe later today, Reese."

Reese loops her arm around Cruz's, and they head back toward the barn.

"She's precocious."

I chuckle. "Yes, she is." The four of us take a seat on the porch. "Please tell us more about you."

Julianne smiles. "I'm blown away by how much we look alike."

Jill and I nod in agreement.

My older sister continues. "I was adopted by Edmund and Caroline Silva when I was three. They were trying to have a child of their own for nearly ten years beforehand. My childhood was simple, and I focused mostly on school."

"Did you go to college?" Jill asks.

"Yes, I'm a high school principal at a private school in Wilmington. What do you do?"

Sheer glee passes over me. In the last eight months, I've met two people who genuinely don't know who I am before meeting me. It's a second opportunity for me to meet someone fresh. "I have a degree in education with a focus on special needs. However, I play professional football right now."

"Oh. Wow! Cool. I know nothing about football. Baseball is more my thing. What about you, Jillian, or do you prefer Jill?"

"I prefer Jill. I'm a special needs teacher. Do you prefer Julianne?"

"Anything is fine, but most of my coworkers and my bestie call me Julie or Jules."

"Sweet. Block your ears for a second, Jordan."

I frown but do it anyway.

"Now that it's just us girls. Significant other?" Jill asks.

She shakes her head. "I can't believe he listened."

Jill grins. "He didn't. He's trying to be respectful though. I'm sure he heard my question. Right, Jordan?"

I shrug and lower my hands.

My sisters laugh. *My sisters.* I'm barely comfortable with Jill, now there are two. It's amazing and scary at the same time. Are there more of us? "Can I ask an off-the-wall question?"

"You can ask," they say at once.

"Are there more of us?"

Four ice blue eyes connect with mine, and we turn toward Joyce.

"As far as I know, there's only the three of you," she shares.

"We can have Jake confirm this, right, Jill?"

"I will," she assures me.

My phone chimes in my pocket.

"It's time, isn't it?" Jill asks.

"Yeah. First though we need to set another time for a sibling get-together and share information," I suggest.

Both of my sisters pull out their phones and swap them.

We rejoin everyone in the barn after planning a time to meet up. We sit down and share a delicious meal with my rapidly expanding family. I have never had a holiday meal with so many people in my entire life. The planner, whether Jill or Norah or both, thought of everything from turkey to ham to stuffing, right down to the fresh cranberry sauce. The guests are smiling, chatting, and enjoying the food and the company.

"Is it time, Jake?"

Jake laughs. "Almost, Cam. I swear you attend only to play in our annual game."

"You know it. Well, and Jill's desserts," Cam replies.

Everyone at our table breaks down in laughter. The army of people clean up from dinner, and we convene in the expansive backyard. Connor and Jake have already separated the teams for two-hand touch football. Using cones, Connor marked the out of bounds and a line for the end zone. Normally, the game is small, but more guests means larger teams.

Reese is on my team, and Jake is the quarterback. Connor was crafty and purposefully separated the couples. Alex and Norah are on his team instead of Jake's..

Joyce, Connie, and Julianne watch the kiddos along the sidelines. Their faces are painted with sheer joy. When I leave the huddle with my team, I glance over and see Callie chatting it up with Julie.

We line up. Connor is defending Cam off to my right. Alex is set up to defend me, and Norah has Reese. Ben, Jake's dad, and Ed are matched up as well. Lane and Cruz are jockeying for position. Jill and Maia are still sizing each other up.

"Are you any good, Jake?" I shout.

Norah giggles.

"I can hold my own," Jake replies.

Apparently, I need to learn more about my brother-in-law's early days.

I take off down the sideline, and so does Norah. She slants to the right, but Reese has her well covered. Jake releases the ball, and Connor hauls it in with minimal effort. He scampers backward and hops over the line for a touchdown.

The spiral was perfection. "Did you play?" I ask in the huddle.

"Yeah, in high school Connor and I were on the same team for football and hockey. In previous years, I played quarterback for both teams during the holiday game."

Reese volunteers to run the offense for Connor's team. "Don't worry, Mr. Jake—or is it Uncle Jake? I can do this."

He glances in my direction. I offer him a curt nod.

"Uncle Jake works."

After a few plays, the score is tied at two points for each team. We take a quick drink break before lining up again. We continue playing for another half hour before Connie indicates dessert is ready.

In our last huddle, I explain the final play to Connor and Reese including Reese taking on the role of quarterback for the final play.

"You know what to do, Reese."

"Same play as in the yard at home, right?"

"Yup. Throw it shallow."

"Got it, Dad."

"Are you sure about this, Jordan?" Cruz asks.

"Yeah, Alex will remember the route and tackle me."

Reese laughs.

I nod to Reese and Connor.

"Gators. One. Two. Hike." She drops back and throws the ball short of the slant route. There's no chance for me to catch it. This time, instead of gunning for me, Alex intercepts the ball.

"Ohmigod! Ohmigod! I did it!"

"Woo-hoo! Yes! Way to go, Mom!"

I curl my arms around her and lift her off the ground, turning in a circle.

"You set me up," Alex accuses.

I allow her to slide down so we're face-to-face. "I admit to nothing. Reese missed the throw, that's all. Besides, this is the first time I've been able to hold you longer than a second or two today. It's barely enough."

"You're sneaky, Mr. Devereaux. Very sneaky."

"Admit it. You love it."

"I do, I truly do." A huge grin stretches across her face.

"Come on, lovebirds, dessert is waiting," Cruz shouts from behind us.

Alex buries her face in my neck. I'm sure her face is bright red.

We don't move for nearly a minute. "Alejandra, it's just us," I murmur.

Before lifting her head, she kisses along my jaw.

"Stop it!"

She looks up at me with a pout on her face.

"Stop. Dessert here, then dessert at home. Deal?"

"Deal." Hand in hand we join the rest of our family in the barn and sample too many delicious desserts.

CHAPTER TWENTY-NINE

JORDAN

Time has been passing rapidly. Christmas was a low-key affair with Jill and Julie at our house. We've been spending tons of time together and learning about each other.

The gym had its soft opening a couple days ago, and for the first week anyone can take a free class. After two whirlwind days, the opening was a huge success. Now were deep into preparation for the playoffs. It has been grueling, but worth it.

As promised earlier in the season, Alex and Reese are joining me for the playoffs even if they're away. The final whistle sounds for the conference championship. "Let's go!" Cam shouts. "Two down, one to go!" Coach receives a Gatorade shower, and now they're coming for me.

"No. No! Not until after the big game."

My younger teammates back off me, but shower Ty instead.

"Guys! Not cool!" Ty admonishes them. Deep down, I know he's not angry.

The guys laugh and walk away from Ty soaked in blue.

"Gators back together again!" Cam throws an arm around each of us.

"Time to get another championship together!" I state.

"Yes, sir!" Ty agrees.

"Yo, Devereaux! Melanie wants you three in the press room," Preston summons us.

"Coming!" we reply in unison.

The press room is buzzing with reporters clamoring for a quote.

"Preston, great game today!" Scott from a major sports show praises him.

"Thank you. This season has been amazing. I put the passes out there, and Jordan or Cam haul them in."

"Next question." Melanie points to Stu.

"You had a monster game, Jordan. How did the drama from early in the season impact you?"

"Stu, as I explained earlier in the season, what happens off the field is separate and apart from the field. Preston is as advertised, and he proved it week in and week out, lofting passes for me to catch. The reality is... we're going to the Super Bowl!"

The rest of the reporters laugh and throw questions at us for the next thirty minutes. Thankfully none of the questions are aimed at me. Well, none are aimed at my personal life. I'm eager to get this over with so I can clean up and get to my ladies. I would much rather their company than being cooped up in this press room.

More than an hour after the game ends, I make my way down the tunnel. Not surprisingly, I find my ladies and Madeleine waiting for me.

"Woo-hoo! I'm so proud of you, Dad!"

I scoop Reese up and wrap my other arm around Alex. "Thanks, peanut."

Alex murmurs near my ear, "I'm so happy for you, Jordan. You worked your ass off."

Ignoring my reaction to her is virtually impossible. Reese saves the day by catching Alex's curse word. I'm grateful. Now I have time to control myself in our surroundings.

"That's $50, Mom."

I laugh, and Alex frowns.

"What are you talking about, Reese?"

"That word is on the curse list Dad created. You owe for saying 'butt' in a different way."

Alex laughs heartily. "You got it."

Unfortunately, I need to let them get to the airport. We fly as a team. "Time to go, ladies," I state and usher them to their car. After an extra-long flight home, I find Reese sound asleep on the couch.

Alex whispers as I approach. "Hey. She tried so hard to wait."

"I'll bring her to bed and meet you in ours."

"Deal."

You would think I'm exhausted from the game and travel. I'm never too tired to study the dips and curves of Alejandra, most of which I've painstakingly memorized with my mouth and hands. When I step into our room, a designation that shifted soon after our dinner out with Cam and

Ty, I find my gorgeous woman sound asleep in our bed. Stripping off my clothes, I slide in behind her and join her in dreamland.

Near seven the next morning, I wake and find her side of the bed cold. Her stealth skills have been increasing. She's been training with Reese each morning before school and running the gym. I allow my thoughts to drift back to a time before she was ours. Yes, ours. Alex is as much a part of Reese's life as she is mine. I don't have much time to revel in my thoughts.

"Morning, Dad."

"Hey, peanut. Ready for school?"

"Yup, but we have something for you first."

I wink at her. "Who does?"

"Mom and me, duh!"

As she finishes speaking, Alex steps through our door with a tray heaping with food.

"You cooked for me?"

"We did," Alex replies.

She doesn't realize it, but this is another example of her taking care of me. Perhaps she does now, but she didn't before. I scoot up and lean against the headboard as she sets the tray over my thighs.

"Be right back." Alex rushes out of our room.

I'm confused until she returns with a cup of coffee in her hands. "Afraid you were going to spill it?"

She smiles at me and steals an all-too-brief kiss. "Yes."

Reese is bouncing with anticipation. "Could you try it, Dad? You're killing me."

I laugh and dig into the omelet. After I finish the bite, I put her out of her misery. "It's awesome, Reese. Why were you worried?"

My daughter shrugs before rising to kiss me on the cheek. "Gotta finish getting ready for school."

"Thanks for the delicious food, peanut."

"Welcome. Don't kiss for too long or I'll be late for school. Principal Platt doesn't care about your win last night."

Alex blushes fiercely and stares directly at me, willing me to answer Reese. "We got you. I love you to the moon. Have a great day!"

"I love you to the moon and back. You too," she answers and hustles out the door.

"She's right." Alex leans forward and skims her lips across mine.

"I know. I don't have to like it though. Want some company at work today?"

"As long as you don't distract me from my job."

I bracket her hips with my hands and tug her closer. "I make no promises, beautiful."

"I'll meet you there after I finish and shower."

She bends at the waist, kisses me again, then rushes out of the bedroom.

CHAPTER THIRTY

ALEJANDRA

The past few days have passed quickly. I can only imagine how it feels for Jordan. "Ready, Reese?"

"So excited! I can't believe Dad is letting me skip school today."

Our flight to New Orleans is early afternoon on Friday. Luckily, her school has a short break early next week. The doorbell rings, and Reese rushes past me to answer the door.

"Make sure you check who it is first!" I call after her.

"I will," she shouts in reply.

I grab our bags and make my way to the foyer to a bustle of noise and people.

"Hey, everyone!" I greet them.

Madeleine, Christoph, Cruz, and Jill are milling in the living room waiting for me to join them. Unfortunately, Julie can't join us.

"Hey," Jill says and hugs me. "Ready?"

"A little excited, Jill?" I ask.

Reese shakes her head. "She's over-the-top excited. Your first Super Bowl is amazing. They only get better after that."

"How many have you been to, Reese?"

"You should know these stats, Mom. This one is Dad's fourth. He's won twice already. I was at the two he won. Trudie agreed to take care of me for Dad, even though she retired a while ago."

Although they try to stifle it, each of our guests dissolve into laughter.

"Well, let's get moving then." Our ride to the airport and the flight are uneventful. We check into our hotel and wait for Jordan to join us for dinner.

Near seven local time, we head down to the private dinner Madeleine set up. Soon after we take our seats, Cam and Ty join us.

Reese is on her feet and running before they have two full strides into the room. "Uncle Ty. Uncle Cam."

"Hey, Little Miss! Did you grow since our last dinner?" Ty asks.

She shrugs. "Maybe. Where's Dad?"

"He's on his way. Coach stopped him in the lobby. Hi, Alex. Nice to see you again."

"You as well. Do you know Madeleine?"

"Yup, she's my agent," Cam admits.

"Mine too," Ty adds.

I introduce everyone else and take a seat beside Reese. Jordan joins us soon thereafter, and we share an amazing meal.

"I'm so happy you're both here." Jordan admits while he walks us to our room. Unfortunately, he's required to room with his teammates. He was lucky this time and is rooming with Preston. "I need to hustle to make curfew."

I giggle and unlock our door.

"Have a great walkthrough tomorrow, Dad."

"Thanks, peanut. I love you to the moon."

"Love you to the moon and back," Reese replies and plops down on her bed.

"I'm crazy happy for you." I admit.

"Thanks." He circles my waist with his arm, drawing me against his hard, lean body.

It's impossible to ignore his arousal against me. "We don't have time for that now."

His skin pinks up. "It's constant whenever you're nearby, especially when I can hold you close." My gorgeous man draws his tongue along my lower lip and kisses me breathless. He sets a light kiss on my forehead and latches the door behind him.

After a whirlwind of fan activities at the stadium the next day, Reese and I take a dip in the hotel pool before a low-key dinner in our room. Near nine, I slip her tablet from her hands and charge it. Picking up my phone, I text Jordan.

Me: Can you talk?

A video chat request blinks on my screen almost immediately. I answer.

"Hey. Nothing to worry about." I turn the camera toward sleeping Reese. "I just wanted to see your face."

"Aww."

I laugh. "I miss you. I know I saw you last night, but it isn't the same."

"It isn't. I miss you too."

"Is wishing you good luck appropriate, or do we just consider tomorrow like another game?"

"I try to treat it like each one before, but it isn't an easy feat. The festivities surrounding this game make it feel bigger because it is. We work our asses off to get here. Having been on both sides, going home the runner-up sucks."

"Understood. Have a great day at work."

He winks at me. "Thanks, gorgeous. I'm aiming for at least four bows tomorrow. I love you to the stars."

"We'll be ready. I love you to the stars and back."

The next morning, we purposely move slowly. The game isn't until tonight. Reese and I did a light training session in our room and then ate a huge brunch. I'm pacing while Reese is reading until it's time to meet with the group in the lobby. We're heading to a pregame reception put on by Madeleine's agency in the owner's suite.

"Ready, Reese?"

She checks out her clothes. "Jersey, comfy kicks, hoodie, and my favorite watching partner, all check."

"Thanks." I scan myself again before grabbing the badges from the bureau. I put both around my neck and tuck them into my shirt. When we emerge from our room, Cruz and Jill are walking in our direction from their room at the end of the hall.

"Are you excited, Reese?"

She shakes her head. "No, I'm nervous for Dad."

"Are you normally nervous?" Jill asks.

"Only for the playoffs."

Cruz nods, and we make our way to the lobby. Madeleine and Christoph exit the elevator beside us. As we exchange our hellos, I freeze halfway to the exit. Fear cascades through me. My hands start to shake, and terror overtakes me. Terror for me but mostly for Reese. I never wanted to be anywhere near him ever again. The trial was close enough.

"Alex, you good?" Cruz asks.

I step to the right, push Reese behind me with Cruz flanking her, wrap one arm around her, and instruct her to stay put. I slip into protective mode for my daughter and a bit for myself. No, a lot for myself. "Tall, Hispanic guy with the red shirt on the right is Ramon."

Christoph turns from my left to face me, blocking my view. "You don't have to do this. I can escort him out of here."

I take a settling breath. "I thought he gave up. I guess not. Escorting him out won't do any good. He'll keep trying. I need to get this confrontation over with and get to the game. I need to close this chapter of my life for good."

Christoph suggests, "Jill, Madeleine, and Cruz can continue to the car with Reese."

"Okay." I turn in a tight circle and ask Reese to continue on with the others. "I love you to the moon, peanut." I press a kiss to the top of her head and fight down the urge to hurl bubbling in my stomach.

"You've got this, Mom. You're the bravest person I know. I love you to the moon and back."

Jill loops her arm with Reese, and they leave. *How does Reese know about Ramon?*

I'm standing with Christoph beside me when Ramon approaches with his hands up in front of his chest. A sense of calm washes over me. I wasn't scared for me. I was terrified for Reese. Terrified for her to witness me revert to the shell of a person I was when we were together. *No! You're not the same scared, dependent girl anymore.* I pull myself out of my head and remind myself I learned the necessary skills to take care of myself and found my family in Jordan and Reese.

Ramon's words start off softly. "I'm the last person you want to or expect to see here. I'm violating my parole conditions being here. I—"

Momentarily, I wonder how he found me here, but realize this hotel is the official accommodations for the team. "What do you want from me? You destroyed so much good in me. It took me years to rebuild and get stronger."

"I know. My counselor put me in a program for domestic violence abusers. I realize—"

"You're here to make amends for some program?"

"Yes. I need to apologize for the pain and anguish I caused you. I don't expect you to accept it, but I need to say it more for me than you. You didn't deserve to wear the wrath of my rage on your body. I'm sorry, Alex."

I'm stunned speechless. This moment feels nothing like I thought it would. I expected to feel relief or pity. I don't. Perhaps choosing me and bettering myself makes his apology... unnecessary, at least for me. I took the shell of myself and made her wiser, stronger, and able to be a solid role model for others, including Reese.

Christoph shifts beside me to remind me he's there. I appreciate the support. "Alex," Christoph's voice filters into my thoughts.

I don't focus on him until he sets his hand on my forearm. I take a settling breath, then shift my gaze to Ramon. "Ramon, I appreciate your adherence to your program. Consider the amends portion met, at least you offered them. Please leave and refrain from contacting me or my family again."

Ramon nods and turns for the exit. Frankly, I expected more of a fight to walk away. He drove hundreds of miles to get here. I stand rooted in my spot for a solid minute before Christoph silently ushers me to the edge of the lobby.

"Jordan *cannot* know about this before the game," I state without looking up.

Immediately, he pulls out his phone and sends a text or two. "Done. What else do you need right now?"

"We need to get to the reception. Madeleine is already late."

Christoph shakes his head. "Don't worry about anything except yourself right now. Madeleine is the president of Scala Talent and Sports Management. They will wait for her. Reese is secure with Cruz. What do you need?"

"Right now, nothing. The sheer number of things I need to unpack from this impromptu meeting is astronomical and likely requires assistance from my therapist. I'm grateful I wasn't alone with Reese, but we need to get to the game."

"Are you sure? I can send the others ahead, and we can meet them there if you need more time."

"Yes, I'm sure," I say the words, and I almost believe them. Examining my feelings will have to wait. I refuse to let Jordan down.

Seemingly convinced, Christoph escorts me to the car and we head off to the reception. As promised, Madeleine's staff waited for her. Reese and I nosh on some tasty snacks until it's time to head to our seats.

If I thought the atmosphere of a regular season game was fantastic, the Super Bowl is off the charts. The fans are ecstatic, and my nerves cause flutters in my belly. The starting lineups have been called, the national anthem has echoed around the stadium, and the coin toss is complete. I hold my breath as the ball is kicked off.

Reese grabs my arm. "This is so exciting!"

"Is it different than the others?"

"Duh! It's a different team, you're here, and Dad's happier than ever."

"Okay."

Reese grabs my hand as the opposing team runs the kickoff back to the thirty-yard line. "Not too bad."

After a three and out, we have the ball at the forty. The DC team converted one first down before losing the ball to a fumble.

Reese scrubs her hand down her face exactly how Jordan does when he's frustrated.

"Don't worry, the game just started."

Reese nods and turns back to the field, riveted by the action. Can't say I blame her; although, currently, my focus is on Jordan on the sideline talking to Cam with a tablet in his hand. The first quarter ends, and neither team has moved the ball much.

"Can we get a drink?" Reese asks.

"Sure."

Cruz swoops in. "What do you want, Reese? I'll get it."

She answers, and Jill and Cruz step away toward the food spread on the far wall. The roar of the crowd increases, and we turn our attention back to the game. Ty intercepted a pass and ran back for nearly fifty yards.

"Woo-hoo, Uncle Ty!"

Preston takes the next snap and hurls a pass on a slant route to Cam. It's complete for twelve more yards. On the next play, I watch as Jordan runs a corner route along the far sideline. Preston releases mere seconds before he's tackled. He twists beneath the defender to see Jordan pluck the pass from the air and fall into the end zone. Jordan scrambles to his feet and bows twice before handing the ball back to the referee. Reese and I high-five.

"That's one!" I shout, which earns me a confused look from Cruz who returned with our drinks. I lean closer so he can hear me. "Jordan said he was aiming for at least four bows today."

Cruz nods and turns his attention back to the game.

"This is crazy!" Jill states, looking at Reese and me.

"Yeah, it is," I offer.

The rest of the second quarter passes without any additional scoring. Jordan and his teammates are up seven to zero at the half. During the halftime show, which Reese nor I have any interest in, we take a trip to the restroom and load up on snacks. We chat with Madeleine and Christoph and retake our seats in time for the second half to begin.

The third quarter starts out like the first until Preston connects with Cam in the end zone for a touchdown with nearly three minutes remaining. The crowd erupts in cheers.

"Uncle Cam rocks!" Reese exclaims, and we high-five again.

"Yes, he does."

The closer we get to the end of this game, the prouder I become. Jordan set a goal for himself, and he's fifteen football minutes away from achieving it. No sooner do I turn my focus back to the field, Preston heaves a deep pass. Jordan is well covered by the opponent's safety. Not once this entire season have I seen Jordan leap as high as he does to snatch the pass out of the air. I'm confident the smile on his face is from ear to ear. He lands near the edge of the field. The crowd waits with bated breath for the score to be reviewed. Cheers erupt in the crowd when the touchdown is confirmed and Jordan bows twice. Reese and I join in the celebration.

I watch him walk to the sideline, except this time he looks directly toward us and makes a heart over his. Reese grabs my arm and points.

"I see, peanut." My gaze is pinned on him instead of the game. As the clock ticks down, elation courses through me. Once the clock expires, we're escorted down to the field for the postgame celebration.

Confetti rains down on the players and coaches. Coach and Jordan receive a Gatorade shower. Reese grabs my hand and rushes onto the field once we're given the go-ahead.

"Reese, where are you going?"

"To Dad. We have a spot!"

"Of course you do!"

Reese laughs and weaves through the crowd as fast as she can. She releases my hand as the crowd parts, and she finds Jordan. He's jumping up and down with Cam and Ty. I stop and take the scene in. Jordan hugs Reese and sets her down on the balloon-and-streamer-covered turf. Reese flies through her handshake with Cam and Ty. Jordan rushes to me, wraps his arms around me, and hoists me off the ground.

"Congratulations, Jordan!"

"Thank you, gorgeous. I couldn't have done it without you. I love you to the stars!"

Before I can reply, Cam, Ty, and Reese join us. Reese is perched on top of Cam's shoulders, an enormous grin on her face with a way-too-large Super Bowl Champions hat atop her head.

"We need to get over there for the trophy presentation," Ty shares.

Jordan kisses me possessively before linking our hands and leading me near the podium. Cam sets Reese beside me before following Jordan onto the platform.

"How you doing, peanut?"

"I'm happy for Dad. My uncles too. Plus, now we get Dad to ourselves for a few months."

I hadn't thought about what happens after the victory parade. "Is having him home as awesome as it sounds?"

Reese grins as wide as possible. "No, it's so much better!"

The trophy is passed around among the players, and Jordan is announced the most valuable player of the game.

Once they're done with the presentation, Jordan bounds down the stairs and quickly asks near the shell of my ear, "Are you okay with being on ESPN?"

"Yes."

The reporter prepares us how to respond and positions us near the logo on the field. Our fingers threaded between us, Reese is beaming up at her father as the cameraman and a reporter focus on our family.

The reporter asks, "Jordan Devereaux, you just won the Super Bowl. What's next?"

In unison the three of us reply, "We're going to Disney World!" He plants a sweet kiss on my lips, then one on the top of Reese's head.

Once we're done with the press, Jordan, Cam, Ty, and another player I haven't officially met named Hillman locate Madeleine and each hug her, thanking her for her hard work as their agent.

The pride on her face is impossible to miss. Good for her. I know she works her tail off for her clients while being an amazing mom to Liz. About two hours later, the guys head into the locker room to clean up, and we head back to the hotel. Reese is passed out when Jordan arrives at our door in the wee hours of the morning. We kiss and grope our way to the bed and curl up until midmorning the following day, waking barely in time for our flight home.

The next few days is a chaotic string of victory events. I'm not able to share my run-in with Ramon until three days later. At first, Jordan is upset with me for not sharing with him immediately, but then he comes around to my reasoning. Now we focus on the off-season with only one more event in a few months for the team to get their rings.

EPILOGUE

JORDAN

Bright and early two weeks later, I slip out of bed, stumble into the kitchen, and start breakfast. Hopefully, Reese's plea for a day off from training today will be successful. Although Alex has been known to train alone anyway. Reese is in on today's secret mission. My accomplice list is long. In addition to Reese, I needed assistance from Maia, Jill, and Norah.

Near seven, a groggy Reese wanders into the kitchen.

"Morning, peanut. I'm just about finished."

A knowing smile grows on her face. "It's today?"

I frown at her. "You forgot?"

She giggles. "No, of course not." She looks over her shoulder to make sure the coast is clear. "I can't wait to be able to spill this secret."

"You don't get to spill it. I do," I remind her.

"True. Let's get moving then."

I set a single rose on the tray and bring Alex breakfast in bed. When I reach the door, I see her moving toward the door. "Go back to bed, please," I call from the threshold.

Alex looks over at me and sees the tray. She does an about-face and jumps back into our bed with a sexy laugh. "What's all this for?"

"Just because," Reese answers before I can.

"Are you both going to join me?" Alex asks.

"Yup. Be right back," Reese dashes out the door.

I pass her on my way to retrieve my tray. She grins at me. I settle next to Alex. Reese chose to sit on the dressing bench at the foot of the bed.

"What are you two scheming?" Alex asks.

"Can't I make a special breakfast for my ladies whenever I want?" I wink at her.

"You can, but usually it's attached to an event or occasion."

"She's onto us, Dad."

I laugh. "Yeah, she is."

"Can I tell her the first part?" Reese asks.

"Just the first part," I warn.

"Did you know Aunt Norah's sister is a big-time dress designer?"

Alex smiles. "I did. Kelly is awesome. Her husband is dreamy—"

"Excuse me?" Jordan asks.

Alex laughs. "Relax, he's a movie star and worth two glances. Besides, he's quite taken, as am I."

"Fair enough."

"As I was saying, her husband is dreamy, and their kids, Nick and Ellie are younger than you, Reese. If I recall, Nick is six, and Ellie is four."

"Well, to spill the first part of the day, we're going to the farm to meet Miss Kelly to pick dresses for the gala."

"Really?"

I wasn't sure about the custom dresses part of my plan. Taking care of Alejandra is a delicate balance. She's fiercely independent, which I love about her, but I have a deep-seated desire to provide for her too. She will think the dress is over the top, and perhaps it is for a regular guy. My profession has provided me with obscene wealth, more than I could spend in my lifetime considering my investment strategy.

"Yup. I'm excited beyond belief. Dad's old team didn't have a gala for the ring ceremony like this one. This is new, but I'm here for it."

I laugh at my daughter's choice of words. A custom dress for her is a bit of a splurge, but the gala is a big deal for me, and I'm treating it as such for my family.

"Jordan, you don't—" Alex begins.

"I want to. Please let me." I lean over and brush my lips over hers.

"Okay," she murmurs as I pull away.

"You two have a little over an hour until your ride will be here to pick you up."

"Do you know who is picking us up, Reese?"

She nods her head furiously.

"Care to spill?"

"It's Miss Maia."

Today, like the last time the girls hung out, Maia's not working. Soon after the win and Alex sharing Ramon's appearance at the hotel, we slowly decreased security. I bring Reese to school and pick her up in the off-season. It allows Alex to teach the early classes and be home in time for dinner. In the fall, we'll make adjustments.

We finish breakfast, and my ladies get ready for more than dress shopping. Norah has arranged for a day of pampering at the farm for Alex and a little bit for Reese while I finish setting things up here. I fully expect pushback like the last spa day.

Maia arrives precisely on time. I'm not surprised. She's glowing in the early months of her pregnancy, but I won't say anything. "Morning, Maia."

"Hi, Jordan."

"They should be out momentarily."

"How reluctant is Alex?"

I shrug. "More than I would like, but—" I glance over my shoulder to make sure she isn't here yet. "—she's going to need to get used to what I want to give her."

Maia tilts her head, indicating she can't answer because my ladies are approaching. "Sounds great, Jordan."

I hug Reese and kiss the top of her head. Then I sweetly kiss Alex before they go. "Have fun." I shoo them out the door.

With only a few minutes to spare, the rest of my crew arrives. Jill and Cruz are on food while I set up the backyard with the guys.

"Thanks for your help," I say after Cam and Ty enter the house.

"We're just helping to steal your ideas for a later time," Ty admits.

"Speak for yourself," Cam scoffs.

I introduce them to Jill and Cruz before sharing my plan. Over the next few hours, we work to set the house for Alex. Maia sends a few progress texts to let me know when I'll run out of time. Cam and Ty knock back a cold one before they head out.

"Alex is good for you, bro. Don't screw it up," Ty offers before leaving.

"Don't listen to him. Alex is awesome. She's perfect for you and Reese. I'm happy for you, man."

"Thanks, Cam. See you on Tuesday?"

"Yup." We've started a tradition of having a late breakfast on Tuesdays to keep in touch during the off-season. I close the door and join my sister and brother-in-law in the kitchen.

"Ready for my instructions?" she asks.

"Sure, lay it on me."

Step by step, Jill explains what needs to be done for the elegant meal she prepared for tonight.

"Thank you so much, both of you."

"Don't mention it. I love cooking for others. Also, you and Alex will be honest when I ask for feedback too."

"We will… but probably not until tomorrow."

Cruz grins and ushers Jill out of the house. I glance at my phone after it vibrates in my hand.

Maia: She will be there in about thirty minutes.

Me: Thank you.

Great job, Maia. Alex will arrive just before six.

Maia: Take care of her. She deserves it.

Me: I will. So do you.

Maia: Thanks. My love life is a work in progress.

Then I hustle through the shower and dress. My next text comes from Alex.

Alejandra: What are you up to, Mr. Devereaux?

Me: I love it when you call me that. Why would you think that?

Alejandra: How many people are going to be present when I get home?

Me: Only me.

She parks in front of the house because she believes we need to pick up Reese from hanging out with Carter later. Instead, Reese is having a sleepover with Maia at the condo, complete with pizza, smores, and a movie or two. Meeting her at the driver's door, I open it and offer her my hand.

"You are up to something, aren't you?"

I shrug, then smile. "Hi, sweetheart. You look gorgeous." She's stunning. Kelly did in fact come to make a custom dress for the gala, but she also brought options for tonight's dinner. Her dress is emerald silk, which slithers over each curve with precision.

"Thank you. You look hot yourself."

"Do I?" I wink at her before kissing her softly. When we reach the front door, I open it for her, then present her with a bouquet of roses.

She lifts them to her nose and sniffs. "Thank you. Now I know you're up to something."

I offer her my arm, then shake my head. "Flowers mean I'm up to something?"

"Usually, yes."

I grin at her. She isn't wrong. "Just dinner and the house to ourselves tonight." I inwardly groan at my partial lie. "Why don't you put those in the vase while I grab drinks and the first course?"

"Sure. Did you cook?"

"No, I had a little help there for tonight. Jill and Cruz cooked."

"That was nice of them," she replies and busies herself snipping the ends of the flowers.

With a bottle of Kanonkop 2017 Black Label Estate Pinotage from Jake's cellar, I pull the appetizer out of the fridge. Jill made spicy cherry tomato and pancetta burrata, which is a fancy way to say bruschetta.

"Can I help?"

"Sure, you can pour the wine and then take a seat."

Alex pours two glasses and takes a seat in the dining room. I set the serving dish in the center of the table and join her.

She serves one portion to me and one to herself.

"How was your day with the girls? What color did you choose for the garnet and gold gala? I need to share again—you look sinful in silk."

Her face flushes pink before she accepts the compliment. "Kelly said something similar. We had a great time. Is Reese's dress a secret, or is the style shareable?"

"My goal was for you to find a dress… or two"—I smirk at her—"and relax. I'm sure you guided Reese to an appropriate dress for the gala."

"You're sneaky and with accomplices nonetheless."

She doesn't know the half of the number of accomplices for today. "Worth it." I lean over and meet her lips in a kiss. We polish off the burrata and move on to the main course, which is a crispy pork with spicy Asian-inspired risotto.

"Please tell Jill the food was amazing. Cruz too."

"I will."

Her plate is nearly clear when I catch her staring at me.

I set my fork down, turn my chair toward her, and pull hers closer, gripping the outside. "Please share, beautiful."

"For the first time in my life, I'm unflinchingly and unquestionably happy, and I'm afraid to embrace it completely."

"I am too. We're going to embrace it together."

Silence falls between us. It isn't uncomfortable; it's reflective of our tacit agreement.

"Are you finished?" I ask.

"Yeah, why?"

I smile at her. "I need to show you something." We grab our plates and set them in the sink. Threading my fingers with her, I lead her down the hall past our bedroom. At the top of the staircase, I request she close her eyes.

"You *are* up to something."

"Maybe."

She smiles. "Not maybe, definitely."

"What if I am?"

"Depends on what it is."

I lean forward and set my lips on hers. "Shouldn't matter. No peeking." At the bottom of the steps, I have her sit. I skim my fingertips down her legs and remove her shoes with a kiss on each ankle. Her sexy sigh indicates I found a new spot on her luscious body to worship.

She rises to her feet with my assistance, and I guide her to the center of the room.

"You can open your eyes."

With tons of help from Maia and Norah, I transformed a portion of the massive family room into a private dojo for Alex and Reese to train each morning. It's complete with a matted floor and each piece of equipment Norah recommended.

"Jordan, it's…. How long have you been working on this?"

"I asked for guidance right before Christmas and started planning soon thereafter. The contractor has been working on it while you're at work since the middle of last month."

"I couldn't have planned it better myself. You thought of everything, down to multiple sizes of gloves and pads. You take…." She pushes out a sharp breath and curves her arms around me. "I love how you take care of me, especially when I refuse needing it."

I kiss her temple and whisper, "I always will. Trust us to do this right."

She eases back and whispers, "I will too," then plants a hard, possessive kiss in agreement on my lips. As much as I would like to christen this room by peeling her dress from her body, exposing each inch of her skin, it isn't time yet.

"Would you be interested in one of Jill's special desserts?"

"Umm, hell yes."

After another round of breathless kisses, I curl my fingers around the ankle straps of her shoes and link my other hand with hers. In the kitchen, I ask, "Can you get two spoons?"

"Sure." She grabs the spoons, sets them beside me, and hoists herself onto the island.

I plate one slice of the dark chocolate cake with red wine ganache glaze. My sexy woman slides the spoon into it and offers the first bite to me.

"Is it amazing?"

I relieve her of the spoon and feed her a small bite.

"Damn! Jill is a chocolate master."

"She is." Rather than eat more, I set my hands on her knees and push the silk up her toned thighs with expert precision while spreading her legs. Stepping between them, I draw her lips to mine and kiss her deeply. Our dessert is forgotten as the world falls away whenever she's within reach. As much as climbing over her and stripping her dress from her subtle curves is rocketing up my to-do list, sharing the rest of my planned evening is more important.

"Ready for the last part of our evening?"

"There's more?"

"My plan was to eat this outside."

"Well, let's go then."

I shake my head. "Please wait here for me. I'll be right back." With nearly two slices and two spoons, I rush down the lighted path and set our dessert in the tent. When I return, I take her hand in mine and lift it to my lips. After a soft kiss, I curl my arm around her, lower her to the floor, then lead her out into the backyard. We approach a series of panels. I created a display with string lights and images of our early life and relationship in a zigzag pattern across the yard.

The first grouping is from my childhood, which arguably isn't much. Joyce came through by sharing images from her file with me. The next panel has images of Alex and Miguel when they were young, as well as one of her parents on their wedding day.

I slide my arm around her waist and grip her hip lightly. The smooth material beneath my hand feels decadent. The fingers of her free hand rest atop the image. We continue despite her being visibly shaken by the image of her parents.

"How did you…?"

"Miguel and Joyce were lifesavers. The guys helped me set this up while you were out today."

There aren't a ton of photos of us together, so I had to get creative. Everyone helped a bit, especially when we were at the same place but not beside one another. Reese, Madeleine, and Jill take photos as often as possible. I included images from each event, happening, or location since we met, such as the Blackthorne office, the gazebo, the shore near the Michelsons', and my games. I also use the image I sent to Miguel while making Reese's cake and a few from the Super Bowl, as well as candid shots she was unaware I took. Specifically, one where she's standing outside on the patio gazing at the sunset.

That one in particular makes her pause. "When did you take this?"

"The evening you told me about Ramon for the first time."

"I look…" The glow of the sun's rays cast her face in the perfect light, and the sheer contentment is heartwarming. "…relieved and happy."

"You do. More importantly, you look open to allowing me and my daughter to share your life."

She turns to face me. I press a kiss to her forehead before leading her to the end of the path. I set up a huge tent complete with a cozy spot for us to finish dessert with a plush blanket or two with coordinating pillows. The best part is the top is open to the sky, allowing for stargazing. My unmatched woman releases my hand and turns in a tight circle.

When she finishes, she finds me on one knee with a blue velvet box in my hand. Her freshly manicured hands fly over her mouth.

"Alejandra, the moment we met, inexplicable sparks passed between us at the most inopportune time. Each day while you cared for and protected

Reese, and indirectly me, my initial feelings grew to a deep, unrelenting love I never expected. Will you grant me the greatest honor of my life and become Mrs. Devereaux?"

She lifts the hem of her dress and lowers down to the ground in front of me. "I have a proposal too."

My heart lodges in my throat.

My exquisite and complicated woman kisses a tear from the ball of my cheek.

"Which is?"

"I want Reese to be mine too."

"She already is."

My almost fiancée shakes her head. "Officially, before we have more kids."

"Are you…?" It would be a dream come true, soon but amazing.

"No, but I don't want to wait too long."

I raise an eyebrow at her. "At the risk of not getting an answer a second time… Alejandra, will you take my name, adopt our daughter, and have a bigger family with me?"

A single tear runs over the ball of her cheek. "Yes, I can't wait to be Mrs. Devereaux."

After swiping the lone tear away with my thumb, I slide a cushion cut center stone with pear-shaped accent stones on her finger and kiss the top of her hand. I lower her to the blanket beneath us where I intend to ravish her beneath the starry night sky.

Thank you so much for reading *Hers to Protect*!

I hope you love the Blackthorne family. Will Maia and Nolan figure out how to parent together… or apart? More details can be found on my website.

Did you love *Hers to Protect*?

Thank you for taking the time to read it. I hope you loved it!
If you liked this book or another one of my books, please consider posting a review.
A short line or two will be perfect! It helps indie authors like me get noticed. I appreciate your support and feedback.

COMING SOON

Two new stories are coming soon!

A York Beach Novel

The Cappellis

Chasing Someday

Blackthorne Security

Protecting Our Family

MY BOOKS

MATCHMAKERS' BOOK CLUB
For Love & Coffee

All my books in one place: www.nicolevidal.com/books

www.ingramcontent.com/pod-product-compliance
Lightning Source LLC
Chambersburg PA
CBHW072341020726

47506CB00004B/956